ONE LIE TOO MANY

ONE LIE TOO MANY

EILEEN COOK

Houghton Mifflin Harcourt

Boston New York

For information about permission to reproduce selections from this book, write
to trade.permissions@hmhco.com or to Permissions, Houghton Mifflin Harcourt
Publishing Company, 3 Park Avenue, 19th Floor, New York, New York 10016.

hmhbooks.com

The text was set in Truesdell Std.

Library of Congress Cataloging-in-Publication Data is available.

ISBN: 978-0-544-82982-4 hardcover
ISBN: 978-1-328-61841-2 paperback

Manufactured in the United States of America

DOC 10 9 8 7 6 5 4 3 2 1

4500749136

ONE LIE TOO MANY

ONE

Destiny is like a boulder. Bulky and hard to move. It's easier to leave it alone than to try to change it. But that never kept anyone from trying. Trust me: I'm a professional.

Reading people is a talent. I've always been a good observer, but as with any natural ability, if you want to be any good, you've got work at it. When I talk to people, I size them up. I listen to what they say and, more important, to what they don't. I notice what they wear, what brands they choose, how they style their hair. I watch their body language to see if it matches their words. The image they work so hard to show off tells me what they're trying to hide.

I make guesses and let them lead me. It's easier than it looks. Then again, most people aren't paying that much attention when someone tells them what they want to hear.

"What do you think, Skye — will it work out?" Sara leaned forward, ignoring the rest of what was going on in our school cafeteria. She chewed her lips. There were sticky pink clots of Sephora lip gloss on her teeth. Nerves. She was worried about what I would say. She'd have been better off worrying about why she wanted to stay with a guy who was a class-A jackass. However, she wasn't paying me for love advice; she was paying for a psychic connection to the universe.

I shuffled the cards. They were worn and faded, more like fabric than paper. My official story was that my grandmother had passed down this deck of tarot cards to me on her deathbed because she believed I'd inherited her psychic ability. This was a complete lie. The only thing my grandma believed in was bourbon. However, no one trusts a psychic who works with brand-new cards. I ordered the deck from Amazon years ago. When it arrived, I soaked each card in a weak tea bath, then put them in the oven, set on low. It wasn't exactly a Food Channel recipe, but it worked. I'd shuffled them over and over until the cards took on the look and feel of a deck that had been in the family for generations. I held the cards out to Sara.

"Cut these," I said. "Make three piles and then stack them." I pulled back as she reached for the deck, holding them just out of her reach. "It's important that you focus on your question as you do this." I fixed her with a stare as if this were a matter of life and death. Sara nodded solemnly. Her hands shook as she cut the deck and then passed it back to me. Part of my secret was making the other person touch the cards. It made them feel complicit in whatever happened next.

I dealt six of the cards into a Celtic Cross spread on the table between us. The cafeteria wasn't the ideal place for a reading. It was hard to feel a connection to something otherworldly when the smell of greasy industrial sloppy joes and overboiled canned corn hung like a cloud in the air. On the other hand, there was no way I was inviting people back home with me. I'd take the overcrowded café and people's judgment that I was a bit of a weirdo before letting my classmates see our salvaged-from-the-dumpster furniture. No thanks. I may be a fake psychic, but I've got *some* pride.

I tapped the table. "The first card represents you and your question. The one over it is what crosses you — got it?" I waited for her to nod and then lightly touched each of the others with the tip of my finger. "This is the basis of your question, the past, what hangs over you, and the final card is the future."

Sara took a deep breath. "Okay, my question is, what's going to happen with Darren and me?"

I flipped over the first card. The queen of cups. This was going to be easy. That is, if I believed in any of this, which I don't. What no one seemed to realize was I could read the tarot any way I wanted. There was no magic. What I had was my ability to memorize the meanings of the various cards, years of watching my mom, and an ability to spin a story. "This card represents you. This is associated with women who are creative and sensitive."

Sara's forehead wrinkled. "I'm not really creative. I mean, I want to be, but . . ."

"You're in the band," I pointed out.

Her shoulders slumped. "Only because my mom made me. She thinks it'll look good on my college apps."

"I suspect you have a creative side that you haven't fully explored," I offered. "Don't think of it as just the arts. The queen represents creativity — someone who sees things in a new way." Her friend Kesha, who was practically seated in her lap, nodded. Her elaborate African braids bounced up and down.

"You're totally the most creative person in cheer," Kesha said.

"The squad always does ask me to do the posters," Sara admitted.

I fought the urge to sigh. Sara needed to broaden her horizons beyond being a good cheerleader. "There you go," I said, tapping the rest of the deck with confidence on the scarred and chipped table. "Now, the card crossing you is the six of swords. That often means a journey or a separation."

Her eyes grew wide. "Like a breakup?"

Only if you're smart enough to dump his ass.

I shrugged. "Maybe, but it could also be a journey of the mind."

Kesha's forehead wrinkled up like one of those shar-pei dogs. "What does that mean?"

"It means that either Sara or Darren is at a stage where their life could go in a different direction. That they're changing. Evolving."

"What if he changes so much that he doesn't want me anymore?" Sara's voice came out tiny and small. Kesha reached over and squeezed her hand. Sara's lip quivered. "He's going downstate for college in the fall. He says we'll date long distance,

4

but . . ." She was unable to put into words what she knew was coming.

I turned over another card. "This is the seven of cups. It means opportunities and possibilities."

"Is that good?" Sara bit her lower lip.

"It's always good to have options." *Like choosing a guy who doesn't sit with his Neanderthal friends and hold up a sheet of paper with a number rating girls as they walk by in the cafeteria.* "You have choices coming up. You could see who else is out there." I saw her expression and switched my approach. She wasn't interested in advice about who to date. "Or another option is figuring out what changes you could make to your relationship with Darren."

"How can I do that?"

I turned another card. Death. The skeleton held his scythe at the ready. Kesha gasped. "That looks really bad," she said.

They're playing cards, I wanted to say, but I stuffed down the urge to ask if she was afraid of Monopoly or Chutes and Ladders. "The death card isn't bad —"

"Death card?!" Sara's voice cracked.

The effort to keep from rolling my eyes was giving me a headache. "It doesn't mean *death*, not like physical death. It means that there's a change coming. Something moving from one state to another. It can be a really good thing." I flipped the next card. "Ah," I said, and nodded knowingly.

Sara looked down and then back at me. "What does *that* mean?"

"It's called the hanging man."

"Oh Jesus." Kesha's hands twisted in her lap.

"See how he's suspended by his feet?" I pointed to the illustration. "His card represents seeing the world from a different perspective. It's not a bad card."

"I don't get it, Skye. What does that have to do with Darren and me?" Sara was leaning so far forward, her nose was practically on the table.

I smiled and spread my arms. "Don't you see? That card gives you the possible solution."

Sara exchanged glances with Kesha to see if it made more sense to her. Based on Kesha's expression, it didn't.

I sighed. "Tarot isn't about any one card. It's about how they work together. Look at what you have here, what cards *you* drew." It never hurt to remind the person that if they didn't like the outcome, they were partly to blame. "We started with you as a creative person. Then what's opposing you at this point is that Darren is undergoing a journey. That makes sense if he's going away in the fall. Then there are two forces — this card meaning change is coming. That tells me this can't be avoided."

Sara nodded. "I feel like I'm already losing him, and he hasn't even graduated yet."

"I understand," I said. "But how the situation turns out will depend on your ability to make him see you in a fresh way. Maybe change your look, or do something out of character that makes him rethink your role in his life."

"He always wants me to go camping," she mumbled. "It's usually not my kinda thing."

"There you go," I said, pointing at her chest as if she'd just solved a really tricky problem. "Doing stuff outside your comfort zone is *exactly* the kind of thing you should be doing if you want to keep him."

Someone a few aisles over tripped and dropped a tray with a loud crash and the shatter of exploding dishes. A cheer went up from the crowd in the cafeteria. Pain and humiliation is always amusing when it happens to someone else. Other psychics never had to work with these distractions.

"So, if I reinvent myself, then Darren and I will stay together?"

I shrugged. "That's what the cards imply. Not that he needs someone different—just that he needs to *see* you differently." At least I was giving her good advice, regardless of Darren. Everyone benefits from shaking up their routine once in a while.

The corners of Sara's mouth started to turn up. "You know what this means . . ."

Kesha let out a squeal. "Makeover!" The two of them hugged. "We'll go to the mall after school. When he sees you he'll already be planning his first visit home before he even leaves." Kesha's face was determined. The woman was on a retail quest to help her bestie.

"There's another way you could read the cards," I said, kicking myself for not just leaving it alone. "Your card is creativity and strength. You could also see this situation as change is inevitable, but you'll be fine no matter what Darren does. That you have the inner strength to move forward in a new direction on your own."

Her mouth pinched. "But there's still a chance for me to work things out with him, right?"

I gave up. If she wanted to waste all that energy on a boy, it wasn't my problem. None of their problems were mine. I had plenty of my own. "Sure."

Sara leaned back in her chair as if all of her energy had rushed out like air from a balloon. Now that she had a plan, she was exhausted.

I shuffled the cards back into a tidy stack. I took my time. Sometimes people decided once the cards were out that they might as well ask a few more questions. Fine with me. I charge for each deal, but after a beat I could tell Sara wasn't going to ask anything else. Now that the great Darren mystery had been put to bed, she wasn't interested. She was too busy plotting how to remake herself into Darren's ideal. She could do better, but that wasn't the question she'd asked.

That was always the awkward moment — when it came time for them to pay. I hated asking for the cash. It felt slimy, but not so distasteful that I was willing to do it for free. My mom made it easy with a sign by our door noting that she accepted both cash and PayPal. I cleared my throat and turned my hand palm up.

"Oh, sorry." Sara pulled a ten out of her wallet and slid it over as if she didn't want to touch me. "Thanks, Skye. That was awesome." I shoved the bill into my pocket. She watched me tuck the deck of cards into the small paisley fabric bag I kept them in. "That was pretty cool."

"The gift chose me," I said with a shrug. I didn't point out that the reason she thought I was amazing was because I told her exactly what she wanted to hear. I knew Darren well enough to know he followed his dick around like a dog on a leash. Sara wasn't done crying over him. I'd have bet money on it. No psychic ability required for that prediction.

Sara wasn't some cheerleader cliché. She was on squad, but she was also an honor student. I'd heard she was in AP chemistry and calculus, and she was only a junior. You would think someone that smart wouldn't be so stupid. But they were all like that.

She waved to me over her shoulder as she scurried across to her friends, and I smiled back. Another happy customer. With any luck, a few of those friends would decide they wanted their own readings. They tended to come in clusters.

My stomach rumbled. Even with the ten bucks, I shouldn't make a Subway run. I was still way short of my goal. I should have saved the money, but it wasn't like ten bucks was going to make a huge difference. Screw it. I could already smell that fresh-baked bread.

TWO

The bright spring sun blinded me, and I had to use my hand to shade my face as I searched the parking lot of the school. My best friend, Drew, honked the horn of her polished silver VW convertible Bug as soon as she saw me. I bolted down the front stairs and into the street.

I held up the ten-dollar bill as if it were a golden ticket. "I've got a hankering for processed cheese that only Subway can satisfy." I smiled as I squeezed into the front seat and pointed to her cheek where a tiny smear of blue pastel from art class could just be seen on her dark skin. Drew glanced in the mirror, licked a finger to wipe it off, and then hit the gas.

"Hi-yo, Silver—AWAY," we yelled at the same time. It was a lame joke, but we'd made it ever since Drew got the car as a sixteenth birthday present. We had a million inside jokes dating back to when we first met in third grade.

I didn't have any siblings, but Drew felt like my sister. I liked how she smelled like oil paints and how she left smudges on everything from the charcoal pencils she used. She was irrationally scared of hamsters, but totally fearless when it came to doing a backflip. She actually enjoyed all the old books they made us read in English class, and swore like a sailor when there weren't any adults around. I knew her better than any person on the planet, and she knew me too.

Well, she knew most things.

When the Subway was just barely in sight at the far end of the street, Drew put on her signal and started to slow down. She was a driver's ed instructor's wet dream. She pulled carefully into the lot and parked near the back.

"Did you look through that stuff I sent you on apartment brokers?" Drew asked.

I made a noncommittal noise as I pretended to fish for something in my bag, hoping she'd drop the subject.

She pulled open the door to the restaurant, and the steamy smell of lunch meat wrapped itself around us. "Look, I know you were set on Brooklyn, but everything I've seen makes me certain it will be easier to find someplace reasonable in another part of town."

Drew and I had been planning to move to New York for years. We talked about how we'd weave through the crowds of tourists in Times Square, past the half-price theater ticket booth and the chain restaurants with their neon signs. We'd know which subway lines to take without having to check the map, and there'd be a guy at the corner deli who would save us a copy of the paper on Sunday mornings when we slept in. She'd be in school, and I'd get some kind of cool job — like working at an art gallery or for a fashion magazine. We knew what it would be like to live there, even though neither of us had ever set eyes on New York except for in movies and TV shows.

It had seemed like a harmless dream. Like picking prom dresses out of a magazine when you weren't even dating anyone. Now it was getting real, and that realization made my anxiety ratchet up several notches.

"Queens is an option," Drew added. She started listing the pros and cons of different areas of the city as we waited in line. She didn't need to worry about where she would be living. She'd been accepted to the School of Visual Arts, and her parents had put down a deposit on one of the dorms. I was the one with nowhere to go.

I stared up at the menu board, considering my sandwich options even though I always got the exact same thing. The clerk shoved the various vegetables I pointed at into my roll as I pushed my plastic tray down the line. "I'm sure I'll figure something out." I passed over my hard-earned ten to the cashier. Now I didn't have the money, but I did have a fresh pile of guilt. And one veggie sandwich.

Drew grabbed her sub and, after a pause, a bag of chips. She looked great, but she worried about her weight. "Yeah. But you don't want to wait too long. Finding the right place is going to take some time."

There was no right place. At least not for me. Her family had plenty of money for her to go. I didn't even have enough to cover first month's rent for an apartment. Not even a tiny studio. Hell, not enough for a *shared* tiny studio. I was going to have to tell Drew the truth soon; there was no way I could move with her. At least not this summer. I kept putting off breaking the news, and the longer I did it, the harder it became to tell her.

"Isn't that a great idea?" Drew said. I nodded, even though I hadn't been paying attention. She would keep brainstorming plans to make the move easier, but it wasn't going to happen.

Well, it would happen for Drew. She'd go to New York. I hated the tiny part of myself that resented her for that fact. It wasn't her fault she was who she was, or that our lives had been on different trajectories since we met, but I'd been able to ignore it until now. Now the division was speeding toward us like an out-of-control truck. The truth was graduation was coming, and I'd be the one still living in a small Michigan town trapped between the touristy towns like Traverse and the less desirable cities in the south. The boring middle. A town that could be exchanged for any other small town, with places like the Kwik Klip Hair Salon, where the *K* was a pair of scissors on the sign, and where the bowling alley still did big business on a Saturday night, and the most exotic restaurant in town was the run-down Chinese place. She'd do all the things we talked about, but I wouldn't. I'd be stuck working at the Burger Barn, or at the grocery store, dreaming about a life I'd never have. My stomach was as tight as a drum. I didn't even want my sandwich anymore.

Subway was packed. We grabbed the last empty table next to a group of the people from our school. I hoped their loud discussion of where to eat on prom night, which they were debating as if it were as important as nuclear disarmament, would take Drew's mind off moving.

"I'm still not sure about bringing my car," Drew said. "My dad thinks it's a waste, but then we'd have it if we ever wanted it. What do you think?"

I took a sip of my Diet Coke, letting the carbonation burn through the lies building up in my mouth. "I bet parking in New York is expensive. It may not be worth it to drive."

Lucy Lam turned around. "You can't drive in New York. It's, like, impossible." She tossed her hair over a shoulder. One long dark hair drifted down onto the table, landing on her salad. I considered telling her and then thought, *Screw it*. She'd moved to our school a year ago. Tragically for her, the role of school bitch had already been filled, but she was doing her best to be a skilled understudy for the part.

Drew arched an eyebrow. "So you're a New York traffic expert?"

"I've been there, like, a million times — my aunt lives there, so basically, yeah," Lucy said.

"I thought your aunt lived in Jersey," Paige Bonnet countered from the far end of the table where she sat as the official queen of the popular people. She smirked at Lucy, and the other people at the table exchanged awkward glances. Looked like there was a battle brewing in Popularlandia. I didn't even bother to try and keep up with the politics of who liked whom and who was on the outs anymore. Allegiances in that group changed more often than I changed my socks.

Lucy's nostrils flared. "Yes, she *lives* in New Jersey, but we go into the city all the time."

"You guys are moving to New York, right? In the city, not the 'burbs." Paige looked at Lucy.

Drew nodded. She was beaming as if thrilled that Paige knew about our postgraduation plans. "We're still trying to find an apartment," she explained.

Lucy snorted. "You're *both* moving to New York?"

I swallowed the lump of bread that had expanded in my throat, cutting off oxygen. I should have eaten in the cafeteria.

"Yeah, Skye's going too," Drew said. She sat ramrod straight, as if daring Lucy to push it.

"You planning to go to Columbia?" Lucy asked, the corners of her mouth curling up.

I shook my head. I wasn't university bound, not even community college. I hadn't applied anywhere. It wasn't that I was stupid, and my grades were decent enough, but I didn't have the money to go, and it seemed pointless to take out a loan when I didn't even know what I wanted to do with my life. I had vague ideas about photography or maybe something in social work, but as soon as I tried to picture myself in the future, the image got blurry and faded away. Drew had always known what she wanted. She'd been drawing since we were kids. "I don't have any firm plans right now," I mumbled.

Lucy drew back as if shocked. "What, here I thought you'd tell us you had a full-ride offer from all the Ivy Leagues and an apartment on Fifth Avenue." She smirked. "I know how you love to tell a good story."

Blood rushed to my face. I wanted to drop under the table and disappear. Just when I thought that people had forgotten the past, someone dug it back up. The joys of living in a small town. The bodies of your mistakes rarely stayed buried. They had a tendency to pop up when you least expected them.

"Hey, take it easy. That's not cool," Brandon said, nudging Lucy with his elbow. He smiled at me. His big sister had some kind of special needs, so he was, possibly, the nicest person in our entire school, but having him stick up for me made me want to puke my vegetarian sandwich onto the table.

Lucy tossed her hair again. "I'm *joking*," she said to the group. Ah, the joking defense. The tried-and-true excuse for bullies everywhere. "I just didn't think she'd have the money for someplace like that. You know the city's really expensive, right?"

"Of course she knows," Paige said. "Skye's not an idiot. She's not going to plan to move to New York without knowing what she's getting into."

Lucy's mouth formed a tight line. "It's no big deal to me. I'd just heard that in the past Skye's confused what she *wants* to be true with what *is* true." She turned to Drew. "All I'm saying is you might not have to worry about getting a moving van that fits both of your stuff."

"I'm not worried," Drew said. "I *know* she's coming with me."

"Uh," I said.

Drew whipped out her phone. "I'd trust Skye with my life."

Her fingers flew over the screen and then she slapped it down on the table. "There. I just cancelled my dorm reservation. Now Skye and I will get a place together. Maybe, if your aunt ever lets you stay in the big city, you can come visit. That is unless you need to get back to bridge-and-tunnel Jersey."

Paige laughed, and Brandon high-fived Drew. He turned his raised palm to me, but my hands lay in my lap like dead fish.

My breath came fast and shallow. *Drew hadn't really sent that email, had she?* Maybe she just wanted to make a point. There was a huge waitlist for residence space. If she'd given hers up, she wouldn't have anywhere to live. Her parents were going to kill her. Or me.

"Whatever." Lucy grabbed her giant leather Coach tote from under the table. "We should get going, or we're going to be late." They gathered their stuff and shuffled back to the parking lot. Paige looked over her shoulder at us and waved as she walked away.

Drew was flushed, and her eyes sparkled. She looked almost high. She'd always had a crush on Paige. She'd never pursued her, or any of her other crushes, but she held her out as that un-obtainable beautiful thing. Deep down, I was certain Drew knew Paige wasn't worth her time, but it didn't stop how she felt. She noticed how I was breathing. Her face instantly turned serious. "Hey, take it easy. Are you okay?"

I tried to say something, but my heart was galloping full speed and I couldn't get enough air into my lungs.

"Close your eyes," Drew said, her voice was calm and firm. "You got this. Breathe in through your nose."

As she counted to three, I forced myself to follow her directions, blowing it out a few beats later. She breathed with me, counting softly several more times until I was breathing normally again.

"Better?" Drew patted me on the back.

I nodded. I wasn't even remotely fine, but I had managed to avoid spiraling into a full panic attack, so that was a positive.

"Don't let Lucy get to you. It was bitchy to bring that up." Drew wadded up the sub wrapper into a tight ball. "She didn't even live here when it happened, and she's got no business acting like she's somehow in the know."

I nodded. I didn't care about that at the moment. "You didn't really just send an email to give up your space, did you?"

"No," Drew said.

My lungs filled fully, relief streaming like cool water through every nerve.

She bounced in her hard plastic seat. "I sent my cancellation email last night! That's what I was going to tell you. I told you I had a plan that you would flip over."

Air stuttered in my chest. "Why?" My voice cracked.

Her face grew serious. "Lately you've been weird whenever we talk about New York, and I know why." She patted my arm. "Money's tight. Even with the cushion you've saved, and even if you get a job right away, you'll have a hard time on your own, and I know you hate the idea of living with a stranger. I know I would. What kind of friend would it make me if I left you to handle this solo? This way we can pool our money and afford a better place. With what you've got saved and the money I'll get from my parents, we'll be all set."

She had no idea. How was I going to tell her that I didn't have any cash to pool anything? It wasn't that I hadn't tried to save, but every time I did, something came up. Stuff like late electric bills and a need for shoes that didn't have a hole.

"What are your parents going to say?" I squeezed out.

Drew stood and dumped the trash on her tray into the garbage. "They're going to be pissed, but there isn't a thing they'll be able to do about it now. I don't want to live in a dorm if I can live with you."

Shit. I had to tell her. "Listen, Drew, you can't do this."

"Too late. It's already done." She laughed and tucked her curly hair behind her ears. "The school sent me an email this morning letting me know my spot has been filled. They also sent me a list of possible apartment brokers." She hauled me up from the seat. "We're going to be New Yorkers together!"

THREE

After school I told Drew I had stuff to do and headed to our town library. It was my favorite place on the planet. Built over a hundred years ago, with its granite blocks, scratched wooden floors, and deep-set windows, the library felt solid and permanent. It had a sense of peace, like a church without the religion.

My chosen spot was the reference room in the very back of the second floor. It was poorly lit and dusty, but it was almost always empty, and there was a cracked dark green leather bench on the back wall, perfect for curling up. I would lie there for hours reading, pretending it was my living room, until the librarian announced they were closing for the night by flashing the lights on and off.

My hand ran over the shelf, stopping at the spine of one of the outdated World Books. The letter *L*. I paused and then instead I pulled the giant maroon map book from the shelf below onto the worn table and flipped to the map of Manhattan. I'd looked at it so often I could have drawn a copy with my eyes closed. My fingers traced the roads, up Sixth Avenue to Rockefeller Plaza and Radio City Music Hall, then across to Fifth Avenue, skirting along Central Park and into Harlem, then across the East River and into Queens.

The sound of my finger whispering across the page relaxed me. I closed my eyes and imagined myself there. Our dream apartment would have an exposed brick wall, and we'd know that you couldn't have the light on in the living room and run the blender at the same time or you'd blow a circuit. Our neighbors would speak Cantonese, Spanish, Russian, and some language we couldn't place, but we'd play a made-up drinking game where we had to guess the subject of their conversations.

My hand shook. There was no way I could afford to go to New York. It wasn't just coming up with the monthly rent. I'd need a security deposit, plus utilities, cable, food, and everything else required to survive. A minimum-wage waitressing job wasn't going to cut it, and I wasn't qualified to do anything else, no matter how many fancy gallery jobs I dreamed up. I couldn't ask Drew to float me.

I should have told her months ago that it wasn't going to work, but I hadn't wanted to let her down. It was easier to pretend graduation was never going to arrive. When Drew asked,

I'd made up a number for my savings account. I liked that she felt proud of me for saving all that money. I wanted to be the kind of person who had that kind of discipline. There were a lot of times I could almost forget it was a total lie, until my bank statement would come in the mail.

Making big plans almost always turned out badly for me. My destiny was set before I was born. My mom was fifteen when she got pregnant and dropped out of school to have me. Then perhaps to punish me for ruining her life, she named me Candi. With an *i*, no less. You know what you never hear? "Let me introduce you to my neurosurgeon, Dr. Candi Thorn." Or, "All rise for the Honorable Judge Candi Thorn." A parent who names you Candi is setting you up to be a stripper, or a Walmart greeter complete with a wrinkled blue uniform vest festooned with various smiley-face buttons and flag pins. Or a lifer waitress at the Burger Barn. I had to go by my middle name, which was still pretty hippie dippy, but *Skye* is light years better than Candi.

When Drew and I became friends, I realized that there was this completely different world possible. At her house there were matching dishes, and their glasses weren't collectibles from some gas station promotion. The heat was never off because the bill hadn't been paid, and their fridge wasn't full of ketchup packages stolen from McDonald's. It wasn't that I didn't know people lived like Drew, but I'd never seen it up close. I knew that was what I wanted. I would become the kind of person who traveled, who went to art galleries and knew people who talked about real things like politics and books.

I wanted to be the kind of person who moved to New York.

But as much as I wanted life to be a certain way, wishing doesn't make things happen. For years I tried wishing my mom into a better job. Or there was the disaster of when I tried to fix her up with my fourth grade gym teacher so they could get married. That ended with the whole school witnessing my mom screaming at him in the parking lot.

Then there was the lie about my dad . . .

I sat in the corner of the bench and pulled my legs up. One reason for wanting to move to New York was to be in a city where every single person I came across hadn't been a part of the most humiliating experience of my life. I don't remember when I started lying about my dad. Early. First or second grade. And I didn't set out to lie as much as I wished the truth — that my dad was a car mechanic who dumped my mom as soon as he found out she was pregnant with me — weren't real.

My mom had always been honest: *I picked a real loser when I picked your father.* I used to wish that she'd told me he was dead instead of AWOL. It seemed better to have a dead dad than one who was very much alive and working at a garage three towns over but had no interest in my life.

So I made up a dad. He was in the military. That explained his long absence from home and why he and my mom divorced. She couldn't bear him being in harm's way. Deployment is so hard on those left behind. His job made me a bit more noble too, gave me a whiff of respectability that my mom's job at the grocery store didn't convey. I was the daughter of a real live American hero. The kind of guy other people thanked for their service. And I might have gotten away with that lie. A distant dad, gone from my life not because he couldn't be bothered, but because he was called to a higher purpose — protecting America.

Then in eighth grade I pushed my luck. I told people my dad had been injured. I can't remember what made me add to the lie. To embroider the story with a roadside bomb, VA hospitals, and countless surgeries. Maybe the original story had become dull. Or people wondered why he never seemed to get leave to visit and I thought I needed to create a reason. But my lie went a step too far. Instead of merely keeping people from asking too many questions, it made people feel bad for me. To want to *do* something.

Without telling me, Drew got the ball rolling when she asked her parents if they would let her take money out of her savings account so I could fly to the veterans hospital in Washington, DC, to visit my dad. Her parents told people at their church, and suddenly the thing spiraled out of control. Weeks later there was an all-school assembly with my mom invited for a big surprise. The mayor of our town was there. A representative from the Rotary Club presented me with a check in front of everyone. Enough cash so I could travel to Washington with my mom. There was talk of the excess money going toward an accessible home for my poor amputated-legs dad. It was a great example of a town pulling together. A bunch of people were crying and waving these tiny American flags the local Walmart had donated for the event. It would have been amazing — made for TV — except for the part where I'd made him up. I'd just stood on the stage and wished for a meteor to strike me dead while my mom looked around confused, trying to figure out what the hell everyone was talking about.

I still remember Drew's face when she realized I'd lied. She was with her parents, all dressed up for the occasion, and her face collapsed. Her response hurt almost as bad as the pitying looks from everyone else and the hushed snickers. The money had to be returned. No more big giant cardboard checks for me. I had to stand there next to my mom as she explained the truth. I knew, even at thirteen, that no one was ever going to let me forget this.

I did get a few things out of the situation, even if there was no dad or trip to our nation's capital. I got a standing appointment with a counselor to get at the root of my "issues," and the development of a full-blown anxiety disorder complete with panic attacks.

Drew forgave me. I felt bad that she'd tried to do this amazing thing for me and I'd ruined it. She felt bad that her plan had blown up so publicly in my face. Or maybe she felt bad because my life was so messed up that I had to make up an entire parent. Either way, we never talked about it much after that. We moved on. But I knew she never forgot.

I wasn't sure we'd move on from this. If Drew discovered I'd lied again, she wouldn't forgive quite so easily. She might finally decide she'd had enough.

Or maybe I'd had enough. Maybe the only way to make the life I'd been wishing for a reality was to do something big. If destiny was going to try and keep me here, I was going to have to do something bold to change it.

I jumped up and crossed the room with jerky steps to the set of World Book Encyclopedias, pulling out the *L* volume with a shaking hand. I flipped through, and the typed note was tucked in between the pages describing the Lindbergh kidnapping.

ARE YOU IN? Y or N?

My pen hovered above the page for just a split second and then I circled Y. I slammed the book's cover shut and put it back on the shelf. One step closer to my new life.

FOUR

Regret, unlike satisfaction, isn't hard to get. And by the time I got out of bed the next morning, I knew that I'd made a huge mistake. I'd tossed and turned all night, the sheets twisting tightly around me. There was no way I could go through with this. The fact of what I'd done filled my guts with wet, heavy cement. I wasn't the kind of person who would do anything to get what I wanted. Or at the very least, I didn't want to be the kind of person who would sink this low.

As soon as I was out of the apartment, I looked over my shoulder to make sure no one was around the bus stop and then whispered into the phone when he picked up. "I've been thinking. I'm not sure I want to be mixed up with this. I can't do it." I held my breath, waiting for the reaction.

He was silent for a beat. "Are you kidding me?"

"You don't need to worry. I won't tell anyone. You do whatever you need to, but I don't want to be involved." My tight chest loosened.

He barked out a laugh, shattering my fragile sense of relief. "That's a shame, because you're already involved. It's too late to back out. Things are already in motion. If I were you, I'd make sure I had an alibi for tonight."

I stared down at the phone. He'd already clicked off. I was screwed.

FIVE

Four days after I left the note at the library, I trudged through the lobby of my apartment building after my double shift at the Burger Barn. The stench of bacon grease and burnt coffee had soaked into my clothes and hair. The lack of sleep over the past few days was catching up, my eyes were gritty, and my legs felt as if they were tied down with weights.

The back wall of our lobby is covered in 1970s gold-flecked mirrored tiles, and there's a sofa covered in some kind of moisture-resistant fabric. The whole apartment building has a worn, past-its-"best-by"-date look. I yanked open the creaky fire door that led to the hall and waved to the closed door of apartment 103 as I went past. Rumor has it Ms. Kowlowski sits on a kitchen stool in her daisy housecoat and slippers looking out her peephole and keeping track of who comes and goes all day long. I guess everyone has to have a hobby.

If I were struck blind, I'd know I was home by the smell. Our apartment building was a toxic mix of moldering hall carpet, the curry Ms. Baskhi cooks in her apartment, stale laundry stink wafting up from the basement, and my mom's addiction to Febreze. Mom is convinced there is no problem that Febreze can't solve. It's like a magical fairy dust that she sprays on anything that doesn't actively move away from her. We might have had a sofa we found out by the dumpster, mostly no-name brands in our cupboards, and closets full of clothes that other people didn't want, but dammit, our place smelled like a fresh-rain-soaked lavender field in Southern France.

I heard the TV before I even unlocked our apartment door. My mom likes the volume loud enough that you can practically see the sound waves as they move through the room.

"Skye, you have to watch this." Mom waved wildly for me to join her. She was still wearing her uniform smock from the Stop and Shop. She must have gotten her nails done on the way home. They were a bright red with a crystal embedded in the thick polish at the tip. My mom lives to BeDazzle everything.

I dropped onto the sofa and tried to figure out what had caught her attention. *Ghost Hunters*, I guessed, based on the night vision shots with people faux whispering, *"Did you hear that?!"* every two seconds.

"See the guy on the left, the one with the thick glasses? He can feel the vibrations of the dead." Mom chewed a wad of mint gum with her mouth open. My mom sees dead people. And angels. And auras. She believes in aliens, fairies, the Loch Ness monster, Bigfoot, and in all those online scams that promise you millions of dollars if you simply click "like" and post a picture of a stack of money on your wall. I used to think it was cool that she saw magic in everything. Then I grew to hate it. Then I hated that it bothered me even more.

"Wow," I said in a flat voice.

She glanced over, scowling. "If you could be bothered to watch, you'd see it's true. He predicted a child died in that house, like, a hundred years ago, and when they researched it — he was right." She pointed at me with one shiny fingernail like she'd made a critical point.

I sighed. It never once occurred to her that the show might actually lie.

"I think I have a bit of that ability too. It's more than psychic readings: it's a sense of those who have been lost." Mom sipped loudly from a can of cola. "There are times when I'm in a place and I can almost feel a humming in my skin, like electricity. They were saying human spirits are basically made up of energy, so that would explain it."

I barely managed to avoid rolling my eyes. "You don't *feel* ghosts," I said, stealing one of the stale Chips Ahoy cookies from the bag in front of her on the coffee table. I had to nip this in the bud or she'd spend the next two weeks wandering around making up stories about the dead people she saw every place we went. It would be like the time she had to wear sunglasses all day and night because the brightness of people's auras was blinding her. She'd fallen down the stairs to the basement because it was so dark she hadn't seen that our neighbor had left his laundry basket outside his door. She'd sprained her wrist on that adventure and had to take a week off of work. Unpaid.

It was bad enough that my mom was convinced she was a psychic. I'd grown up with her reading tarot cards in our living room to people who never seemed to wonder why, if she was capable of seeing the future, she didn't make some investments that would lead to us living better. If she'd picked Apple stock years ago, we'd be living in a mansion by now.

Mom leaned back, pouting. "Oh, and you know everything, I suppose. Just because you treat psychic readings like a joke doesn't mean everyone does." The first time my mom found my tarot cards, she'd been thrilled. She thought it was great we could have this in common. Once I convinced her it was nothing more than a scam, she was appalled. She felt I was courting "dark forces" by pretending. At least I admitted I was pretending. My mom actually *believed* she had some kind of special abilities. I wasn't sure which was worse — to know you were a liar or to believe your own bullshit.

"I don't know everything, but I know no one has ever scientifically proven psychic skills," I said.

"Of course it doesn't work with all that negativity and skepticism." Mom waved off my logic. "There has to be a supportive atmosphere."

"Reality doesn't require emotional support," I pointed out. "It just is. You don't see gravity asking for validation."

"You'll see; they have a scientist interviewing him in the next section." She crossed her arms over her chest.

I was willing to bet that any scientist on this show had obtained his degree from a school he'd found advertised in the back pages of a comic book.

The program broke for a commercial for our local news. "Tonight we'll be bringing you some breaking news—"

Mom rummaged through the pilled crocheted afghan looking for the remote. "You want to watch a movie after this?"

The picture on the screen stopped my heart. I grabbed her hand to keep her from clicking it off. *Oh shit.* This was it. No more theory. This was really happening.

"The Bonnet family has filed a missing person report on their seventeen-year-old daughter, Paige. Paige hasn't been seen since Thursday, when she didn't return home from her classes at Pine Hill High School." The anchorwoman's face attempted to fight through the Botox filler to look concerned.

"Do you know her?"

"Shhh." I waved off whatever she was going to say so I could listen.

"Judge Bonnet's daughter has run away in the past. While police don't believe Ms. Bonnet is at any risk, they, along with her family, would like her found as soon as possible to confirm her safety. Police are asking that if anyone has information about Paige Bonnet, or her whereabouts, to call the hotline number below. Stay tuned to tonight's broadcast for any developing leads."

"She's pretty. Is she in your class?" Mom leaned closer to

the screen, inspecting Paige's picture before it turned to another commercial for laminate flooring.

"Yeah, I don't really know her." I tried to swallow, but all the saliva in my mouth had evaporated. Paige was really gone. I knew exactly what happened to her. However, I wasn't going to be calling any hotlines. *Oh god, what had I done?*

Mom rubbed her temples as if she were trying to pull a message from the air. "I have this bad feeling that someone did something to her."

"You don't have a feeling," I snapped. I jumped off the sofa. I couldn't stand to be in the living room anymore. The air felt too hot and close.

Mom's eyes widened. "I didn't mean to upset you, it was just a flash, like a vision. It might not mean anything. You know how these things come to me."

"It wasn't a flash of anything." I grabbed the remote off the cushion next to her and jabbed the button so the TV clicked off. I didn't want Paige's face to pop up on the screen again like some kind of freaky missing-girl jack-in-the-box. "You shouldn't talk about things you know nothing about."

Mom grabbed the remote from my hands. "What in the world is wrong with you?"

"A girl is missing; don't you get that? You making stuff up, or having magical feelings, or wanting to consult the great beyond for advice, doesn't help." I bit off the rest of what I was going to say. It wasn't going to make a difference. What was done was done.

"Seems to me you have a sense something is wrong too."
Mom sniffed dismissively. "Or someone needs to get some more
protein in her diet because she's getting a little cranky." Her
voice came out in a singsong tone.

I stormed out of the living room and slammed my bedroom
door. I'd convinced myself that I wasn't really involved, that I
was more like a bystander, but that wasn't completely true. I'd
known this would happen when I left my answer in that book.
I'd thought waiting was bad, but this was worse.

My heart raced and adrenaline Ping-Ponged around my system. I wanted to pace, but my bedroom was barely large enough
to hold my twin bed and the card table that I used as a desk. *Holy
shit. Paige Bonnet was actually missing.*

I took a few deep breaths in and out. The police were looking for her, but it was clear from the news report that no one
believed anything bad had happened to her. She'd cried wolf
too often, taking off for spring break, running away to stay with
some guy she met on a Christmas ski trip. She might be a judge's
daughter and from the right side of town, but she had a reputation for being a wild child. No one would look for her seriously.
Not yet.

Getting them to do that was my job.

SIX

I shifted in the seat, which had been designed with anything other than the human butt in mind. The waiting area for Mr. Lester's office was all glass. As people streamed by on their way to class, I could tell they were all looking in and wondering what problem brought me there this time. I slunk down in case Drew went by. She'd managed to get an open slot first period, so unless she felt like coming early, she should still be at home tucked into bed.

Mr. Lester and I went way back. All the way to the "dad incident" of grade eight. This morning when I told his secretary I needed an emergency appointment, she looked me up and down with her overtweezed eyebrows arched, trying to tell if I simply wanted to get out of class, or if I really needed help. After a beat, she let out an exhausted sigh and told me to take a seat.

The original plan had been that I would go to the cops, but I'd known from the start that wouldn't work. I hadn't argued because I knew Pluto wouldn't want to be second-guessed. I shifted again in the seat. I was sweating, and the plastic of the chair was making it worse.

Despite what Pluto thought, the cops wouldn't listen to me. My brain stuttered on the name Pluto. I was still trying to get used to it. He'd insisted on fake names. And it wasn't just his name. Pluto had come up with an entire alternate biography — down to his hobbies and hair color. Everything about him was a lie, and it was my job to keep those lies straight, even in my own head. I was to forget everything real and replace it with what Pluto dreamed up so that the two could never be confused. It was probably a good idea. Not that I had any clue — I wasn't exactly a criminal mastermind. What I did know was that while Pluto might be right about names, I was right about the cops.

Mr. Lester was a better choice. First off, he was a huge believer in woo-woo, which meant he'd already be inclined to believe my story. He always talked about signs and trusting your gut. He wore a bracelet made of woven leather and rocks that some shaman gave him when he went to California on a meditation vacation. A man willing to wear magical rocks as an accessory was *exactly* the person I needed to disclose the whole thing to. Secondly, the cops would listen to him when he came forward. They could ignore me, but they wouldn't take the chance with a school official. Lastly, as much as I teased him about his bracelet and motivational posters, he was one of the few people in this town I trusted. He'd help me. Even if he didn't know exactly how he was accomplishing it. I'd volunteered in his office for years, and while I wouldn't say we were friends, he liked me.

Another minute slowly ticked past. "Do you know how much longer he'll be?" I asked Ms. Brew.

She looked up from her ancient computer monitor, mildly shocked to still see me there. I was willing to bet she was surfing some TMZ site and reading diet secrets of Kate Middleton instead of working.

"His phone meeting should be over soon," she said, then resumed ignoring me.

I flicked through the brochures on the table. Support groups for LGBTQ students, info on how to identify addiction, and a helpful top ten list on how to deal with bullies. First bell rang, and the halls emptied out as everyone else hustled to class. A part of me wanted to forget the whole thing and go to history. Once I talked to Mr. L, there would be no going back. If I walked away now, I could avoid being involved any more than I already was.

Not that I was involved, I reminded myself for the thousandth time since I'd seen Paige on TV. If anything, I would help the situation resolve more quickly. There was no point in feeling guilty about it. Paige would be home safe and sound before she knew it. She would have been abducted regardless of what I did. It wasn't like it was my idea — the entire scheme had already been planned, down to the tiniest detail, before I knew a thing about it.

There had been a *spreadsheet*, for crying out loud; it was going ahead with or without me. I just had to do this small thing and then I'd have the money I needed for New York. Drew, and everyone else, would never know I'd lied, and I'd be out of this town forever as soon as the graduation ceremony ended. It would be worth it once it was over. Besides I couldn't go back in time and change anything. Paige would be fine. More than fine. For people like her, everything always turned out.

I rested my palm on my belly and took a deep breath to ensure I was using my diaphragm the way Lester taught me freshman year when my anxiety had been really bad. Lester was always on me to stop imagining the worst. To focus on what really happened, not some worst-case scenario. Paige had disappeared Thursday after school. Now it was Monday morning. Basically four days. That was little more than a long weekend. I crossed and then uncrossed my legs. Paige would be found, there would be a tidy ransom, and then she'd be home. Easy peasy. Depending on how you looked at the situation, it wasn't even really a crime, more like a political statement.

"Skye?"

My head jerked up. From the way Mr. Lester and the secretary were looking at me, I sensed he'd said my name more than once.

"Sorry."

Mr. Lester winked. "The way you were ignoring me made me think you'd decided to go back to calling yourself Candi."

I smiled weakly at his lame joke because that was what was expected.

His face morphed into his somber expression. "You needed to see me right away?"

Deep breath. Showtime. This was my last chance. I could burst into tears and plead panic over looming graduation, let him talk soothingly to me for a half hour and then walk away, or do what I'd promised.

"I need to talk to you about Paige Bonnet."

SEVEN

Mr. Lester's brows furrowed at the mention of Paige's name. "Of course." He stepped to the side so I could go into his office. I'd spent so much time in this space, I knew it like it was an extension of my own home. The back wall was floor-to-ceiling dark IKEA bookcases filled with books and odds and ends like a signed Lions football helmet and a stone Buddha. His desk and a large filing cabinet were tucked into the corner.

He'd replaced the industrial office furniture with two comfortable mismatched wingback chairs that took up the bulk of the space. It was supposed to give you the sense that you were simply having a casual conversation in someone's living room instead of spilling your guts to a school counselor. It worked, too.

There'd been plenty of times I caught myself forgetting that he was paid to be nice to me.

I crossed my legs, and he did the same, mirroring my posture. I did that too when I was doing a reading. It was supposed to make the other person feel more relaxed.

"Would you like some tea?" Mr. Lester nodded toward the bookshelf where he kept his electric kettle. "I've got some of that creamy Earl Grey you like." He tugged on his short red hipster beard as if encouraging it to grow.

"No thanks," I mumbled. I stared down at my hands. I was too queasy to get anything to stay down.

"If you're worried about your volunteer obligation with exams coming up, we can cut back," Mr. Lester offered. He'd arranged for me to work in his office for school service hours years ago. This meant I got free hot lunch without having to volunteer in the cafeteria. The only thing worse than being the kid with no money is having everyone know you're a charity case week after week as you dole out applesauce and extra helpings of undercooked Tater Tots.

I rubbed my hands on my jeans. Instead of looking directly at him, I focused on counting some of the millions of rust-colored freckles on his pale arm. "That's not really what's bugging me."

"You mentioned Paige," Mr. Lester said. "I didn't think you two were friends."

He knew I didn't really know her. Anyone who had met either of us for more than five minutes had to know we didn't hang out. Paige was as likely to be my friend as I was to sprout feathers, fly to New York, and live in the trees in Central Park. "No, we're not friends, but I'm worried about her."

He nodded slowly. "That's understandable. However, there's no reason for people to jump to any conclusions. Paige has a tendency for . . ." He searched for the right word. "Drama. I suspect she's fine, just off on an adventure."

I wondered what Paige would think of the fact that even our school guidance counselor assumed she had taken off on her own. The fact she'd run away last spring break worked against her. She was pretty and privileged. She wasn't the kind to cause any real damage. But she *was* trouble.

I even knew exactly what kind of trouble. I'd looked up Paige's student file. The fact I volunteered in Lester's office meant that I had a unique opportunity to know more about my classmates than they might imagine.

The first time I'd peeked, I'd done it because I wanted to know what was in my own record. I had to see what had been written about the "dad incident." But once I'd read about myself, I'd gone back to Lester's file cabinet to read about other people. I collected tiny details, like the name of someone's dying grandparent, who had an eating disorder, where they hoped to go to school, and any family drama that they dragged with them to school. All of it made my readings a bit more accurate. I knew Mr. Lester would have been disappointed in me if he knew, but I'd never used the info to hurt anyone. And I figured that since my deep dark secret had come out in a school assembly, it was only fair if I knew a part of what they kept hidden.

When the plan for Paige's abduction came together, I pawed through her file looking for information. A few incidents of drinking, shoplifting; she'd skipped a class here or there; an inappropriate relationship with her club lacrosse coach; she'd had a fight in the gym with one of her friends. She got caught breaking into the mini-golf fun park on a dare in grade ten. As the news reported, she ran off to Florida last spring. The cops picked her up at a hotel. She'd been drunk and had to have her stomach pumped. That little tidbit never made the hallway gossip rounds. Lester had written he thought she had issues with wanting her parents' attention and approval. In particular, her dad. Turned out we had that in common. Hers had high expectations; mine was missing in action.

Based on Paige's history, the idea that she might have taken off without telling her parents where she was going seemed completely reasonable. Pluto had guessed right. No one would take the fact she was missing seriously. They wouldn't even suspect she'd been abducted.

Pluto insisted I was needed to make the abduction work, but I didn't see why. There was no reason to believe I was being told the full truth. I certainly wouldn't have told someone else all the details if it had been my idea. It didn't really matter. Everyone had a part to play, and this was mine. The sooner I did it, the sooner I could be done with this. Paige could take care of herself. For once I was going to do what I needed for me.

"What if Paige isn't okay?" I paused. "What if something . . . bad happened to her?"

"Her parents are in touch with the police. I'm certain everything that can be done is being done." Mr. Lester leaned back, giving his beard another yank. "Sometimes it's easier to be upset about something happening to someone else than to admit what might be going on in our own lives." He gave a meaningful pause, complete with another beard pull. It was like his personal whisker safety blanket. "Is it possible that your worry over Paige is because of the uncertainty in your own life? Graduation's coming. Lots of changes ahead."

Great, now he was going all Dr. Freud on me.

"The past couple of nights, I've had what I'd guess you call a vision." I looked into his eyes. "About Paige."

Mr. Lester's bushy eyebrows drew together, like two ginger caterpillars mating above his nose. "Vision?"

"You know that I have . . . I guess you'd call them hunches."

He nodded. I noticed he was leaning slightly forward. The hook was in the water, and he was ready to bite. He'd always wanted to ask me more about my tarot card readings, and I usually avoided or changed the topic.

"I'm not really sure how to describe it — sometimes I just know things." I shrugged like it was no big deal. "It runs in our family. Both my mom and grandma have the same gift."

"Some people think that intuitive ability is a genetic trait, like blue eyes or big feet."

My shoulders relaxed. "So you believe me?" I blinked a few extra times, trying to make sure my eyes were wide and innocent-looking. If I could have worked up a tear, I would have let it hang there for a beat before falling gently to the ground.

"Of course. I think there are a lot of things that we don't

fully understand." He raised a finger. "However, that doesn't mean that if you had a hunch about Paige, it portends anything in particular. Maybe she had a fight with her parents, or was upset about something else, and that's what you sense."

"In my vision, she's screaming."

That shut him up.

"The images are clipped, like a slide show going by too fast." I shook my head as if to clear it.

Mr. Lester took a deep breath. "What have you seen?"

I lowered my voice as if I were about to tell a ghost story over a campfire. "It's Paige. She's crying. I think she's in a car, but I'm not sure. She's scared. I'm sure of that. I can *feel* the terror coming off her. I get the sense someone is making her go somewhere."

"Let's not assume it means anything. It could be a projection of your own stress. In this . . . vision . . . can you tell where she's headed?" His hands were clenched.

I bit my lip. "No. There are flashes of things. Some kind of sign, but I can't read it, a large red barn or maybe a farm, and I see this woman with long blond hair and a huge smile."

He yanked on his beard. He was going to have a bald patch at this rate.

"A woman? Is she in the car with Paige? Is she the one in the back seat? Maybe that's what you're seeing." He was no longer talking about hypotheticals. He may not have wanted to, but part of him believed.

"No." I shook my head. "At least I don't think that's what she means." I grimaced as if trying to force the knowledge out.

46

Mr. Lester grabbed a pad of paper from the shelf behind him. He tore off the first few sheets until he had a clean page. "Okay, tell me anything you saw or felt. We'll make a list."

"Paige doesn't know what to do. She wants someone to help her, but she's alone." I grab my own head to give the scene some action. "They pull her by her hair to make her get out of the car. I think they hit her too. That's when she screams."

Mr. Lester let out a breath. His hand shook slightly as he wrote down each thing I told him into a tidy bullet point list.

"And it makes no sense, but I keep seeing a number. It has a six in it. Maybe a two." I sighed. "That's not exactly right, but I don't know anymore."

He looks up. "Is it like a room number? Like in a hotel, or could it be part of an address?" Mr. Lester leaned forward, ready to Sherlock Holmes the shit out of this problem.

"I'm not sure. It's just the numbers in my head. Over and over. That's it. That's all I saw." I threw up my hands. "I don't even know if it means *anything*. Like you said, it might just be a nightmare, or worries about the end of the school year." I snuck a quick glance at him to see his reaction. It'd been my experience that people were more likely to believe me when I questioned what I was saying. If I did it, then they didn't have to. They would be free to believe. People don't trust others who are too certain. "I told myself it was nothing more than a weird dream, but then it kept happening, and I felt like I had to tell someone, you know?" I let my voice catch, as if I was overcome with emotion. "What if she needs help, and I didn't do anything?"

"You were right to come and share what you experienced."

47

He sat up straighter. "You know you can always talk to me. About anything."

"I thought about going to the police, but they wouldn't believe me." I waved my hands in a limp manner. "I mean, I don't really *know* anything. The cops might assume I was making it up for attention or something." I paused. My past history lay between us. He knew exactly what I was thinking. You make up one injured war vet parent, and no one ever forgets. I needed him to believe me. "Or maybe they'd think the reason I knew anything was because I did something to her."

Mr. Lester patted my hand. He was shifting into action mode. Guidance counselors so rarely get to feel like superheroes. "You leave this with me. I'll talk to some people. Don't worry, I'll make sure everyone knows you weren't involved. If you were, you'd have no reason to come forward. Besides, I know you, kiddo. You'd never hurt anyone."

I blinked away an image of Paige cowering in a basement, tied up and terrified. She wasn't hurt. She was fine. I didn't need to imagine something horrible. I wiped my nose and sniffed. I had an airtight alibi for when she went missing, but I wouldn't mention it now. I'd let that come out later, when people had more questions. "Thanks, Mr. Lester. I appreciate you didn't call me crazy."

He tapped me softly on the tip of my nose. "You're not crazy, Skye. This is likely just a dream, but better to check it out just to be sure."

I stood slowly. "I should get to class. Thanks again for helping."

Mr. Lester beamed. I felt a stab of guilt. I almost wished he wouldn't be so nice. If the truth came out, he'd be disgusted with me.

He scribbled his name on one of the pink late passes and handed it to me. "Of course. That's what I'm here for. I've got it under control."

I paused in the door. "You'll tell me what you find out, won't you?"

"I sure will, Skye."

In the end, I wouldn't need him to tell me. Once the ball got rolling, things happened pretty quickly.

EIGHT

The news that the police had found Paige's car was everywhere by Monday evening. It was parked in the long-term garage at the County Regional Airport. More important, it was also clear that she hadn't gone anywhere willingly. Instead of sleeping, I'd spent most of the night trolling around different social media sites looking at what everyone was saying. Theories were multiplying faster than I could keep up. People decided that a stalker had taken her, or she'd been sold into an underage prostitution ring, and a few were floating the idea that aliens had sucked her into a spaceship. It was easier to read about hypothetical Paige than lie there picturing her tied up, blood crusted on her forehead, her eyes wide with fear.

The next morning a group of Paige's friends clustered together hugging and crying by her locker. No one knew any real details, but that didn't stop anyone from speculating about what happened to her.

I paused by the bulletin board so I could listen in, faking an interest in the notices: a sign up for the senior party being organized by the Parent Action Committee, a flyer for a bake sale fundraiser for the band, and a reminder that if people didn't order their cap and gown by the end of the week, they wouldn't be allowed to participate in graduation.

"I heard the police are sure she was forced out of the car," Lindsey whispered. "Someone took her."

"What was she even doing at the airport?" Lucy shook her head as if she were annoyed.

"Like she told you everything?" Lindsey sniffed. No doubt Lindsey hated Lucy acting like she was the center of this drama, when as Paige's official BFF, that role belonged to her.

"I'm just saying, I thought she was grounded, so she would have gone directly home after school," Lucy explained.

"The kidnappers probably made her drive out there," Lindsey said.

"Are the police totally sure she didn't just take off?" Lucy asked.

Lindsey's nose twitched in annoyance. "The police said there were signs of a struggle, and besides, if she'd taken a flight, there would be a record. No one gets on a plane without picture ID anymore. My mom said because of renovations to the parking lot, the surveillance cameras are disconnected, so there's no way to see what happened."

"How would someone know that?"

Lindsey shrugged. "Anyone who worked at the airport would know, or the construction guys, or even someone who flew a lot likely could have noticed."

"Maybe your mom took her," Dougie Winsor suggested. "Could be she was afraid Paige was going to steal your prom queen title, so she decided to take her out."

His comments lay flat and dead between everyone. I shifted by the bulletin board, taking a step closer to them, not wanting to miss a word.

"That's not remotely funny," Lindsey finally spit, breaking the silence. "Paige is in serious danger, and you're making lame jokes." Her eyes filled with tears, and the other girls closed ranks around her, patting her back, shooting death stares at Dougie.

He held up a hand in surrender. "Hey, I was just trying to lighten shit up. Everyone's so serious."

"It is serious. Maybe you should keep your lame-ass jokes to yourself." Lindsey crossed her arms over her chest. "I can't believe you'd accuse me or my mom of something like that, even as a joke."

"Look," Greyson said, playing the peacemaker, "everyone has to know if something happened to Paige, it's because of her dad."

The crowd nodded. Paige's dad was known as Hanging Bonnet for his harsh way of dealing with people who appeared before him. The judge made the national news for his "shame sentences," where he would make criminals do embarrassing things in public to teach them a lesson. Now they were saying he was a possible Republican candidate for a Senate seat.

"Do you think someone he sent to jail is getting revenge?" Emily asked. She looked nervous, as if she expected a horde of criminals to rush down the hall toward her for merely being Paige's friend. I pretended to copy down the information from a flyer so she wouldn't notice me.

Greyson shrugged. He was on the football team. I could never remember what position he played, but he wasn't exactly known for his problem-solving skills. "I don't know, maybe. I bet her parents are freaking out. She disappeared last Thursday, and it wasn't until yesterday that they found her car. That's a long time for an evil dude to have someone."

Everyone was silent, as if pondering just how many bad things could happen. "Did you see the public plea her family did on TV? Her dad told Paige to stay strong and know that he'll come find her," Lindsey said. Everyone nodded. Anyone who missed it live had seen the clip over and over online. "Her dad even cried. You could see he didn't want to, but he totally teared up. I mean, seriously, *her dad*."

"Whoa."

Dougie snorted and shook his head. "I feel almost bad for the guys who took her. Can you imagine how pissed she must be? Paige can be a real bitch when she's crossed."

Lindsey and her friends glared at him, and he backed up a step. "Geez, all I'm saying is that she can take care of herself."

I coughed, trying to bury a nervous laugh that was about to break free. Lucy spun around and glared at me.

"You have a problem?" she asked.

"No. No problem."

"Then maybe you should move on." Lucy's hands were on her hips. I could picture her fifty years in the future yelling at kids to get off her lawn while wearing her perfectly matched floral Lands' End outfit.

I'd heard everything I needed to know anyway. I might as well go to class.

"That girl creeps me out," Emily said in a loud whisper.

I felt another laugh burbling up. She had no idea. I spun around and slammed right into Drew, making me drop my bag. She grabbed my elbow to keep me from stumbling.

"You okay?" She picked up my bag and handed it back. "What was that all about?"

"Nothing."

Drew watched the group move down the hall. "Did you hear about Paige last night?"

"Um, yeah."

"Weird, huh?" Drew shuddered. "You don't think stuff like that will happen around here."

That was an understatement. Our town was the very definition of boring. Big excitement around here was the opening of deer season. Anyone who was a criminal mastermind had moved on to more exciting pastures. Before this, the only crime in our town was people selling weed or breaking into someone's garage to steal power tools.

I jerked my head at the retreating group of Paige's friends. "Yeah, I overheard those guys saying that it's most likely related to her dad. It's not some random thing." I nudged her with my elbow. "I don't think you have to worry. They'll find her." The last thing I needed was Drew getting sucked into this story. She'd always been fascinated by Paige.

She smiled. "I know. I hope she comes home soon."

I threw my bag back over my shoulder. "She will."

"You sound so certain," she said.

I crossed my fingers. "Call it a hunch."

NINE
Paige

I've been here five whole days. At least I think it's been five days.
The first day was really fuzzy. Since then I've been making a mark
each morning so I don't lose track. Not knowing how much time
has passed makes it worse. Like my real life is less and less real.
I keep pinching the skin just inside my elbow so I feel the pain.

They took my phone. They left me my backpack. I decided I
should start writing things down. It's something I can do. And I
need to do something, because if I don't, I know I'll completely
unravel.

First off—I don't know where "here" is. I'm pretty sure they
drugged me at the airport. I remember struggling with one guy
as he pulled me out of the car, then nothing. I woke up here. My

head hurt so bad, and I was really nauseated. I vomited into the sink, and when I saw the blood, I was afraid something inside me was broken, but when I calmed down, I realized I must have bit my tongue when he hit me.

This place is a cabin. It's like the bunkhouse I stayed in when I went to camp. They only left one blanket on the saggy double bed. A polyester bedspread, like the kind you find at cheap motels. It smells. At first I refused to use it. I got over that pretty quick. It gets cold at night.

All the windows are boarded up, except for a really narrow one near the ceiling. It's way too small to crawl out. I tried for an entire afternoon to pry the boards off the other windows, but they didn't budge. All I managed was to rip a fingernail and bury a bunch of splinters in my hands.

There's what used to be a kitchen, but no fridge, although there's a space where one might have been before. There's a kettle and a hot plate. The cupboards have drifts of dried-out mouse turds in the corners. There's a small bathroom—just a toilet and sink. At least I have electricity. I'd rather have that than heat. I don't think I could handle it if I had to sit in the dark. I leave the light on at night. If the bulb burns out, I don't know what I'll do.

The strangest thing is how silent it is. It's almost like what it must be to be deaf, except I can hear my own heart beating. I started singing out loud just to have some noise. The second day I tried screaming for help. Nothing happened. Not that I expected it to.

If they didn't care if I yelled, it meant there was no one to hear me, but at the same time I couldn't shake the feeling that I'd disappeared into some kind of alternate reality. Someplace where I'm the only person left in the world.

They left me a case of bottled water, along with a loaf of Wonder Bread and a jar of Jif peanut butter. They didn't leave me a knife; they weren't that careless. All I have is a couple plastic spoons.

The first day I tried to figure out what I'd do when the kidnappers came back. I want to be the kind of person who comes up with some kind of plan for when they come in, a way to save myself. But, the truth is I don't know what to do. I tried to fight back at the car, and all it got me was a hard slap across the face.

I always thought I was brave, but now I realize it was only because there was never anything I really needed to be scared of.

If I'm honest I'm less afraid of what they'll do when they come back and more terrified that they won't come back at all. The first couple of days I ate two or three sandwiches, but then I moved to one, and today I had just a half. I started doing the math to figure out how long I can make the food last, but I'm not even sure how much I need to eat to stay alive. Maybe they left just enough food to give me hope, but not enough to survive. I think that's the most horrible part of all of this—not knowing if I should hope or just give up.

◆ ◆ ◆

If this note is found after I'm gone, I want someone to tell my parents that I loved them. Let them know I'm doing everything to keep hoping this will work out. Tell them that I stayed strong. My dad is always saying that—stay strong—it's a Bonnet family motto. I don't know what I can do to get away, but I'm not going to stop trying. Maybe being brave is what happens when you don't have a choice.

Paige

TEN

"Don't be nervous," Mr. Lester said.

Easier said than done. The windowless interrogation room in the police department wasn't exactly set up to make a person feel comfortable. Not that they called it an interrogation room; the tiny plastic plaque outside the door labeled it INTERVIEW ROOM #2. The table and chairs weren't bolted to the floor, but there wasn't a single thing in the room to give it personality or comfort. Nothing on the walls, not even a pro–seat belt or anti-drugs poster. It was painted a flat, industrial, oatmeal beige that looked washed out. There was a long mirror on the side wall that years of watching crime TV had taught me was a two-way mirror. The space felt oppressive, which I guessed was the point.

The door opened, and the detective poked his head in. "Sorry to keep you folks waiting. Skye, we're still trying to reach your mom. You have any other ideas of how we might find her? We've left messages at the places you suggested, but so far we haven't heard anything."

My mom never remembered to charge her phone. She might as well carry around a plastic brick. "Maybe we should just talk without her," I said.

The detective frowned. "We'd prefer to have a parent present. I know you're eighteen, but you're still in high school. What about calling your dad?"

Mr. Lester squirmed in his seat. "Skye's dad isn't involved in her life at this time."

That was an understatement. The last time my dad was involved in my life, I was a fetus. Unless you counted my imaginary father, and I was hoping the police wouldn't connect that ancient story with me.

"It could be a long time until my mom shows up. Mr. Lester's here. I'm okay talking to you as long as he stays." In a perfect world, my mom would keep out of the whole thing. Besides, I wanted this conversation to be over. The longer I sat, the more it seemed as if they would somehow be able to tell I was guilty. Like the stink of what I'd done would leak out of my pores.

Mr. Lester sat a bit straighter, taking on the mantle of parental responsibility. He raised his chin in the air. "I could step in, assuming this isn't any kind of formal statement?"

"No, we're just gathering some information." The Asian

detective wore a suit. There was a tiny brown spot on his white shirt collar. A burn mark from an iron. I focused on that to keep my nerves in line. What did that tell me? I was willing to bet he was single, and while it wasn't important for him to look stylish, he wanted to look professional and in charge. He didn't have the money for dry cleaning, or at least he didn't spend his cash that way. He waved to someone in the hall to join us.

Once the other detective came in, it was snug. If my mom showed up, I'd have to sit on her lap. The first detective opened a notebook. "I'm Detective Chan, and this is Detective Jay. We're overseeing the Paige Bonnet case. The things you told Mr. Lester yesterday were helpful. We wanted to talk to you further to see if we might be able to learn more."

"Sure." I cleared my throat.

"Can I get either of you anything to drink? We got one of those fancy pod machines that pretty much makes up anything —latte, cappuccino, tea?" Detective Jay had a tiny divot in his earlobe. At one point, most likely long before he was a cop, it had been pierced. He was a few years older than Chan, but I was willing to bet light years more fun.

"No, thanks," I said. Mr. Lester also declined.

Detective Chan opened a file and spilled some photos onto the table. There was a shot of a Dairy Queen, the sign out front reading DILLY BARS 2 — 4 — 1! Then a shot of a barn, a couple of cows posing by the fence, and the picture I'd been waiting for.

A large billboard with the giant face of a woman smiling out, her blond hair tossed over a shoulder. She looked like she was about to rupture with joy. WELCOME TO COUNTY REGIONAL AIRPORT! YOUR GATEWAY TO THE WORLD!! Clearly, whoever designed the airport's marketing materials believed if one exclamation point was good, two was better.

"Detective Jay is the one who put your clues together," Detective Chan said.

Jay shrugged. "I'm addicted to the fish and chips at that tiny restaurant right by the airport. The Flying Moose. You ever been there?"

Mr. Lester and I shook our heads.

"You should try it. Friday nights you get the second dinner half off. Anyhoo — yesterday afternoon I was headed out there. I passed the Dairy Queen, then the farm, and when I saw the billboard as I rounded the curve, I thought —" *Bam!* We all jumped in our seats as his hand smacked down on the table. "It just fell into place. It had to be the airport."

"And then you found her car," Mr. Lester said.

Detective Jay nodded. "Here's the interesting thing. They number the spaces there, and when you pay for parking, you have to put in your stall number. Care to guess which stall we found Paige's car in?"

"Something with a six in it," I said. Giving them an idea of the number had been risky. It was a specific detail, but because it was so clear, it would have been hard to ignore. Almost impossible to chalk it up to being lucky. In general, it was better to give vague information, but once in a while you needed a home run. Something that stretched the concept of coincidence. Something that made people believe you.

Detective Jay made a finger gun and shot me to indicate I'd nailed the number with one guess, which struck me as completely inappropriate, given the situation. "Six twenty-four, to be exact."

Mr. Lester gave a low whistle.

"We looked into where you were the night she went missing," Detective Chan said.

"What?" Mr. Lester's mouth dropped open. He looked back and forth between the two detectives as if he expected them to declare they were joking. I kept my face blank. I'd always known they'd check out my story. They'd have been stupid not to. It was far more likely that I was involved in some way than that I was a real psychic. At Pluto's direction, I made sure I worked Thursday night. I dropped a full tray of burgers and milkshakes on purpose. People would remember that. A long list of witnesses who could verify my alibi. Even on the way home, when it was late enough to not matter, I stopped into the 7-Eleven for some gum and collected a receipt, smiling directly into every security camera I saw.

"I thought I'd been clear when we spoke that I was confident Skye wasn't involved in anything," Mr. Lester protested.

"Just standard procedure," Detective Chan assured us, his look telling me he didn't trust me an inch. "Everything checked out. You were working that night. Your boss confirmed it."

My boss, Gerry, must have been thrilled to have the cops visit. He and the dishwasher Ben had a thriving weed distribution business running out of the kitchen of the Burger Barn. In the cooler behind the giant tub of mayo, there was a Doc Martens shoebox full of marijuana measured out in Baggies and rolls of cash. I hoped the sight of the two detectives made him shit his pants. It would have been sweet revenge for all the times he "accidentally" brushed past me behind the counter, his hand lingering on my ass.

Mr. Lester tapped the table with his finger. "I want it to go on the record that while Skye may be forgiving, I find your reaction offensive. Skye didn't have to come forward. If she was involved, what possible reason would she have to share this information?"

Detective Chan shrugged and turned back to me. "It's our understanding that you don't know Paige Bonnet. Is that correct?"

"I guess." I bit my lip, trying to look frightened, which wasn't exactly requiring too much effort. I'd read somewhere that most innocent people are nervous around the police. If you act too calm, it makes them suspect you. I shifted in my seat and looked up at the detective through my bangs. "We go to the same school, and I see her in the halls and around town. Everyone kinda knows Paige, you know?"

"But you two didn't socialize or have any classes together?" Detective Chan pressed.

"Nope. I doubt she knows who I am." I made a self-deprecating smile. "I'm not exactly in her league."

"Remember, no person is better than another," Mr. Lester said, interrupting. "You're as good as anyone else in that school." The rest of us glanced at him and then ignored what he said.

Chan didn't break eye contact. "I'll be checking with people at your school. If you two ever had a fight, or if she bullied you, you'd be better off telling me now."

I shook my head.

Mr. Lester snorted. "I assure you Paige and Skye don't have a history of any sort. Negative or positive. If I'd known she was going to be treated this way, I would have brought her concerns forward anonymously."

Detective Jay waved off Mr. Lester's umbrage. "Detective Chan is just being thorough. Let's focus on Paige and how we can help her. So these images and the number—" Detective Jay pointed to the photographs on the table. His fingernails shone in the light, and I was willing to bet he buffed them. "These details just came to you."

I nodded.

Mr. Lester patted my hand. "As I told you when we spoke yesterday, Skye has always had a gift."

"Tell me more about this gift." Detective Jay leaned forward.

"I get feelings about things, stuff I have no way of knowing about, but I do. I always have." I held his gaze just a beat into being uncomfortable and then went back to staring at my hands. There was a tiny scab on the side of my index finger. I really needed to stop chewing on my fingers. Every few months I would make a stab at growing out my nails, but it never lasted.

"So you know things," Detective Chan said, making finger quotes around the word *know*.

I smiled as if I hadn't noticed his sarcasm. "It's not magic or anything. My mom says lots of people have the same skill, but they don't always realize it. They call them hunches, intuition, or lucky guesses. I wouldn't be surprised if you had a bit of the ability. I bet a lot of police officers do. It could be what made Detective Jay go out to the airport yesterday." Detective Jay nodded thoughtfully. He was a believer; I could smell it on him.

Detective Chan chuckled. His thick dark hair looked almost wet in the overhead light. "He does make some pretty good intuitive leaps. We'll have to start calling him the Psychic Detective." The two cops shared a glance, like a long-term married couple used to teasing each other.

"Nothing years of experience won't teach you too." Detective Jay pushed his sleeves up.

"There's some interesting research being done on psychic phenomena," Mr. Lester added. "I read an article last night by a fellow out of Cornell University who thinks, neuropsychologically, psychic abilities make sense."

"Is that so," Detective Chan said.

"Can you get me a copy of that article?" Detective Jay shot Chan a look. "It's important to keep an open mind. Worst thing for a detective is tunnel vision." He and Lester exchanged emails. Detective Jay was my best bet. I glanced over and realized that Detective Chan was scrutinizing me.

"Have you had any other . . . hunches?" Detective Chan tapped his pen on the pad of paper in front of him. "Anything else you can tell us about Paige?"

"I've been trying. Ever since I heard about her car, I've been freaking out." I wrung my hands. "Do you think she's okay?"

"Hard to know. We've released to the media that there were signs of a struggle and some blood in the car."

I pulled on the hem of my shirt. The room was growing too

hot with all four of us crammed inside. The idea of how the blood got there made me cringe.

"I haven't had any other visions, but I'm pretty sure there were two people involved," I offered. I was about to shift again when I caught myself. I couldn't afford to look too uneasy. Trying to constantly guess how I should come across left me feeling like I was balanced on the tips of my toes every second.

"Can you tell us anything about those two people? Men? Women? Black, white, Hispanic? Age? Shabby or well dressed, anything?" Detective Chan asked.

I shook my head sadly. "I'm sorry. No."

"But knowing there are two of them might help, right?" Mr. Lester pulled on his beard.

"Sure," Detective Chan said. "We'll put out a BOLO for two people with no other description. That should narrow it down."

Detective Jay shot Chan a dirty look. "Of course it helps. At this stage in the investigation, we don't know what will be useful. What's important is that we keep this communication channel open. If you think of anything, Skye, anything at all, you can call me. I'm the lead on this case, and it's my number one priority." He slid his card across the table. There was a number scribbled on the top. He tapped it with his finger. No wedding band. However his ring finger was dented, like he used to wear a ring all the time. "That's my cell. You can reach me anytime if you've got something. It might seem irrelevant, but we still want to know."

As I took the card from his hand, I turned my head to the side. "Your wife recently left you?"

Detective Jay sucked in a breath. Bingo. It wasn't a huge leap. I'd read a lot of cop marriages didn't last. Now it was time to throw in another guess for a big win. "She's with someone else now. It's still hard for you."

Detective Jay's hands shook slightly, and he put them under the table so we couldn't see. I felt bad picking at a clearly sensitive subject, but I needed them to believe I was something special.

"Sorry," I mumbled. I tucked the card into my pocket. "Sometimes things just come into my head." Jay nodded, but I noticed he was careful not to touch me again.

"What can you tell about me?" Chan thrust his hands across the table. Unlike Jay, his hands were slight and smooth, almost like a mannequin's. I lightly touched his palm, then pulled away as if his skin were hot. "You believe Paige is dead. That in the end, if you find her at all, it will be too late."

He didn't jump, but I saw the corner of his mouth twitch. Nailed it. Not that it was a hard guess. Chan was a cynic, and Paige was a missing girl whose car had been found with blood in it. Statistically that didn't bode well.

The door flew open, and my mom stood there, the receptionist a few steps behind. It must have been raining. Her shirt was damp, and her mascara had smudged under her eyes. She looked rumpled, like an irritated homeless woman who would yell at you for not giving her a quarter.

"What's going on?" she demanded. She looked back and forth between me and the cops trying to figure out just how much trouble I'd gotten myself into this time. I knew when they called her that she might show up. What I never knew was how to predict her reaction.

Mr. Lester stood as if he was about to start formal introductions. "I'm Mr. Lester from school. We've spoken on the phone a few times."

Mom crossed her arms over her chest. "My boss told me this was about that missing girl."

Detective Jay also stood. "Sorry. I left a message with your employer when I couldn't reach you. Skye isn't in any kind of trouble. We wanted to ask her more about the premonition she had about her classmate Paige Bonnet."

"She had a premonition?" Mom's eyes sparkled and she stood a bit straighter. "Our family is *very* gifted in connecting with the spiritual plane. I'm not surprised. Candi was always special."

"Skye," both Mr. Lester and I said at the same time. My jaw was tight.

"The real tragedy is that most people aren't willing to listen to advice from beyond this world," Mom said.

Oh shit. She was about to climb up on her "*I'm a magical person and the rest of the world doesn't treat me special*" soapbox.

Detective Jay's arms were wide, like he wanted to give all of us a hug. "I'll admit your daughter is making a believer out of me. Her hunch about Paige has been vital to the investigation. If not for her, we wouldn't have found the car."

"We would have found it eventually." Chan sounded annoyed.

"But time is of the essence in these kinds of cases, isn't it?

What with that poor girl missing." Mom thrust her chin in the air. "Maybe this is something I could help with too."

Oh god. No. I tried to catch my mom's eye so I could mentally scream at her to shut up.

Chan's eyebrows shot up. "You have something you can tell us about the case?" He looked around the table to see if he was the only one who was confused. "You're a psychic too?"

"Oh, of course, our whole family has the ability. Let me try." Mom touched her temples and closed her eyes. "The girl is in great danger. I can see her, but she's surrounded by negative energy. It's all olive green and a dark, almost maroon around her."

"She's in a green and maroon room?" Chan asked, trying to make sense of what she was saying.

Mom's eyes flew open, annoyed. "No, of course not. Those are her aura colors."

Detective Jay nodded, but Chan looked like he was ready to fit my mom for a tinfoil hat. I was clenching my jaw so tightly that I heard it click.

"Can you see what kind of danger she's in? Or anything about where she might be?" Detective Jay picked up his pen, ready to write down whatever words of wisdom spilled from her mouth.

Mom massaged her wrists. "They have her tied up. The rope, or maybe it's some kind of wire, or cord, is cutting into her skin. I can feel it."

"Maybe it's those plastic zip ties," Jay suggested.

Mom's shoulders slumped. "I don't think I can tell you anything more — the connection's lost."

Mr. Lester was gaping at my mom, his mouth open in awe. He'd never seen her in action before. Detective Chan pushed his seat back. "Well, if the connection is lost, we might as well call it a day. Both or either of you need to get in touch if you get any other . . . hunches. Otherwise I'm going to ask you to keep your involvement quiet."

"Of course," I said at the same time that my mom asked, "Why?"

"We typically keep certain details out of the public eye," Detective Chan said. "We don't want to get a bunch of wackos who pretend like they know something when they don't. We want to make sure we can focus on finding Paige."

It might have been my imagination, but he seemed to be staring right at me as he spoke. My heart picked up speed. If he guessed what I was up to, I was dead.

ELEVEN

Mom practically bounced in the driver's seat. "When I woke up today, I knew something special would happen. There were three crows on the telephone line above the parking lot. All in a row, all facing the same way. That's a sign, you know. Birds don't naturally flock that way."

Suddenly she was an avian expert. "Mmm," I mumbled. My mom saw signs in everything. Changes in the weather, which direction the wind blew, dogs howling, bells ringing—you name it. In her reality, coffee grounds on the counter were never just a mess—they were messages from the beyond. It was just a matter of time until she discovered the face of the Virgin Mary in one of her grilled cheese sandwiches.

"Why in the world didn't you tell me about this prediction?"

"I don't know." I rested my head on the passenger-side window.

"This is serious. It's not the kind of thing you should keep hidden." When I didn't answer, she continued, "You're always keeping secrets. You know you can tell me anything."

"I know," I said.

"And you wonder why I snoop." She shook her head. "If you just told me what was going on, I wouldn't be blindsided. Imagine how I felt when I got a call from the police." Her fingers were tapping out a drum beat on the steering wheel. "We should light a candle when we get home and see if the tarot can tell us anything more."

"I don't feel like it." I slouched further in my seat. When had this become an "us" project?

Mom looked over. "That girl is at risk. I think we have an obligation to do what we can."

"I can't *do* anything," I said.

"Don't be silly, Candi. You've already done something. Tell you what, I'll swing through the drive-through at McDonald's and get us some dinner." We were crossing from the west side of town, with its Panera and Starbucks, to the east side, which was full of dollar stores and fast food joints.

"I don't want McDonald's," I said. "That stuff isn't even food."

She snorted. "You used to love it. Remember how you thought you were related to Ronald McDonald when you were little?"

"The key word there is that I *used* to like it. I'm a vegetarian —I've told you a thousand times."

74

Mom waved me off. "I saw you eat a hot dog last week."

"It was a *veggie* dog," I pointed out. The truth was I wasn't a great vegetarian. I did my best to at least avoid beef, pork, or lamb, but chicken was a weakness, and I'd pretty much convinced myself that fish wasn't even really an animal in the same way. I was always able to find an excuse when I wanted something bad enough. My morality was more flexible than I liked to admit.

"You could get a salad, or — oooh, I know, one of those apple pies." She whistled, her mouth a perfect O of Revlon Colorburst Candy Apple red.

"Whatever you call that thing, it isn't a pie. It's fruit paste wrapped up in a fat-and-sugar-coated-cardboard crust."

"Mmmm, now I want one of those too." A truck horn blared as she crossed into the other lane without looking or signaling, our ancient rust-spotted Ford sliding across the wet road with a squeal. I grabbed the armrest in the door. A mud-splattered UPS truck whipped by inches past my side of the car. The bottom of our car scraped against the speed bump as we pulled into McDonald's like we were rogue NASCAR drivers. She glanced over. "You sure you don't want one?"

I crossed my arms over my chest. "Positive."

She paused in front of the buzzing neon menu board, ordering a Big Mac combo meal with a pie for herself. "How 'bout fries? They're vegetables."

The smell of fresh fried food mixed with the scent of rain on pavement wafted through the open window, and my mouth watered at the idea of salt. "Small," I said grudgingly.

She pulled to the window and turned down the radio while we waited.

"I know why you're upset." Mom checked her lipstick in the rearview mirror, adding another spackle-like coat. "You think I don't get it, but I do."

"I'm not upset," I lied.

"Sure you are. You're picking at your fingernails. You always do that when you're worked up about something."

I glanced down and realized that I'd just torn a thin sliver of skin down the side of my thumbnail. I slid my hands under my thighs. I couldn't have my fingers looking bad. Who'd want their tarot cards read by someone who looked like she got a manicure by putting her hands in a paper shredder?

She giggled. "Remember when you were in fourth grade? I put duct tape on your fingers to keep you from tearing them down to bloody stumps. You walked around with tape gloves."

"It wasn't that bad."

"You remember it your way, I'll remember it mine." She wagged her index finger in my face, the crystal chip in her nail polish winking at me.

I felt a flash of annoyance and had to restrain myself from slapping her hand away from me. "You can choose to remember things any way you want, but it doesn't change reality."

She tapped me on the nose. "See, you *are* cranky and upset. Some fries will do you good. You probably got low blood sugar." She leaned out the window into the speaker. "Can you make it a large fry instead?"

I bit my tongue. There was no point telling her what I wanted.

"You're upset because, as much as you try and act like these abilities aren't real, now you're being confronted with the fact that there *is* something to them. Otherwise you never would have gone to the police. In your heart, you know you're special. I've always told you that you have a gift."

"What you always talk about is how *you* have a gift." I slumped down, trying to disappear into the seat.

"Where do you think your ability comes from?" She shook her head like she couldn't believe how thick I was. "I've always had these feelings. I haven't taken it as seriously as I should either. Psychic ability is like any skill; you've got to practice if you want to be good at it."

"You don't need to practice." I watched an empty paper cup skitter across the parking lot in a wind gust. The clouds were starting to break up. The storm was over already. "I had one *tiny* prediction, but the cops can take it from here."

I wanted to kick myself. I should have known my mom wouldn't be able to resist sticking her nose into this. My mom was supposed to be the adult, but at times she was more like an annoying little sister following me around, sneaking through my things, complicating my life.

"How can you say that? The police all but admitted if it weren't for you they wouldn't have found that girl's car. I tell you, I got a hunch. We're going to save her." Mom patted my knee.

I pulled on the seat belt, letting it snap back tighter across my chest. I was going to have to figure out how to manage her. If she wanted to fake psychic ability, that would be one thing, but my mom actually *believed* she had abilities. She would fret and pace about readings she gave people, worried if she'd gotten it right. She used terms like *not wanting to let the universe down*. She never seemed to wonder why the universe had dropped the ball when it came to us.

For me, at first, it was a bit of a joke, something to do at a party. I liked how everyone would gather around with their red Solo cups full of cheap beer and watch, their voices low and respectful. Then people started to ask for readings. There were plenty of people who vouched that I'd known things I shouldn't have, that I'd predicted everything from college acceptances and breakups to meeting someone special. Between good guesses and being able to peek at Lester's files from time to time, I had a pretty impressive rep for what was basically a party trick.

My phone buzzed, and I jumped. I fished it out of my pocket. It was a text from Drew.

U ok? Haven't seen u all day.

I couldn't share the truth with Drew, which meant I didn't want to tell her about it at all if I could avoid it. I typed a response quickly. *Sick. Left school early.*

Drew answered right away. *Sick sick? Or other stuff? Heard u left with Lester. Things ok?*

Shit. I should have known Drew would worry. My panic attacks freaked Drew out. The only thing worse than a panic attack is trying to act like you aren't having one because it upsets your BFF. The last one happened in the middle of the mall in Traverse City. For a second I was certain I was going to drop dead outside of the Sunglass Hut right next to a display of discontinued Ray-Bans, which seemed like a really shitty way to go. Most of the time the techniques Lester taught me, from deep breathing to imagining myself at a beach to calm myself down, worked, but other times the anxiety kicked my ass.

Just cold sick.

U sure? U seem off.

I leaned back in the car seat. Mom was singing with the radio. The Smiths.

Yep. Just cold. Maybe allergies. Lester gave me a ride home. See u tomorrow.

The smell of fried food filled the car as Mom passed the hot, steaming paper bags over to me. "Keep the top folded so everything stays warm until we get home. Then we can bust out some cards." She winked at me. "We're going to find that girl."

She was right. I would find her, but not until it was time.

TWELVE
Paige

The bread's gone, even the heel bit that I throw away at home. I never realized what it meant to be really hungry. I can feel my body beginning to eat itself for energy. Cannibalization at a cellular level. It's exhausting.

I've had nothing but time to think. Just time to realize how many stupid things I've done for attention or to fit in. Now I wonder if I'll have a chance to do things differently. I'm so scared that everyone will remember me the way I was—not the way I planned to be at some point. I was going to be nicer, work harder, all that stuff, and now I may not get to.

I wish I could tell my parents that I'm sorry. This notebook might be the only way I can let them know.

If I get out of this, **When** I get out, I'm going to make it up to my family.

I'm writing all of this down in case I don't get out. In case I die. I know that might happen. Maybe it's even likely. I want my parents to know how sorry I really am. I love you all so much.

Love,

Paige

The kidnappers came back! When the door flew open for a second, it was as if I'd imagined them into reality.

The one guy tossed down this plastic bag from Walmart with underwear, some T-shirts, and a pair of sweatpants inside. The other guy had two other sacks crammed with soap, shampoo, and food. My stomach grumbled, and my mouth watered when I saw the apples. When the guy nodded, I took it as permission, and I snapped up the food like they might take it away. I shoved one of the apples in my mouth. I hardly even chewed.

The tall guy stood by the door while I ate, and the other guy wandered around. They both wore black knit ski masks so I couldn't see their faces. If they're worried about me seeing who they are, that must mean there's a chance they'll let me go—right? But at the same time, the masks made them seem almost not human. Part of me wanted to tear them off so I could see their faces, and another part of me was terrified of what might be under there.

The one guy checked the boards that closed up most of the windows. He touched the scratch marks where I tried to pry them off. He picked up this pad of paper and read what I'd written. I wanted to snatch it out of his hands. The apology on it was for my family. But there was no point. The paper was his, the food was his, the new clothing was his, heck, I'm his. If he wants to read this, he can.

I finally got up the nerve to ask them what they were going to do with me. The short one licked his lips with this thick slug-like tongue and asked me what I wanted him to do. My mouth went completely dry. Everything I was thinking must have shown on my face, because the short guy laughed. A hacking laugh, like "hock, hock, hock." He told me to relax, he wasn't interested. He told me I stunk, and I was embarrassed because I knew it was true and then I was disgusted that I cared what he thought of me. The tall one told him to stop messing around. I get the feeling he's in charge. He told me that it didn't matter what they had planned—it wasn't any of my business. He pushed the bag of clothing closer with his worn Timberland boot and told me to clean myself up.

Then they headed for the door. When I realized they were leaving, I panicked. I'd been frightened when they showed up, and now I didn't want them to go. I couldn't stand the idea of being buried under all that quiet. I leapt up and moved toward them. The short one shoved me back hard. Maybe he thought I was trying to run for it. I stumbled and cracked my tailbone on the floor.

"Please don't go," I begged.

They didn't answer—they just slammed the door behind them. I heard the padlock snap shut, and I was alone again. I'm ashamed to admit that I sat there on the floor and sobbed, tears and snot running down my face.

My dad would tell me that crying is a waste of time and energy. He believes emotion gets in the way of action and that the difference between leaders and followers is the ability to put your emotions in place when you need to. If he was here, he would give me a hug and wipe my face. He'd want me to be strong. He wouldn't waste time crying, so I made myself stop. I made myself focus on what action I could take. Thinking of what to do next kept my mind from wandering off to places I didn't want to think about. I went into the bathroom and washed my face. I pulled out the new clothes and yanked off the tags. The fabric felt cheap and thin.

The underwear they brought me was a six-pack of Jockey for Her. Cotton granny panties in bright colors. I wondered if the fact it was a six-pack meant anything, that they'd set me free by day seven, or if they expected me to wash them, or if they didn't think it would matter after that. I made myself pull each item out of the bag slowly and inspect it. I acted like it was my Christmas stocking, where every item had to be oohed and ahhed over.

I pulled out the tube of Crest Pro-Health and the new toothbrush. I squeezed out a tiny dollop of the sharp mint paste onto my tongue. Then I carefully folded the box down. I put the toothpaste on the shelf in the bathroom next to my new deodorant, toothbrush, and comb. When I reached into the bag again, I realized what else was there—a newspaper. My heart slammed into my ribs.

I laid the paper out on the bed, the sheets rustling. My face stared up at me. Next to my senior picture was a smaller photo of my parents and sister. I devoured the article, tasting each of the words. My family had made a public statement. They were doing everything to find me. They wanted me to know they loved me. My finger traced the letters, turning black with ink, before I began reading the rest. There wasn't much else. The police representative didn't say much, but the paper said there were leads. Witnesses. Someone thought they heard me scream. Someone else was pretty sure they saw me in my car with the two guys in the back. The article didn't say who it was, but there was an "unnamed source" who had led the cops to my car at the airport.

There would be evidence in the car. They'd worn gloves, those thin plastic ones that people who work in delis wear, and knit masks over their heads, but they still must have left <u>something</u> behind. A few stray hairs or some DNA. I needed to have faith the police will do their jobs. I looked down at the picture of my parents.

I haven't had many interactions with the police, but I know my dad. He <u>will</u> find me. I just need to do my part—stay alive until he comes for me.

I know you'll come, Dad. I love you.

But please come soon. I don't know how much more I can take.

THIRTEEN

Judge Bonnet stared across the dining room table. I made sure to hold eye contact. The end of his nose was practically twitching as he searched for a weakness. Like a rabbit hiding from a hawk, I did my best to be very still until his gaze went elsewhere. I was on his turf, and I needed to be careful.

The Bonnet house was decorated like a Pottery Barn catalog, all tasteful neutrals, varied textures, and natural fabrics. Everything looked like it had been carefully placed, even the casually tossed knitted blanket on the sofa. The house wasn't as large as I'd expected—just another McMansion on the west side of town doing its best to be more impressive than it really was—but I still felt nervous to be inside. When I sat in the fancy dining room chair, I almost slid off the slick silk fabric, as if the house and its contents wanted to reject me. I tried to take in as many details as I could in case I needed them, but it was hard to focus. My gaze kept flying around, pulling in the wallpaper pattern, the reflection off the glass-fronted cabinet, the silver bowl in the center of the hutch, but I was unable to settle on any one thing, to put the pieces together to make a picture I could use.

"May I get anyone some iced tea?" Ms. Bonnet offered from the doorway.

"No thank you." Judge Bonnet waved his hand dismissively, and then remembered his manners. "You should feel free to have something of course."

My glance slid over to Paige's mom. Her outfit was perfect, crisp, clean, ironed into sharp pleats. A pink and blue floral shirt with a matching cotton sweater. Talbots, if I had to guess. The only sign of upset was the thick smear of concealer under her eyes, doing its best to hide the dark circles.

I turned back to the judge. He was the one I needed to read. I wasn't going in cold. I wouldn't have to count just on lucky guesses today. Pluto had made certain I had enough inside information to pull this meeting off, but now that I was here, I wasn't completely sure I could do it.

"Pay attention," Pluto had snapped. "The judge isn't a joke. You need to take him as seriously, no, more seriously, than the cops. He'll want to look you in the eye. He thinks that after years on the bench he can tell if someone is lying just by being across from them. You need to be sharp for that meeting. Don't trust him. He may try and suck you in by being nice."

"Great," I'd mumbled.

Pluto smiled, but it didn't reach his eyes. "Don't worry. I'm going to tell you everything you need to play that bastard like a violin."

I looked the judge over to see what else I could glean now that we were actually across from each other. I'd heard and read so much about him, the meeting felt almost anticlimactic. He had on a suit, but the jacket was tossed over a chair and he'd rolled up his shirtsleeves as if he was ready to take some kind of action, like fix a tire, or single-handedly rescue a plane by taking control of the cockpit when the pilot dropped dead. He was fit, like he worked out. He had the body I imagined a military dad might have.

He drummed his fingers on the polished table. That was when I noticed it. Faint, but there, a tinge of yellow. Nicotine stains on his fingers. I'd read an interview with him where he mentioned how he'd quit years ago and talked about the importance of willpower and focusing on health. I also know nicotine stains fade with time. I pressed my lips together to keep from smiling. He was a secret smoker. One of those people who keep a pack hidden in the glove box of their car. Who puff away out of sight and then pop Tic Tacs to mask the smell on their breath. Or maybe he was smoking again because of the stress — either way, I filed away the detail.

Detective Jay and Detective Chan smiled as Ms. Bonnet came back in the room carrying a silver tray with glasses of iced tea, complete with a sliver of lemon balanced on the crushed ice for each of us. It was like I was in *Downton Abbey* all of a sudden. The judge stood quickly and took the tray from her and placed it on the table.

Detective Jay smiled at me. "As you might imagine, the Bonnet family wanted to meet you. We appreciate you coming here with us and answering some of their questions."

"I'm not sure if I can help, but I'm happy to try." I folded my hands into my lap. My throat was dry, but I was certain my hands would shake if I tried to pick up the glass of tea.

"I should start by saying I have zero belief in any kind of psychic whatever," Judge Bonnet said, almost as if he were apologizing. "I asked you here because my wife and I will do anything to get our girl back." His voice caught, and he looked down for a second, then cleared his throat.

I kept my breathing even, forcing myself to count to three with each inhale. The last thing I could afford was a panic attack. I had no interest in meeting Paige's parents, but it would have looked weird if I'd refused. When the cops ask you to help with something, it's pretty much a command performance.

"We want to assure you we've checked out Skye's story." Detective Jay looked down at his notes. "There're no indications that she and your daughter had any kind of interaction. She has an alibi for the date in question. And our interviews with people who know her haven't led us to anything unusual."

"Fair enough, but it's possible that she has some kind of connection to what happened even if she didn't do it herself?" The judge raised his hands. "I'm not trying to accuse anyone, but I am skeptical by nature."

Detective Chan shook his head in agreement. "I understand, sir. I'm skeptical myself."

"But," Detective Jay interrupted, "we've checked out Skye and her mom. They have no connection to Paige or your family.

There are no links to anyone with a criminal history. We've got no motivation for Skye to be involved, and if she were, there's no compelling reason we can identify why she would come forward." Detective Jay glanced at me, then quickly away again. "And to be honest, we don't think Ms. Thorn has capacity to pull this off. To grab your daughter and keep her hidden takes resources and planning. This isn't something a high school kid is able to mastermind. The people behind this have specialized knowledge. The FBI agrees. Whoever is behind this is very likely a pro."

"FBI?" I sat up straighter.

Detective Chan nodded. "There's a chance Paige's been taken out of state. That would make it a federal offense. They're acting as a resource for us and can step in if we need them to."

I smiled like I was happy about the idea of interagency co-operation instead of breaking out in panicked sweat. Pluto had never mentioned that the FBI could be involved. I pinched my thigh under the table. I was an idiot. *Oh Jesus, I was going to end up in jail.*

"How does it work?" Ms. Bonnet leaned forward. "Your visions, I mean." Her giant emerald-cut diamond engagement ring winked in the sunlight from the window as she twisted it around her finger. She'd lost some weight; the ring was loose.

"I'm not sure," I said. "Sometimes I just know things." I had to keep things vague. Details could be checked. But it was hard when people kept pushing, wanting answers. I had to fight against the urge to fill the void, to provide answers that could damn me if I wasn't careful.

"You saw my daughter's abduction," Ms. Bonnet said. "Can't you tell us *anything* else? Any detail may help." Her voice shook.

I frowned. "I want to, but it's not like a TV that I can turn on or off. Sometimes there are clear images, but other times it's fuzzy." I shrugged to show how it was all a mystery to me. "The detectives were the ones who put it all together, that the woman was a billboard picture and what the number meant. They should get the real credit." Praising the cops was important. I needed to keep them on my side. "Sometimes it is easy for me to guess what I'm seeing, and other times it's just a feeling."

"So you don't even know if what you tell us is useful," Judge Bonnet said.

"No." I said it simply with no apology. My answer took him off-guard. He'd expected excuses.

Ms. Bonnet reached into a drawer on the base of the china cabinet and pulled out a tiny, formerly white, stuffed bunny. The fabric on its ears was worn to a shiny pale gray texture. She also held a necklace, a tiny sapphire pendant, that swung back and forth above the table on a fine gold chain. "You told us to have a few things of hers for you to look at."

"Thanks." I reached for the bunny first. "It might not help, but sometimes having something that belonged to a person is useful."

Paige's mom nodded. She gestured to the stuffed animal. "She's had that thing since —"

"It's better if you don't tell me," I said, cutting her off. "That way anything I say isn't influenced by information you gave me."

Her mouth closed quickly. I held the bunny and let my gaze turn soft and unfocused.

I snapped my eyes open. "The bunny has a name — it starts with a vowel." I frowned. "An *A*, I think," I said. "No wait, an *E*."

Her mom gasped. "Elliot. She calls him Elliot."

I nodded as if I wasn't surprised, which I wasn't. Pluto had told me the rabbit's name. "She was really sick once, when she was young. She was in a hospital, but I don't have the sense it was an accident." I cocked my head to the side. "It wasn't anything serious, nothing like cancer. She had this toy with her."

Paige's mom covered her mouth with both hands, her ballerina pink polish glinting in the light from the large windows.

"She had her tonsils out," Judge Bonnet said. "She was five or six at the time, but she was brave as buttons." His Superman chin was thrust out like he was grinding his teeth. "Our family knows to stay strong when they're scared."

"She'd never been away from family before — she was just so young," Ms. Bonnet said, looking around the dining room table at the rest of us. Her lower lip quivered. "We got her the bunny to keep her company. She hasn't held on to any of her other stuffed animals, but this one's still on her bed. Her sister teases her about Elliot all the time."

Detective Jay regarded me, impressed. He should have been, but not because I was psychic, rather because of how many things I had to commit to memory to pull this trick off. Pluto had sent me lists of possible objects Paige's parents might bring out. I had no idea what they would actually pick, but Elliot the bunny had been one of the first things I'd memorized.

I wasn't as lucky with the other item. I'd told Paige's parents to select things Paige kept close to her. I'd counted on them picking some item of jewelry. I'd guessed they would choose the pearl ring Paige had inherited from her grandma, not some pendant that hadn't even been on the list.

I'd have to go more general. Use other information I had, to distract from the fact I didn't have a clue about this particular necklace. The room was silent while I let the chain puddle in the palm of my hand, the cool metal links warming to my body temp. There was a chance it was a ringer item. Something that didn't belong to Paige that was being used to see if they could suss out if I was lying, but I didn't think so. Her parents were entirely too interested.

"I get the sense that she wore this a lot." I let the necklace pour from one hand to the other. Now to connect it to something I didn't have to guess. "There's an image of all of you traveling. Italy, I think." I could see the judge wanting to chalk that one up to random chance, but he shifted in his seat with discomfort. It unnerved him that I'd guessed the country correctly.

"I'm not trying to insult you, but she probably told everyone in school about where we went," he said.

"Was there some kind of accident on that trip?"

Paige's mom's face screwed up in confusion. Powder had settled into the fine lines by her eyes, making her look older. "Accident? I don't think so." She turned to the judge. "Donald?"

"There wasn't any accident," he confirmed. "I think you must be getting crossed signals." He leaned back.

I stared at the wall with intensity, as if I were trying to look through the plaster at something a long distance away. "There was water, a sense of falling."

Ms. Bonnet laughed. "Oh my god, I know what you mean. When you said accident, I thought you were talking about with a car or something. Do you remember, Donald? You tripped into that fountain in Rome and came up spitting and spouting water. Everyone was laughing, but you were so mad."

The judge looked annoyed. "Of course I remember. In case you forgot, it ruined my Nikon camera."

She wiped the smile off her face, but you could see it hiding there, under the skin.

"Did Paige get the necklace on the trip?" Detective Chan asked.

The Bonnets shook their heads in tandem. "No. It was a gift on her thirteenth birthday. My family always believed a young lady should get her first piece of real jewelry at that age, something you'll have forever," Ms. Bonnet said. I nodded like it made sense to me, as if everyone I knew also got expensive keepsakes for birthdays, destined to be treasured for a lifetime.

I can't even remember what I got for my thirteenth birthday, but if I had to guess, I'd say it was a board game my mom picked up at a garage sale — it didn't even have all the pieces.

"I can't even recall if she had the necklace with her on the trip." Judge Bonnet stroked his chin as he thought. "I wouldn't have wanted her to lose it. The girl can barely keep track of her own head half the time, and that's attached. All I needed was for her to leave a thousand-dollar pendant in some Italian hotel bathroom."

There was an awkward pause, and he flushed, the red creeping up from the collar of his starched shirt. I wanted to wag my finger in his face. Tacky, tacky, criticizing your missing kid. "I have no idea if she had the necklace with her or not, just that an

93

image of Italy comes through when I touch it." I said. "I sense the trip was important to her." Let them come up with some reason the items were linked. All they would remember is that I knew about the fountain accident. The fact I didn't know about the necklace would be forgotten. I cocked my head to the side like a dog hearing one of those supersonic whistles. "She felt connected to Italy. She wanted to live there."

That was the final straw. Ms. Bonnet began crying. "She did! She always said that." The judge reached over and took her hand into his giant fleshy grip. "We always teased her about it, how she must have lived there in another life. And after that murder case last year, that high school girl who everyone thought killed her best friend? She was obsessed with going again."

Judge Bonnet was pale. He didn't want to believe me, but he didn't know how to explain what I knew.

"Are you connected to her now?" Ms. Bonnet asked, leaning forward. "Have they hurt her?" She swallowed hard.

Judge Bonnet squeezed her hand again and then covered his face. "She must be so very scared. She tries to be brave, but she's actually a very sensitive young woman."

Ms. Bonnet was now the one to comfort him, placing her arm around his shoulder. "Paige was always a daddy's girl. Neither of us has been able to sleep not knowing if she's okay."

I shook my head. "I'm certain she's alive. Scared and frightened, but she's okay." I had to turn away from her mom. I couldn't face how upset she looked. The back wall of the dining room was full of framed pictures of the family. Paige stared back at me from one of the photos as if judging my performance. My throat tightened.

"Oh, thank god she's safe." She wrapped her arms around herself as if it was cold.

"Why did they take her?" Detective Chan asked.

"I don't know." I shrugged. "I have no sense of the kidnappers. Why they did it, or even where they are now, is a big blank." I wanted to end the meeting, but I needed to put the final nail in the coffin. Something that would make the judge certain he couldn't afford to ignore me. I turned to him. "I have this image of Paige worrying about you. Her giving you a hard time about something. Smoking, I think."

His already pale face turned a whiter shade.

"But Donald doesn't smoke." Ms. Bonnet looked confused. "He hasn't for years. Paige would have been a toddler when he gave it up."

His Adam's apple bounced up and down in his throat. Busted. Detective Chan noticed it too. He glanced down at the judge's hands.

"It probably doesn't mean anything." I let him off the hook. He'd know it was accurate, that's all that mattered. He was the one I needed to convince.

"We're going to need you to come back to the station to look at the list we asked you to draw up of anyone who might have cause to do you harm," Detective Chan said. "We've pulled the records of people you've sentenced over the years."

"Oh god," Ms. Bonnet mumbled. "If one of those monsters has our baby —"

The judge sniffed. "I know my work has a cost, but I never dreamed my family would pay the price for my service. If something happens to my baby girl . . ." He shook his head rapidly, like a dog shaking off after a bath.

"I wish someone would just ask for money, then we could just pay it and get our little girl back." Ms. Bonnet started crying again.

I blinked, watching her fall apart, but it felt like it was happening at a distance. My skin prickled, each nerve twitching. Of course there was a ransom request. That was part of the plan — heck, it was the entire *point* of the plan. Pluto would have asked for the money by now. Yesterday at the latest. If he didn't, he would have reached out to me. This was supposed to be ending soon. I'd assumed part of the reason the cops had brought me in today was to try and figure out if Paige was still alive before the cash was handed over, but I was pretty sure they weren't playacting for my benefit — they had no idea that there was a ransom.

Judge Bonnet didn't meet my eyes. My internal antennae went on alert as I studied his face. If he knew about the ransom request, why hadn't he told his wife or the cops? Why would he keep it a secret? The hair on the back of my neck stood up.

Jay leaned forward. "Don't worry. We've got the full support of the FBI on this case. We can pull them in if needed, but the most important thing is Paige's safety. Everyone in the department has her as the top priority."

"It's also possible that some other random nutjob will ask for money to take advantage of the situation," the judge pointed out. "Someone could see the story on TV and try and figure out what they could gain."

Ms. Bonnet shook her head sadly. "Who would do something that sick?"

"Lots of sick people out there." Detective Chan tapped his pen on the blank pad of paper he'd brought with him. The faint *thwack, thwack, thwack* was driving me crazy.

I wanted to tell them that the ransom was legit. I could have a vision about it. I realized I was sitting at the edge of my seat and forced myself to ease back. I shouldn't look too invested in the money. Getting the payout wasn't my responsibility. That was Pluto's job.

"I'll do whatever it takes to bring my girl home." The judge surveyed the table as if he expected one of us to argue with him. "Anything. I'll have my people arrange a few more media opportunities. We need to make sure we keep this front and center in the news, in case someone knows something. You never know when someone might choose to come forward with information if their memory is jogged. I want to meet again with the FBI reps; if we need more federal support, I want it brought in as soon as possible, but I also don't want this to be a case of too many cooks in the kitchen and no one running the show."

I mentally scrambled to figure out if there was any way I could bring up ransom. He had to know about it. Maybe he was afraid that if he told the police or his family, they would somehow screw it up. He was the kind of guy who thought he was the only real genius in the room. Maybe he wanted to handle the situation by himself.

Jesus, what if he went all Rambo and tried to capture the kidnappers on his own? He probably had a handgun. He seemed like the NRA type who might have illusions that he was some kind of action hero with a well-oiled 9mm hidden in his desk. Maybe he thought he was Liam Neeson.

I swallowed hard. Guns would be bad. Real bad. This was supposed to happen without any trouble. My heart raced, and I refused to let myself consider all the ways it could go south. Imagining disaster wasn't going to help. The Bonnets had the money to pay. The ransom was stupid low just so it would be easy for them to come up with the money. I had the sense that the walls were creeping in. The smell of lemon Pledge furniture polish mixed with Ms. Bonnet's perfume was giving me a headache.

Ms. Bonnet hugged me when we stood to leave. "Thank you," she said softly. "Talking to you made me feel better." She wiped her eye with a linen handkerchief. "Closer to Paige. Even for just a second." She squeezed my hand.

Guilt poured over my heart like a layer of thick, sticky tar. "She'll be home soon," I said. The only problem was I wasn't sure if I was trying to make her feel better or myself.

FOURTEEN

The detectives drove me back to the station from the Bonnets'. I cringed when I saw my mom in the waiting area. She hadn't been invited to the house, but it didn't stop her from getting as close as she could. After being with Ms. Bonnet, I was struck by the contrast between them. My mom's clothes were pilled and baggy. One wash, and they were already giving up the battle to stay together. It was like the atoms in her clothing were less cohesive than Ms. Bonnet's. Ms. Bonnet had done her makeup so she didn't look like she was wearing any. My mom's makeup was too heavy, and you could see where her hair color was growing out. I was torn between wanting to defend her and wishing I could walk past her like I didn't know her. The fact that she embarrassed me made me hate myself.

My mom smiled when she saw us and came over. "How did it go?"

"Fine."

"Were you able to tell them anything?" She glanced at the officers. "If you want me to try too, just let me know. Skye's new at this. I've done readings for years."

"Mom, it's time to go." I took her elbow and tried to direct her to the door, but her feet were glued to the floor.

She drew out a business card. There was block print on the front: PSYCHIC SOLUTIONS and our phone number. My face flushed red-hot. They were made out of cheap paper too, from a copy center. You could see the tiny perforations where they had been punched out from a larger sheet. They would fall apart in your pocket or wallet in no time.

Mom passed cards to each of the detectives. "You can call us for anything. There might be other cases where we can help."

"You guys are in business?" Detective Jay's eyebrows went up.

I shook my head no when my mom answered, "Yes, but we'd give the police a discounted rate. We want to be helpful."

"We'll keep this close by." Detective Chan tucked the card into his jacket pocket. "You never know when you might need some extra help," he said with a tight smile.

"Exactly." Mom finally let me drag her out into the parking lot. Once outside, she practically skipped back toward our car. "I had the cards made up this afternoon," she said. "I got a couple hundred. You can have some too." She was like a kid at Christmas.

The smell of hot asphalt and exhaust filled my head. I thought

I might get sick. "We're not going into business together." I spoke slowly in case the spring heat had melted her brain.

Mom pouted. "I knew you'd have a bad attitude. You hate to be wrong."

"About what?"

She crossed her arms over her chest. "You always made fun of psychic abilities, but it's not a joke now, is it? You had a real prediction about that girl, and if you had one, you could have another."

"This was a one-off thing," I said.

I turned and started walking the rest of the way to our car. I should have known she would glom on to this. It was dramatic, and there was nothing my mom loved better than some excitement. She was like a moth — when there was a bright light, she would bolt toward it without stopping to figure out if it was moonlight or a bug zapper.

"The people I spoke to today were interested," she said.

My heart seized into a tight fist in the center of my chest. I turned slowly around. "Who did you talk to?" I sent a mental prayer to the universe that I could wind time backwards and take back whatever stupid thing she'd done. A headache built up behind my eyes like a troupe of Kodo drummers.

She stuck her chin in the air. "I called a few radio stations and some newspaper reporters."

My blood turned to ice water. I did my best to remain calm. "What did you tell them?"

"About our family's abilities."

"Just that?" I wanted to feel relieved, but I knew there was no way I was getting off that easy. My head pounded harder, the vise around my brain tightening, squeezing out rational thought.

"And about the predictions you made that led to the police finding Paige's car."

The impact of what she'd done exploded in my mind. *Oh shit.* "Why would you do that? The police didn't want any of this to be public. They told us to keep it quiet."

She sniffed. "So they get all the glory."

I threw my hands in the air. "What glory, Mom? There's no glory. Just a girl who's missing."

"What do you want me to do? People want answers."

I kicked a chunk of loose pavement and sent it spinning across the parking lot. "So you're trying to make an opportunity for you out of someone else's tragedy?"

She rolled her eyes. "First off, I'm making an opportunity for *us*. Secondly, the tragedy isn't our fault. It's not like we took her."

My stomach threatened to hurl its contents onto the ground. She had no idea how wrong she was. And now she was dragging the media into the situation. They were going to dig. Look for a story. And if they found anything—I was dead.

I pinched the bridge of my nose. I had to think. My phone buzzed. I pulled it out, already dreading what it would say.

WTF? U had a vision of Paige being abducted?!

That hadn't taken long. The news was out. I texted Drew back and asked her to pick me up. The last thing I wanted was to spend one more minute with my mom. Then I tried to think of what lies I was going to tell Drew. Pretty soon I was going to need my own spreadsheet to keep everything straight.

FIFTEEN

Drew's bedroom was straight out of a teen movie. She had a queen-size bed from Restoration Hardware with huge plump pillows and a puffy duvet, like the Princess and the Pea. There was a single trundle mattress that rolled out from underneath her bed when I stayed the night. One wall was covered in cork so she could hang stuff without leaving holes, and the other walls were painted a frosty pale pink and decorated with silver-framed black-and-white photos of Paris lined up like at a gallery. I sat on her bed, stacking the various throw pillows around me like a fortress.

Drew faced me. It felt more intense than being across from the two detectives. I'd put her off on the drive here, but there wasn't any avoiding it.

"How did you hear?" I asked.

"Paige's story is big news, like CNN-holy-shit-a-pretty-white-girl-is-missing big." Drew's voice sounded like she'd been sucking helium.

I cringed. "It's on CNN?"

"Not yet, just the local channels, but I bet CNN picks up the story if they haven't already. They don't mention you in particular, just that a teen psychic gave the police critical information about the kidnapping." Drew was flushed with red splotches staining her caramel-colored skin.

I pulled a paisley pillow to my chest. "I hope they keep my name out of it. Can they say my name on the news if I'm still in high school?"

"You have to tell me what's going on." Drew leaned forward.

I bit a tiny bit of skin by my thumbnail and peeled it away, liking the sharp pain. "I had a dream about Paige, and I told it to Mr. L. Next thing I knew, the cops were involved, and apparently it helped them find her car." I paused. "It was probably just some kind of freak luck."

"Your mom always said your whole family could do that stuff." Drew had always been slightly in awe of my mom, who couldn't have been more different than hers if she tried. Her mom was some bigwig health care administrator at our hospital, but she looked like an African princess. She piled her braided hair on top of her head like a crown, making her even taller and, if possible, more imposing. And she had this way of gliding rather than walking that meant she could sneak up on you before you even suspected she was there. She was super strict with Drew and her brother. There was never any confusion that she was their mom and not their best friend. Whenever my mom would flounce into my room and plop down on my bed with us, or come dancing into the living room when we were watching TV wearing something of mine, Drew would stare at her like she was a creature from another planet.

"Yeah."

"I still can't believe you knew where her car was. That's just freaky." Drew's hand flew to her mouth. "Oh my god, what if the kidnappers come after you? They might want to, you know, shut you up."

I had no idea how my life had turned into a mobster movie where I had to stress over having people on my tail. "They're not going to worry about me. I don't really know anything." I picked at the raw skin on my thumb. I wished we could talk about something else.

Drew's hand dropped softly onto my knee. She smelled like the Clinique Happy perfume she was addicted to. "You didn't — I mean, you did see *something*, right?"

I stiffened, pulling the thumb away from my mouth. "What are you trying to say?"

"Is it possible you just imagined what you saw?" Drew wouldn't meet my eyes. "Given, you know, your past."

Her words fell with a *thunk* between us. So much for thinking she would never drag this back out. My mouth went dry. "I didn't make this up."

"I'm not saying you would do it on purpose." Drew's hand waved away my concern. "But maybe your mental health situation clouds how you see things."

"I don't have mental health *problems*," I bit out. She made it sound like I heard voices or needed a straitjacket. "It's just anxiety."

"There's nothing wrong with having mental health issues. It's the same as any other health condition." Clearly she'd been paying attention to the various public service announcements her mom was always making. "Is it possible that the anxiety made you see stuff?" Drew shrugged. "I don't know much about it, but maybe when the news came out that Paige went missing, your brain sorta wanted to *think* it knew something."

"What would be the point?" I asked. "Do you think I'm doing it for attention?" I had the urge to throw one of her J. Crew pillows at her. Or a book. Maybe a brick. She was supposed to be my best friend. Not second-guessing everything I did.

"Maybe your subconscious mind was reaching out."

"Then how did I know the parking stall number?" I stopped myself from saying anything further by biting down on my lip.

Drew threw her arm around me. "Hey, don't get mad. I always have your back. I don't want, you know, things to go bad like they did before. You've never hinted that you ever had any real ability in that area. I thought you did readings for fun. If it was just a guess, now would be the time to come clean, before stuff gets worse."

Drew had no way of knowing this could make what happened in eighth grade look like nothing. Every second I stuck with this story, I got in deeper and deeper, but I couldn't see any way out other than to keep moving forward.

"I don't need you lecturing me," I said. Drew and I had been friends for years, but there were times when she crossed the line from being my friend to acting like my mom. Worse than that — she acted like *her* mom.

Drew shrugged.

"Seriously, I have this handled," I lied.

"All I was trying to say is that maybe this wasn't some big psychic moment. Maybe it was just you noticing something the rest of us missed. You're good at that. You see things a different way."

"You mean I'm a freak." I wanted to blow up at Drew, but she wasn't making it easy. She kept deflecting everything, staying calm, which somehow annoyed me even further.

"I didn't say that. I'm worried because I can't figure out why you didn't tell me when you had this vision," Drew said. "This is a huge deal. Like, huge *huge*. We're best friends — we're supposed to share everything."

I sighed. We were best friends, but Drew didn't see it. That our lives were spinning off into different directions. It was one thing when we both lived here, when we went to the same school, but things were going to change in a few weeks, and they would never go back. Guess it turns out I can see the future.

"I don't know why I didn't talk to you about it." There was no way to explain I'd hoped to never tell her. The urge to laugh hysterically was a tight ball in my chest. I'd actually thought at one point that this would be easy. That I'd say a few things, Pluto would get the money and pay me, Paige would come home, and I could go on with my life like nothing had happened. I was pissed at myself for being stupid. How had I not realized what a big deal all of this would become? I'd wanted the cash so bad I didn't think it through. "The situation was weird. I wasn't sure what to make of it, so I told Lester, he told the cops, and the whole thing sorta snowballed from there."

Drew nibbled on the corner of her lip. "Was it freaky talking to the police?"

"A bit," I admitted, my anger melting away. Maybe if I told her what I'd done, she could help. Or her parents could. They weren't lawyers, but they were the kind of people who were friends with lawyers. Her mom and dad had the responsible adult thing down. If Drew had started talking about psychic skills and missing girls, they wouldn't have made business cards. In her house, there were chore charts and curfews. I tried to pull more air into my lungs and think of how to even start that conversation.

Drew jumped off the bed, shocking me into silence. "You know what makes me feel better? Ice cream. If my idiot brother didn't eat it all, there's some in the freezer." She pulled me up and hugged me. "Don't worry, it'll all work out."

I followed her downstairs and tried to work up some hunger for Breyers Cookies & Cream. The moment had passed. I floated with the anxiety, riding it instead of fighting, the way Lester had taught me. I just had to stay calm. I had to be smart.

SIXTEEN
Paige

I've never been so aware of how many hours, minutes, and seconds fill every day. I've taken to doing everything slowly. Staying focused keeps me from losing control, from letting the panic take over. I keep my fear locked up, but I can feel it straining to get out. Its thin fingers scratching at the door, breaking it down, like something from a zombie movie. You know it's going to get out, and when it does, it'll eat you alive.

I wash my hair, concentrating on making sure every strand is lathered from my scalp to the tip. I brush my teeth, counting to twenty for each tooth. I chew every bite thirty times, until it stops being food and becomes mush that I swallow, and then I make myself wait for sixty seconds before I take another bite.

I'm even writing this slowly. I think about each sentence before I write it down. Because what I write down next matters. It's the last barrier before my terror breaks completely free.

They told me what happened—

I had to stop for a minute because I didn't want to put that in writing. As if that somehow would make it more real. Then I realized that it doesn't matter if I write it down or not—it's still true. So here it is: My dad refused to pay the ransom.

It's not even much of a ransom. I could almost understand it if they were asking for millions of dollars, but all they wanted was $25,000. The kidnappers are pissed. They want to know what kind of game my dad is playing. The tall guy hit me. Not a smack, either, but a hard slam across my chin, rattling my teeth and making me bite my tongue. They want to hurt him, but they can't.

They can hurt me, though.

At first I didn't believe the kidnappers—but they played a recording of him on the phone. He said he wouldn't be "held hostage to someone's demands."

That's a direct quote. I wrote it down as soon as they left, as if I'd ever forget. Last time I checked, I'm the one locked up, not him. He's not stuck in some room counting out squares of toilet paper wondering what he'll do if he runs out. He's not making himself eat only tiny amounts in case the kidnappers don't come back for days. He's not left wondering what will happen if they become even angrier or if he'll ever get out of this hellhole.

My dad hung up on the kidnappers. **He hung up.** Like he

couldn't even be bothered to talk about it anymore. As if the conversation were <u>boring</u> him. Perhaps he had more important things to do. Like run for office.

His official stance is that he isn't sure he wants to run for the Senate seat. That he worries about the amount of commitment, the <u>curse</u> of having to spend more time away from his family. That's a lie. I've heard him talk about it on the phone. Planning. Coming up with strategies. He wants that job so bad he can taste it. He's already picturing himself hustling off to important meetings where the president awaits his sage advice. He's planned his office, down to moving the giant desk that used to belong to my grandfather to Washington. The desk will give him the excuse to tell the story of how my grandfather came to this country with little more than a few dollars in his pocket and a determination to work hard. Nothing my dad likes better than making it sound like our family is basically a Hallmark movie of rough-and-tumble immigrants with hearts of gold.

He's probably enjoying that I'm here. He's in the spotlight. He can go on camera and sound sympathetic. No wonder he doesn't pay the ransom—the longer I'm gone, the more free TV coverage he gets for his campaign. He doesn't care if I'm scared, or cold, or hungry, or if these guys will break an arm or leg to make their point. He's not dissecting each second into a manageable piece because he knows he might not be able to stop if he starts to cry and scream.

Everyone thinks my dad is the best guy ever. There's a lot they don't know.

The kidnappers haven't told me what they're going to do since he didn't pay. They could send him something like my ear or a finger to show him they mean business. They didn't go to this much trouble to just walk away. If he won't come up with the cash, they'll make him pay up another way. They'll take it out on me.

I'm so scared.

SEVENTEEN

I got off the bus. I was running late. This was the last stop on the very edge of town. The movie megaplex had been built out here so it could have a parking lot the size of Maine with the idea that people from the smaller towns all around would flock here to go to the movies. Sometimes it worked, but most of the time the place was empty because people stayed home to watch Netflix.

I paid for my ticket, resenting what this escapade was costing me. Pluto was either paranoid or way too fond of thriller stories. The insistence on the alter egos, fake names and bios, the burner phones. All the subterfuge. It wasn't that I didn't appreciate being cautious, but at the same time, I couldn't help feeling that this was all because Pluto loved the game. Well, I wasn't going to sit back passively any longer. I made sure to fold the receipt up and tuck it into the zippered pocket of my bag. The whole point was to make sure I had proof of where I was.

Pluto had suggested that I buy something, a drink or some Twizzlers, to "look the part." My mom had brainwashed me for years that only idiots pay what theaters charge when all you have to do is smuggle in your own candy. I couldn't eat anything anyway. The acid levels in my stomach had been so high since Paige disappeared that I was pretty certain I was developing an ulcer.

The theater was almost empty. The trailers were showing, and I had to stumble to a seat in the half dark. I slumped down. Pluto had told me to avoid looking around, but I couldn't resist peeking over my shoulder to see if I recognized anyone. Nope. At least one lucky break. I checked my phone again. I had to wait another twenty minutes. I tried to focus on the movie, but I couldn't keep the story line straight. It didn't matter: I'd already looked up reviews and summaries of the plot so I could talk about it if I needed to.

When the time came, I slipped out of the row and headed for the exit. *Nothing to see here, just someone going to the bathroom.* I tried to walk casually, but my movements were jerky, like I was moving at one speed and reality was moving at another. I paused just outside the restrooms and drank out of the water fountain. The emergency exit door was where Pluto said it would be, next to the men's room. I hoped he was right and that the theater staff had disabled the alarm so they could use this exit to take the trash out; otherwise, things were about to get real interesting.

I pushed the panic bar, half expecting buzzers and lights to go off, but it clicked open without a sound. I slid out into the night, shutting the door quietly behind me, wedging the tiny piece of cardboard I'd brought in the latch so I could get back in later. It took a moment for my eyes to adjust to the dim light. I was behind the theater next to three giant dumpsters with the sour smell of garbage wafting up. I could just make out the line of trees ahead that made up the back of the park, like tall black sentinels. I shook my head to clear away irrational thoughts. It was a park. There was nothing to be scared of.

I jogged over to the trees. The ground was spongy from the thick layer of fallen pine needles. My feet slid on the uneven path. I slowed down—I didn't want to fall. I fished through my bag and found the flashlight. The park was beyond dark; it was like I'd dropped into a vat of black ink. The beam bounced around until I spotted the path. I took one look over my shoulder at the back of the theater and then turned the flashlight off and hustled through the woods. Without a light, no one would be able to follow me.

Pluto told me it should take about ten minutes to come across the cabin, but it felt like I'd been walking much longer. *Jesus, what if I got lost?* Clammy sweat prickled under my arms, and I started to grow lightheaded. I stopped and counted to ten. I was forgetting to breathe. Classic anxiety mistake. I couldn't afford to let my imagination get the better of me. I was fine. There was nothing out here. I clicked the light back on. I was still on the path. No monsters. I wasn't going to get lost. It was a worn groove of pounded dirt. As long as I moved slowly, I'd stay on the trail. The park was only so big. It wasn't like I was going to wander into Canada or something. Worst case scenario, all I had to do is turn around and go back the way I came.

I whipped around when I heard a sound, but there was no one. Adrenaline flooded my system like bees buzzing through my veins. I hated everything about this place. I couldn't believe Pluto had talked me into meeting here. There was no way I'd missed the cabin, so that meant I must not have gone far enough. I pulled out my phone to check the time. I'd walk for another five minutes and then go back. And I'd keep the flashlight on too. At this point no one from the theater would see the light anyway.

I had to walk only a few more minutes before the cabin appeared out of the dim. I paused at the bottom of the stairs, listening to the wind whistling through the trees. I couldn't hear anything coming from inside. Pluto had told me what to expect, but seeing was believing. The windows were boarded up, with only tiny slits left open. The building seemed to lean forward, like it was hungry. The cabin looked straight out of a horror movie. And I was the dumb girl wandering around.

The one who gets killed early.

A cough from my right made me spin around, dropping the flashlight, my heart lunging up my throat.

"Paige! Jesus, you scared the shit out of me." I bent over to get my breath. My heart slammed against my ribs.

She whacked me on the shoulder. "Don't call me that! What the hell is wrong with you?"

I stepped back, rubbing my arm. "Fine. *Pluto.* You scared the shit out of me."

She bent over and picked up the flashlight, handing it back. "We talked about this a thousand times. It's not just calling me Pluto — it's *thinking* of me as Pluto. It's making your brain see me as that person. Different name, different gender, different everything. It has to be instinct, so if anyone ever overhears you talking, or if they surprise you into saying something, they won't connect the two of us." She snapped her fingers in my face. "Instinct."

"I've done what you said. I just wasn't expecting you to sneak up on me."

Paige pulled the hood from her sweatshirt down. "That's exactly why you have to do it *all* the time — look how easy it was to throw you. Besides, I hid because I wanted to be certain it was you." She looked down pointedly at the flashlight. "Since I told you to come with no light, I had to be sure."

It creeped me out that she'd been standing there watching me the whole time I walked up. I could picture her peeking around the trees, tracking every move I made. This wasn't about being careful; it was about Paige liking that I was scared.

"Did you bring me anything?" Paige looked at my empty hands. "Nothing? Not even M&M's? Or those Sour Patch Kids? I love those things."

I bit my tongue. "What's happening with the ransom?"

"There's been a hiccup." She ran the zipper on her hoodie up and down.

I paused, waiting to see if she was going to say anything else. Each nerve in my body was lighting up with annoyance. "What *kind* of hiccup?"

117

Paige jammed her hands into the pocket of her sweatshirt. "You don't need to worry about it. I've got it under control."

"Really? Because it doesn't look like it."

"At least out of the two of us I can keep our names straight." She blew her breath out in a huff. "I can't believe you demanded a face-to-face meeting to tell me you don't think I'm doing a good job. You couldn't do that over the phone? This is a waste of time and a pointless risk." She started to walk back to the cabin.

Oh hell no. I grabbed Paige's elbow. "Listen, if you can't control your dad, that's not my problem."

Paige's hand whipped out and slapped me. I was so shocked I dropped her arm. I touched my face — it was hot where she'd hit me. I'd never been hit before. Ever.

"I told you, we are not discussing the details. This is my plan; don't you get it?" Paige's nostrils were flared, and her breath came in fast pants. I was suddenly aware that no one knew I was out here. With her.

I nodded.

"You have one job, feed the info I give you to the cops. That's it. And for that you're being paid very well. You can use that money for whatever you want — that's not my business — and how I get the ransom isn't any of yours. You don't need to worry about anything other than your role. It's not your problem. Is that clear?"

"It is my problem if I'm not going to get paid."

Paige huffed. "Don't worry, he'll pay."

"I know you're pissed at your dad for some reason, but he really is upset." I thought of his expression when I'd met with him.

How I'd seen all this emotion just under a thin, brittle layer of control. "You didn't see him. He's trying to be brave and tough, but he's worried. Maybe he's not paying the ransom because he thinks the kidnappers will kill you if they get their money."

She rolled her eyes. "I think I know my dad better than you. People are way more complicated — they've got an outside view and then the inside that almost no one knows. Take my friend Lindsey for example. Do you know why she dropped the debate team right before state finals?" I shook my head. I didn't care what her BFF did. "C'mon, guess."

"I heard she didn't get along with the advisor."

Paige nodded, smiling like I'd gotten a tricky question right. "That's what everyone thinks. Truth is she's terrified to fly, and they have to take a plane to get to nationals if they win. She doesn't want anyone to know, so she came up with a stupid excuse to quit."

"Who cares?"

"The point is, no one at school knows the truth; they know what she wants them to hear. My dad's the same way, only about a million times better at playing the game."

"Look, you don't need me anymore." My feet shuffled in the dirt. "They found the car. I did my part and —"

"Stop right there. You agreed to do this, which means seeing it out to the end. You can't just decide you want to quit now."

I'd demanded this meeting to get some answers, but I'd lost control. "You can't *make* me do anything."

Paige smiled, her teeth bright in the darkness. She leaned forward and kissed my cheek. "You're cute when you're angry."

I wiped my cheek with the back of my hand. It felt like she'd marked me. A wave of disgust rolled through my stomach. I wanted to push her to the ground then kick her until that stupid smug smile was off her face.

"Like it or not, we're partners now. If you back out, you'll be sorry."

"What is that supposed to mean?"

"It means you'll be sorry." Paige patted my shoulder. "You don't want to miss out on the ransom when it comes. And it will come, trust me. You just have to hang in during this rough patch. My dad will pay. I'd invite you in for tea and cookies, but we can't take the chance that you'll leave any hair or fingerprints inside. Remember, you will have only seen this place in your mind." She winked.

I hadn't even thought of the fact I might leave evidence behind. I hated that I'd missed that obvious point and hated even more that she knew it. Paige was one step ahead of me. She spun me around so I faced the path again.

"Remember to stay until the end of the movie. Just in case anyone remembers you being there if it comes up." She gave me a tiny push. "Get going. Stick with me, and we'll be just fine. You worry too much."

I took a few shambling steps back into the dark. The damp smell of rotting pine needles and leaves filled my head. I was an idiot for getting messed up in this, but not so stupid that I didn't hear the threat loud and clear. If I bailed on Paige, she'd make me pay. I had no idea how long she'd been planning this. Months at least. I'd been impressed with how she seemed to have thought of everything. I'd underestimated one very important point—she must have also thought of how she'd get out of it if she got caught. She wasn't going to be the one left holding the bag. I was willing to bet that was going to be my job.

Paige might be my partner in all of this—but we were also enemies—and I wasn't going to forget that for another second.

EIGHTEEN

I pressed my ear to the cold metal door of the theater. I couldn't hear a thing. My heart clenched when it looked like the cardboard was gone, then I realized it had simply slid down. I cracked the door a tiny sliver, and when I didn't see anyone in the hall, I yanked it open and slipped inside.

Someone reached out and clutched my upper arm as soon as my foot hit the carpet. I froze.

"What were you doing out there?"

The guy who held me had dark curly hair and looked like one of those Greek statues we studied in art history. He also looked pissed.

I forced out a stilted laugh. "Funny thing. I had to pee so bad that I wasn't paying attention and I pushed open this door instead of the bathroom." I smacked my forehead like I couldn't believe what an idiot I was.

His glance slid over to the giant orange and yellow sign in the center of the door that declared EMERGENCY EXIT ONLY.

The guy's dark blue eyes held me in place as firmly as his hand. His fingers dug into the flesh of my upper arms. He was going to leave bruises. "If you were just going to the bathroom, why did you prop the door open?"

Oh shit. I was so busted. "I have a ticket," I mumbled. "I'm not sneaking in or anything." *Did movie theaters call the cops for this kind of thing? How the hell was I going to explain what I was doing?* That was when I noticed he wasn't wearing a uniform.

I pulled back on my arm trying to free myself. "Do you even work here?"

He ignored my question. "You're Skye Thorn."

I blinked. My tongue seemed to have swollen, filling my mouth and making talking impossible.

He knew my name.

I made myself focus and look at him more carefully. I'd seen him before. My mind scrambled to remember why I knew him. Then it hit me. He was Paige's on-again, off-again boyfriend, Ryan Denton. I'd seen his picture on the news. He was a couple years older than us, but I couldn't remember if he had graduated or dropped out.

Great. Just my luck that Paige's ex-boyfriend was some kind of Hardy Boy wannabe.

I tucked some of my hair behind my ear, trying to look casual. "The cops told me about you. The last thing you need is more trouble. You shouldn't be following anyone — that's harassment."

Ryan blinked quickly. "What did they tell you about me?"

I shrugged. "Not much." I didn't tell him that the only reason I knew his name at all was that Paige's dad asked the police about him when I was at his house.

His jaw was tight. "They want to blame me for this."

"Why?"

He laughed, but it was bitter and brittle. "Why not? Isn't it always the boyfriend? We have a fight, I lose my temper, and before you know it, there's a missing girl. I've got a record and no alibi for the afternoon she dropped off the planet. For cops I might as well have a neon sign over my head saying guilty." He rubbed his hands on his jeans.

Was this part of Paige's plan? Maybe she thought if she went missing, her boyfriend would come running back to her — like some kind of tacky romance. Or maybe Paige wanted the police to question him. If he was the one who broke up with her, she struck me as the kind who might like to get a sweet bite of revenge. I'd thought this was just about her dad, but there was no guarantee she'd told me the whole truth.

"For what it's worth, I don't think the police really think you're guilty. They told me they thought it was too well planned for someone who wasn't a pro."

"They have a funny way of thinking I'm innocent, then. The cops have searched my car and my place in Cherry Fields, twice." His face was pale with dark circles under his eyes, and despite his tough guy act and tattoos, he looked shaken.

"I'm sorry, but I have to go." I felt bad, but he wasn't my problem. I had plenty of my own.

He seized ahold of my arm again, his anger returning. "I didn't have anything to do with Paige going missing. Which means something else happened to her, and I'm going to figure it out before I end up taking the blame for all of this."

"You can do whatever you feel like." I tried to yank my arm back, but he didn't let go. "What the hell do you want from me?"

"I don't believe in any of that psychic stuff, which means if you knew where to find Paige's car, you know something, and I want to know what that is. I went to your place and followed you out here. Who goes to a movie by themselves and then doesn't even stay to watch it? I want to know why you're sneaking out of this theater."

"I needed some fresh air." I tossed my head, flipping my hair over a shoulder. I hoped to sound tough, but my voice cracked.

He stepped closer, his nostrils flaring. "Bullshit. Tell me what's going on. Did Paige put you up to this?"

"Hey!" a voice called out. Ryan and I both spun to see a thin, pimply kid wearing the orange and navy polyester uniform of the theater workers. "Is everything okay?" He was shaking slightly. "Is that guy bothering you?" His hands hovered over his hips as if he were an Old West gunslinger ready to do battle for my honor. A nervous, ill-prepared gunslinger. "You need me to call a manager?"

Ryan took a step away from me. "It's fine. I was just leaving." He pushed open the emergency door and looked back. "This isn't over," he promised me. Then he slid out into the night.

NINETEEN
Paige

The idea of a ransom first occurred to me when my sister, Evelyn, came home from college unexpectedly for the weekend. She wanted us to meet her boyfriend. This was declared a "very big deal" by my parents, and the entire house went into a flurry of excitement as if the queen of England had announced she might pop over for a social visit.

Mom rushed out to get everything to make her squash risotto (Evelyn's favorite) with chocolate ganache cake for dessert (apparently the new boyfriend's favorite). Dad popped his head into my room Friday night to let me know I was expected to cancel my Saturday plans to clean the house before the royal couple arrived and graced our sad, humble lives with their presence.

I've always known Evelyn was the favorite. I grew up listening to stories of how she slept through the night as a baby, learned to walk early, and had naturally perfect pitch. Teachers fought to have her in their class. Evelyn always got good grades, she made her bed in the morning before school, she never dyed her hair an unacceptable color, and she was never once late for curfew. And now she was dating the perfect guy.

Perfect being a matter of opinion.

I observed Charles as we made our way through dinner. The light from the chandelier in our dining room wasn't doing much for him. His skin tone was fish-belly white, made worse by the fact that he had near black hair and was wearing a dark gray sweater. He looked like one of those Puritanical preachers from the 1700s who farmed their land, went to church when not raising a barn, and burned the occasional witch for not knowing her place. The kind of guy who talked about how minority groups should stop asking for handouts and didn't notice the irony as he climbed into the BMW that his daddy had bought him.

"So Evelyn tells us you're studying engineering." My dad topped up Charles's wine. He'd opened a bottle of Châteauneuf-du-Pape from the cellar in the basement. He'd determined within minutes of meeting Charles that he deserved the good stuff. This was likely due to the fact that Charles shook my dad's hand firmly and called him sir. I'd seen my parents exchange glances, like they could hardly believe their luck, when they met him. I tried to score a glass of wine, but my dad told me *not to be ridiculous*. I suppose I should consider myself lucky that he hadn't counted the bottles, because I've taken more than one in the past.

"Yes, sir. I'm doing a dual major in computer engineering and business. Ideally I'd like to work in the aerospace industry after graduation."

Dad's eyebrows went up a millimeter. "Interesting choice."

"My father works with NASA," Charles explained.

I managed to avoid rolling my eyes. I could see my dad already envisioning his next campaign ad with an astronaut son-in-law-to-be at his side.

Charles took another sip of wine and then smiled at my mom. It looked to me like he bleached his teeth. "The dinner is amazing, Mrs. Bonnet."

Mom blushed and waved him off with a flick of her pressed napkin. "It's nothing."

We ate in silence for a beat. Just the sound of the silverware tinkling against the Haviland china plates and the faint sound of soft classical coming from the speakers in the living room. We'd all dressed up for the occasion, and it felt fake. Like we were onstage playing a happy family having a fancy dinner party, only there wasn't any audience. We were pretending just for ourselves, which struck me as even more pathetic than if we were doing it to impress anyone else.

I had this sudden urge to yell out something really vile. Maybe the C-word just so I could watch the shock in all of their faces. I wanted to stand up and sweep the bottle of wine off the table or chuck the bowl of salad at the wall. Let's see how perfect Charles handles a bit of reality.

But I didn't. Instead I carefully used the back of my knife to tap a tidy portion of risotto onto my fork the way I'd learned as a kid. I didn't fit in, but I knew how to look like I did.

"I hear we may be mortal enemies come next year," Charles said to me.

I dropped my fork onto my plate in surprise. My mom winced at the clatter. "What?"

Charles laughed. "Sorry. I just meant that Evelyn said you were planning to go to Michigan State next year." He mimed boxing. "That makes us arch football rivals."

I pressed my mouth into a shape I hoped looked something like a smile. "I guess so."

"Oh, do you play?" Mom asked.

"No, ma'am. I played in high school, but not with Michigan."

"Paige didn't have the grades for Michigan."

"Donald." Mom's voice was scolding. "You know that's not true."

"Oh, Paige knows I'm teasing her." Dad winked at me, then turned back to Charles. "Both Ms. Bonnet and I went to Michigan as well. Paige is going to be the first Spartan in the family."

"Guess we can't all be Wolverines," Charles said. "At least she's not going to Ohio State." The entire table laughed as if he'd said something remarkably witty. I imagined tossing my sparking water into Charles's smug sluglike face.

Dad raised his hand. "Ah, this is one of my favorite pieces." We all paused to hear the sounds of Ligeti's Violin Concerto coming from the other room. Dad closed his eyes for a beat. All that was missing was him raising a conductor's baton over his head and guiding the music in. "Charles, did Evelyn ever tell you that she used to play the violin?"

"Dad." Evelyn blushed.

"No." Charles nudged her softly. "Look at all the secrets I'm learning."

"She really had a gift," Mom added.

I could feel my spine stiffening. The risotto I'd eaten started to twist in my stomach. I prayed he wouldn't ask.

"Why did you give it up?" Charles asked.

I winced even though I'd known the question would come. Evelyn held up her left hand, wiggling her pinkie finger. "I told you I had an accident, years ago." The tip of the little finger was gone, not quite down to the first knuckle. It was the kind of thing you might not even notice about her until she started waving it around. "It wasn't much, but it was enough to make it so I couldn't play the really challenging pieces. Besides, no matter what my parents say, I wasn't *that* good."

Evelyn was right. She had been good, but I don't remember at the time anyone in our family talking about her being Juilliard bound. After the accident, however, descriptions of her talent grew until she was practically a budding young female Mozart taken out in her prime.

Cut down by yours truly.

Not that I did it on purpose. It had been an accident. We'd been in the kitchen, helping my mom with dinner. I was eight and was thrilled to be in charge of chopping carrots. Evelyn kept saying that I was doing it wrong. Making the pieces too big. I kept insisting right back that I had it covered. She put her hand down on the cutting board to point out a piece that was the wrong size, and *thwack*. The tip of her finger came off before I'd even realized what happened.

I'd cried inconsolably at the hospital. I didn't always get along with Evelyn, but I'd never wanted to hurt her.

"Daddy thinks this is all my fault," I wailed.

Mom patted me on the back. "Your dad knows this wasn't your fault."

Even at eight, I'd known she was partially right. My dad knew it wasn't my fault, but at the same time he *believed* it was. It wasn't that my dad didn't love me — he did — but he didn't really like me.

I stood to clear the table. My dad passed me his plate without looking at me. He was deep in conversation with Charles on the merits of various golf clubs. And it occurred to me I was sick of feeling blamed. Sick of feeling second best. And if I couldn't change how he felt about me — maybe I could make him pay. The plan to go missing was already in motion, but this would be a new wrinkle. That was the first time the idea came to me, but it had been brewing for longer than that. He had always underestimated me.

TWENTY

I peeked through the blinds. Two reporters were camped outside the apartment complex right next to the road. The woman
was wearing high heels and enough mascara that I swear I could
see each individual lash from my bedroom window. The other
guy was the cameraman. He looked like a frumpy football coach
with ill-fitting chino pants and thick-soled white sneakers. I
would have to walk right past them to catch the bus for school. I
wanted to kill my mom. This was entirely her fault.

As Drew had predicted, the story had expanded beyond the
local news. I'd woken up to CNN talking about how the police had used an unnamed psychic in Paige's investigation, a student from her school. As far as I knew, I was the only one at my
school who did tarot readings. It wasn't going to take a huge leap
for someone to figure out it was me and blab it to the media.

If I was honest, there was also a shiver of excitement when I saw the news. Part of me wanted everyone to know it was me. To realize that maybe they'd made a mistake when they ignored me all these years. I knew it was dangerous to think this way — if there was ever something I shouldn't want to be connected to, this was it, but a little thrill was there.

Last night I'd lain awake trying to convince myself that there was no real way to link me to the abduction. We'd been careful. Even if Ryan went to the police, he didn't *know* anything; he just had suspicions. And who was I kidding? The police had suspicions of their own. They'd checked out my story. But the longer Paige was gone, the greater the odds that they would keep digging.

I paced around my tiny room picking things up and putting them back down. Ever since I got back from the theater, I had the irrational fear that someone had been in my room going through my stuff, though nothing seemed to be missing. It wasn't hard to figure out where the paranoia was coming from. I had no way of knowing how long Ryan had been following me, or how far he'd go to figure out what was going on. My anxiety meant I was better able than most to imagine the worst-case scenario. Like one where someone who didn't like me pawed through my things looking for dirt. I checked the window again. The screen was loose, but I was sure it always had been like that. At least I was pretty sure. My fingers spun the screws that held it in place, trying to tighten them.

Would Ryan really have broken in to search my stuff, looking for answers? He was doubtful that Paige had been abducted. That left me wondering what had happened between the two of them and what he knew about her. If the police put enough pressure on him, he'd do whatever he needed to in order to make sure he didn't get into trouble. Throwing me under the bus wouldn't even make him blink.

I knew the kidnapping had been a bad decision, and now it was getting worse. This was turning into prison-level bad. If I thought being stuck in a small town sucked, I was willing to bet being stuck in a jail cell would suck a whole lot worse.

I hate hindsight.

My phone rang, and I checked the screen. Drew. "Hey," I said.

"Oh my god! Have you seen the TV this morning?"

"Yeah." I grabbed my history book from the floor and stuffed it into my backpack, trying to remember if it had been at the bottom of the stack of books yesterday or on the top.

"You're totally going to be famous."

There was that shiver of excitement again, and I pushed it away. I hunched over the phone as if telling her a secret. "There are reporters outside my place."

Drew whistled. "Serious?"

I peeked through the blinds. They were still there. "Yep."

"Are you okay?"

I took a shaky breath. Lester was always on me to breathe, saying how oxygen is nature's relaxant. "I guess. It's a bit weird."

"You want me to pick you up?"

"You've got study first period. You don't have to be in," I reminded her.

"It's okay, I don't mind. I'm up anyway. It wouldn't kill me to go to the library. I'll be there in ten minutes."

"The way you drive?" I managed to joke.

"Okay, twenty. But I'll still be faster than the bus. I'll pick you up in the back lot. I'll text you when I get there."

I hung up and peered out of the blinds again. The female reporter rubbed her arms against the morning chill. If Drew was right, it was only a matter of time until there'd be more. I was glad she was picking me up, but I couldn't shake the idea that she also liked having a front-row view of everything happening.

This had to end. I couldn't sleep. I was chewing the flesh off my thumbs. Every sound made me jump, and my stomach was full of acid every minute of the day. If it didn't come to a close soon, I was going to snap.

I opened the bedroom door and peeked out, making sure my mom wasn't up yet. It was unlikely she'd be awake without me knowing it. My mom was connected to the TV. She couldn't stand to be in a room and not have it on. No TV was almost a certain indicator she was still dead to the world, but I wasn't taking a chance. I tiptoed down the hall and pressed my ear to her door. I heard her breathing heavily in tandem with the fan she ran for white noise.

I slunk back to my room and lifted the mattress, scrambling to find the disposable phone where I'd hidden it. For a split second I couldn't locate it, and panic flooded my system. Stolen! Then my fingers brushed the cool plastic. I made myself grab it and pull it out—part of me didn't even want to touch it. I could picture a SWAT team crashing through the front door as soon as I turned it on—drawn by the phone's GPS or some magical CSI technology I couldn't even imagine. I punched in the number. It rang for a long time before she picked up.

"Why are you calling?"

"Nice to hear your voice too," I said. "Listen —"

"Remember, don't use my name."

My hands squeezed the phone harder. "I got it."

"It's not a joke. One mistake, and we're both in deep shit."

"Fine, listen *Pluto*, the situation is bad."

An annoyed sigh came through the phone. "I thought we settled this last night."

"We need to end this now."

"Not yet. He'll pay. I've got a plan to turn up the heat."

My intestines knit themselves into a knotted snarl. "No, we don't need to turn up the heat, we need to end it. It's not working." I pulled my thumb from my mouth. I was bleeding. "The press is involved."

"So? We knew they would be."

"No, I mean involved with me." I thumped my chest. "I was trying to explain this last night. My mom sort of outed my role in everything."

"Jesus, what an idiot." Even Paige's breathing sounded irritated.

I flushed. My mom had done something stupid, but everyone knew the unwritten rule was that you could call your own parents every name in the book, but everyone else should shut their mouths. Or maybe it was that Paige hated the idea of me getting any of the attention she'd worked so hard to get. She wasn't the kind of person who liked sharing.

"It's not like my mom knows anything," I stressed. "She

thought she was doing a good thing. She's . . . I guess you would call it proud."

She snorted. "Well, it's *not* a good thing. It's a distraction, and it's not a part of the plan."

"I *remember* the plan," I said. "I don't need you to remind me. Look, your dad isn't going to pay, so just come home." If she came back, we wouldn't get a ransom, but I might still be able to carve out a win. I would have helped bring her home. People would find that fascinating.

They would find me fascinating.

"I'm not ready for this to be over," Paige said.

"Too bad. This isn't your decision. Half of the ransom was supposed to be mine, and I need the cash a whole shit pile worse than you do. If anyone should be whining, it's me. You threatened me last night, but you need to remember that anything you can do to me, I can do to you."

"I never threatened you," Paige said. "Don't turn into a drama queen. You always knew this wasn't a guarantee."

Bullshit. All I'd heard about was how this scheme couldn't miss. The term "money in the bank" had been tossed around. Now all of sudden there was no guarantee. "Every day this goes on, the bigger the chance it blows up in our faces." I couldn't believe she didn't get it. "I tried to explain this to you last night, but you wouldn't listen. I'm going in tomorrow and telling them about the cabin."

"No."

I snorted. "It's not up to you. I'm ending it. I called to give you a heads-up so you've got a day to prepare. The cops will be there tomorrow, and you need to be ready."

"Give me a couple more days. I'm telling you — he'll pay. He isn't going to want it to come out that he wouldn't pay to get his daughter home safe. That's an election killer."

"Worrying about your dad's electability isn't my problem. Getting my ass arrested for this is. If all of this comes out, I'm looking at serious problems."

A bitter laugh came through the phone. "You have no idea of real problems. If you think you are in ass deep, then I am in waaaaaaay over my head."

I softened my voice. "Your boyfriend talked to me. He knows something is up."

"Ryan?! How did he —" She stopped talking for a beat. "Ryan's my ex. What did he say?" Her voice was clipped and all business.

"He was at the movie theater. He followed me there. He heard about me on the news."

"Shit. I told you to pay attention. How did you miss him trailing after you?"

I felt a flush of annoyance. "I *did* pay attention. I didn't know I was supposed to be looking out for some guy you used to date. Ryan knows something is up."

"I have to think," Paige said.

There was silence on the phone.

"Are you still there?" I asked.

"Where else would I go? Don't you do a thing until we talk again." Then she hung up.

TWENTY-ONE

"Hey, Skye!"

I turned, and a bunch of junior girls waved at me. They were at least the fifth group of people to call out to me as we came into school. I raised a hand back, and they giggled and scurried down the hall. I watched them round the corner in a tight cluster.

I turned to Drew. "What the hell is going on?"

"Everyone knows you're the psychic the media is talking about." She nudged me with her elbow. "Welcome to being famous."

"Great," I mumbled under my breath.

"Maybe you can parlay this newfound fame into getting a killer date for prom." Drew took a careful sip of the coffee we'd stopped to get on the way. Not that she was drinking real cof-fee: it was some kind of dessert in a cup. If you don't like cof-fee, fine, but don't pretend to like it by making it into a sugar smoothie.

"The last thing I need to worry about is a date," I said.

"You could go out with that guy from your apartment building. He was hot."

I stopped. "What guy?"

Drew looked over her shoulder at me. "The one with the dark hair."

The spit in my mouth turned sour. "I don't know who you're talking about." I'd lived there since second grade. I would know if there was a hot guy living within a ten-mile radius of the building.

"He was in the parking lot when I picked you up." She laughed at my expression. "Don't freak out. He was just some guy. I'm not setting you up or anything."

"Have you ever seen him before?" I grabbed her arm to make her slow down.

Drew arched her eyebrow. "No."

"Was he watching me?" It had to be Ryan. He was following me, hoping I'd lead him to Paige. Was there any way he could tap my phone calls?

Drew motioned for me to keep walking. I was going to be late. "I'm sorry I said anything. I was joking. He was just some boy. Probably waiting for a friend. It was no big deal. I only no-ticed him because he seemed like your type."

"I think he might be following me," I said.

Her eyes widened. "Do you think he's a journalist?"

My mind raced back to yesterday. "I think someone might have been in my room too." People streamed past us in the hall. The first bell was going to ring any minute.

Drew held her hands out motioning for me to slow down so she could make sense of what I was saying. "Okay, are you listening to yourself?"

"I know it sounds weird, but I'm serious."

"Was anything stolen?"

I shifted from foot to foot. "No. But I'm sure stuff had been moved around."

The corners of her mouth turned down. "Skye." Her voice was slow and measured, like she was trying to talk me off a ledge. "Why would someone slip into your room to move stuff around?"

"He's not some *guy*. He's Paige Bonnet's ex-boyfriend," I said, louder than I meant to. I glanced over my shoulder to make sure no one was paying attention.

Drew's mouth made a tiny O. She grabbed my arm and pulled me into the bathroom. She checked under the stalls to make sure we were alone. "You need to talk to the cops if you think he's following you. I've heard he's trouble."

I dragged my foot on the tile floor, making it squeak. "I don't know."

Drew leaned against the sink. "I know for a fact he's got a criminal record." Her eyes grew wider. "For breaking and entering."

I let that fact sink in. It shouldn't have made a difference. It's not like it would have taken a skilled professional to get into our apartment, but it still made me uneasy.

"Do you want me to drive you to the police station?" Drew offered. "Or we could go to Lester's office — he could call them. They can take fingerprints or something."

I tried to slow my thoughts down. If the cops talked to Ryan, he might tell them about the movies. They would want to know what I was doing wandering out behind the theater in the dark. And if they found the cabin —

"Skye?" I jolted. I'd half forgotten that Drew was there. "We should go to the police. If Ryan did, you know, something to Paige and he thinks you might see him in a vision or whatever, he could be after you."

"He didn't do anything to Paige," I said. "He's probably harmless."

"You can't be sure," she said.

The sink behind us had a steady drip. The plinking sound was drilling through my brain. "I'm sure. Ryan wasn't involved."

"What are you talking about? A second ago you thought he might have been in your room. I heard they broke up because he was cheating on her."

"That gives her a reason to want to hurt him, not the other way around." The bell rang. "You're right. I'm just letting my anxiety get the best of me. There's no reason he'd break into my apartment. I'm not going to involve the cops because I'm a nervous wreck. You know how I get — imagining all sorts of things." I forced myself to laugh like it was no big deal. I pulled my bag over my shoulder. "Thanks for picking me up."

She stopped me before I could leave. "You sure you know what you're doing?"

I gave her a thumbs-up. It seemed better than saying I did and adding another lie to the pile.

TWENTY-TWO

I checked the rearview mirror for the millionth time to see if anyone was following me. I'd told my anatomy teacher I was needed in Lester's office, but cut instead. Skipping class wasn't the end of the world, but I'd also snuck into Drew's locker, grabbed her keys, and taken her Bug.

Once you've done kidnapping and fraud, you might as well add auto theft.

If I'd asked Drew, she would have lent me the car, but I didn't want her to grill me about where I was going. I pulled into the Walmart parking lot and found a spot near the side of the building.

Our town was split down the center, with the river acting as a dividing line. The west side, where Drew lived, had the two blocks of Main Street with the old-fashioned light poles and flower boxes in front of all the stores. The nicer restaurants were clustered nearby, and the whole thing was surrounded by tidy subdivisions. The east side had my apartment complex, strip malls, car repair shops, and our version of a cathedral — the Walmart.

It was time I took some control of the situation. Ryan might have been following me, but I could find him just as easily. I jogged across the parking lot, crossed the street, and went into Cherry Fields, the trailer park.

For a trailer park, it was nicer than I expected. Decades ago it had been a farm, and there were still fruit trees lining the driveway. It wasn't like there were pit bulls chained to the bumpers of broken-down cars and people hanging Confederate flags in their windows the way I'd imagined it. The trailers were mostly in good shape, and lots of people had planted flowers or stuck garden gnomes around their tiny yards, but it still wasn't a place I'd dream of moving to. I stopped near the entrance at the giant community mailbox. As I'd hoped, someone had busted out a label maker and put people's names on the numbered boxes: DENTON #15.

I walked down two rows before I figured out the numbering system, then spotted his trailer. It was painted a yellowing white with faded red trim. I held the palm of my hand over the tiny peephole and then pounded on the door.

The door flew open, and there stood Ryan. He hadn't shaved and his sweatpants rode low on his hips. He looked shocked to see me. Good.

I crossed my arms and leaned against the doorjamb. "Not so nice when someone just shows up, is it?"

He looked past me to see if I was alone. "How did you find me?"

"I'm a psychic, remember?"

His mouth twitched. "You wanna come in?"

"I came to tell you that you need to leave me alone."

He turned and went inside. "You might as well yell at me in here. I got water and beer." He looked over his shoulder with a smirk, watching me hesitate in the doorway. "Unless you're afraid," he added.

I stepped inside after him. The trailer smelled like a mix of fresh-cut grass and stale cigarettes. It wouldn't have taken magical powers to figure out Ryan was a hockey fan. There was a giant Red Wings poster on the far wall, and a hockey stick was mounted like a rifle above the doorway to the kitchen. He followed my gaze. "I used to play."

"Were you any good?"

"Not good enough." He went through into the kitchen, opened the fridge, and held out a can of Budweiser. I couldn't tell if he really wanted to drink this early or if he was yanking my chain. I shook my head no. He pulled a couple glasses off the drain board. He poured us each a glass of water. I took a sip and then put it right back down on the counter.

When he stood so close, I was reminded how solid he was. Not much taller than me, but broad across the shoulders. He was only a year or two older than the guys in my school, but he didn't look like them. He looked more like a grown man. Ryan motioned to the sofa.

I shook my head. "I'd rather stand."

"Suit yourself." He stepped past me and plopped down.

I'd wanted to stand because I wanted to come across as in control, but instead of feeling powerful, I felt awkward. My arms felt too long and floppy, and I suddenly didn't know what to do with my hands.

"So, you came to tell me something?" He leaned back, his legs spread.

I stood straighter, hating how I felt prim and stuffy. "I know you broke into my apartment. I don't know what you're looking for — but I'm telling you now. Cut it out. I don't want to get you in more trouble, but if you do it again, I'll call the cops." I was bluffing, but I was hoping he wouldn't guess.

He sat up, the smirk wiped off his face. "What are you talking about?"

I blew the hair out of my eyes. "I know you've been in my room."

"I've been to your apartment complex, but I never went inside." He held up a palm as if swearing an oath. "Promise. If someone's been in your space, it wasn't me."

I tried to read his body language to see if he was lying, but I couldn't tell. He likely wouldn't admit to it. I wasn't even completely sure anyone had been in my room.

"Have you thought it might be Paige?" He scratched his elbow, his eyes never leaving mine.

I jumped, and my face grew hot. "What? No."

Ryan rubbed the condensation on the side of his glass off with the bottom of his T-shirt. "Okay. Just a thought."

I had to focus on what I knew for a fact. "You need to stop following me."

"*You* need to tell me what's going on."

I wanted to scream. The conversation was devolving. "I don't know what's going on. Look, it's simple. I had a vision. I had no way of knowing if it meant anything or not. I shared it with the cops because I felt like I should. That's it."

Ryan propped his feet up on the coffee table, pushing aside a stack of library books and a pizza box. "If it was just a vision, then why is your mom on the news all the time?"

I pulled my hair away from my neck, trying to cool down. "She's not on the news *all the time*. She thinks she has these abilities, and she wants to help."

He cocked his head. "*Thinks* she has them — so she doesn't."

"I didn't say that." I wanted to kick something or grab the glass out of his hand and smash it on the floor. He was doing a better job at reading me than I was at reading him.

Ryan stared at me. "Look, I don't know what you're messed up in, but if Paige is involved, you better be careful."

"Of Paige?" I said skeptically.

He nodded. "That girl — hell, her whole family — they are seriously messed up."

"So you don't believe she's been abducted. That the whole thing is some big . . ." I waved my hands in the air as if trying to conjure up the right words. "Some big lie?"

Ryan shrugged. "Maybe. I do know nothing with that girl is easy."

"So why did you go out with her?"

He smiled. "I liked the idea of a challenge."

"Liked, but not like. You don't like it anymore?" I wondered how he'd enjoy someone pulling apart each of his words for their secret meanings.

"Maybe there are some things that are so challenging they aren't worth the hassle." He smirked up at me. "I'm betting you're worth a fair bit of trouble."

I could feel myself blush. He was trying to throw me. He still wanted her. At least part of him did. I watched the dust move through a sunbeam coming through the window. It looked almost like glitter. "If she's not worth it, why are you worried about her?"

He shrugged. "Who said I was worried?"

"You spend a lot of time on stuff that doesn't worry you."

He rubbed his eyes. "I will tell you that nothing with her is the way it looks. Maybe you had a vision, maybe you didn't, but you seem like a nice girl, and if I were you, I would watch your back."

"I will. But I better not see you behind me anymore."

Ryan stood and I retreated quickly, almost tripping on a bump in the carpet. He rolled his eyes, and I felt foolish for overreacting. He slid past me and through an accordion door at the rear of the trailer, then returned. He handed me a thick-linked gold ID bracelet.

"What is this?"

He smirked. "Aren't you psychic?" He nodded toward the bracelet. "Paige gave it to me. Said it was like a promise ring, only for a guy. She wanted it back when we broke up, but I wouldn't give it to her. I told her it belonged to me now. Take it."

I tried to return it to him, but he wouldn't let me. "I don't want this."

He moved past me and opened the door, letting me know the conversation was over. I walked out, the sun outside seeming hotter than it had just minutes ago when I went inside.

"If you happen to see Paige, you give her that and let her know that I'm done for good. She wanted it, and now she has it. She can leave me the hell alone, and we'll go our separate ways, but if she tries to get me in trouble, I'll tell all her secrets." He leaned closer to my face, and his breath smelled like bitter coffee. "Tell her that's a promise."

TWENTY-THREE

The cabin door flew open, and Paige stormed out. "What the hell are you doing here?"

"We need to talk," I said. I took a stance with my legs wide. She wasn't going to push me around this time.

"Tell me you didn't drive here." Paige looked around as if she half expected to see a car parked on the trail behind me.

"You don't need to worry about it." At least I hoped she didn't. I'd left Drew's car outside the park on the street and hiked in, just in case there were security cameras hiding in the trees or in the parking lot. And, despite risking heat stroke, I'd worn my hoodie to hide my face until I was well down the trail. I figured I had less than an hour before Drew had lunch. I didn't think she'd notice her keys missing before then.

"I *said* I would call you," Paige said. "You shouldn't have come here." She looked behind me again, and I heard the crack of a branch.

I spun to look over my shoulder. Someone had been there right before me. Someone I'd just missed. "Who's out there?"

"No one."

I turned back to her. When she stepped away from the shadows near the cabin door, I saw her face and gasped. I pointed to the giant black eye, the dark purple bruise spreading across her face. "Jesus, what happened?"

Paige lightly touched her face, blinking rapidly. "This? Nothing."

"Are you kidding me?"

She thrust a hip out, striking a pose, as if daring me to look at her. "Not bad, huh?" She turned her head from side to side. "You told me I'd better prepare to be found. This will look suitably tragic in the photos."

"You did that to yourself?" The idea repulsed me.

She nodded, but her glance slid past me. I turned to look again, but couldn't see anything. I traced the outline of the trees, searching for anything out of place. A few branches waved in the wind. "Was someone here? Did they —" I motioned to her eye.

Paige shook slightly, but I couldn't tell if it was from the cold or if she was afraid. "Who would be out here?"

"You tell me." Was someone else involved — someone who wasn't too happy with how things were going?

Paige took a few steps down and sat on the bottom riser. She patted the wood for me to join her. "Don't freak out. I hit myself.

You shouldn't be surprised. I told you I was in one hundred percent." Her voice hinted at the contrast between us, that she was doing her part but I wasn't doing mine.

"Why are you doing all of this?" I asked. I waved my arm around toward the cabin and her face. "You don't need the money. What did your dad do to piss you off?"

"Why does it matter?"

"It matters to me."

Paige picked up a stick and drew in the dirt at her bare feet. "Parent stuff. The usual." She broke the stick over her knee. "How pathetic is that? Even my problems are ordinary and unoriginal. No wonder he's disappointed in me. I figured if I went missing, maybe it would remind my dad that he did love me." She smiled sadly. "You know how it is. You never really appreciate anything until it's gone. Think of the ransom as, like, a late fee, for not telling me he loved me enough."

"Promise me that this whole thing isn't about a boy. No guy is worth it."

Paige's eyes narrowed. "Ryan said something to you."

I pulled the gold bracelet out of my pocket, and she snatched it from me, inspecting it carefully. "He wanted me to give that to you," I said.

"I hope you weren't so stupid that you told him what we're doing."

I ground my back teeth together. "I'm not stupid."

Paige snorted. "You certainly aren't smart enough to follow directions. Every time you come out here, you risk getting us caught." She tossed the bracelet from hand to hand.

"Ryan thinks you might be doing this to get him into trouble." I took a deep breath. "You're not, are you?"

"Aw, did you fall for those deep blue eyes of his too? You rushed out here to protect him from big bad me?" She laughed. "Damn, he's good." She shoved the bracelet into her pocket, and I could see there was grime under her fingernails. "No. I didn't do this to get Ryan in trouble." She looked up at me. "Not that I'd mind if it did. Jesus, it's hot. Who thought it would get this hot in May?" Paige lifted the bottom of her shirt and waved it up and down to make a breeze. "The first thing I'm going to do when I get back home is have a Diet Coke in a glass with about a thousand ice cubes."

My jaw creaked with tension, but I wouldn't give her the satisfaction of asking her to say more.

"My dad tried to make me break up with Ryan, you know. He was all 'his reputation hurts your reputation, blah blah blah.'" She snorted. "What he meant is that it hurt *his* reputation. Can't have a senator's daughter dating one of the common people."

"Or maybe he was worried. It's possible, you know. Or is that why you went out with Ryan?" I asked. "To piss off your dad?"

Paige threw her head back and laughed. "Yeah. That was part of it. You should have seen his face the first time Ryan came over." Her mouth pulled into a sexy pout. "And besides, Ryan wasn't terrible in bed either." She laughed at my expression. "Who knew you were such a prude?"

"You have to come back," I said. "This is getting crazy."

"Yeah. Maybe." She poked my foot with her stick. "You worry too much. Trust me."

"It's not you, it's everyone else I don't trust. If this comes out —"

She stood and brushed the dust off the back of her shorts. "Give it a rest. We'll do it your way. You want me to admit you're right. Fine. You win. Give them a vision tomorrow morning about the cabin."

The feeling of relief was so strong my bones turned to liquid. I felt as if I could pour in between the pine needles on the ground and disappear, but I also wondered what had made her change her mind. If someone had been out here, someone who was willing to hurt her, she might realize how dangerous all of this could be.

"Are you sure you're okay?"

She thrust her chin in the air. "No one scares me. But whatever you do, don't tell Ryan anything," Paige warned me. "He might seem nice, but like most men, he can't be trusted."

TWENTY-FOUR
Paige

I took a deep breath after Skye left. I had a headache that radiated through my face and even into my teeth. I touched the skin below my eye and winced. All I wanted to do was take a nap. Being out here had been exciting at first, an adventure, but I was tired now. Days of doing nothing hadn't been restful; they'd been exhausting.

I forced myself to stand. There was a lot to do before tomorrow. I reached into my pocket and felt Ryan's bracelet. I hadn't thought he would hunt down Skye. That was unexpected. And here I didn't think anything would surprise me anymore.

Skye wanted a clear reason for everything — that X happened and resulted in me doing Y — but things are rarely that cut-and-dried. The idea of the ransom started when Charles came for dinner, but the idea of wanting my dad to pay had been festering for long before that.

He was eating up all the media attention with this abduction. I bet his campaign staff felt like Christmas had come early. They might not even want me to be found. Not like last time I was gone.

When my parents wouldn't let me go on spring break last year, I simply took off without their permission. What I hated more than anything was having to call them for help three days later from the police station. I called crying, and they came to get me, but if I thought there would be sympathy, I was wrong.

My dad paced back and forth in the tiny room. "Get your stuff, and let's go."

"What about what happened?"

He rubbed his face. "I've told them not to go forward with charges."

I sat up straighter. "Why? I want to."

"Trust me, you don't want to. Let's just get you home."

I crossed my arms. "I want to file charges."

Mom sat rubbing my arm, looking back and forth between us. "Donald?"

"I know what I'm doing, and we don't want to do this. You know what will happen, right? Let's figure out the questions they're going to ask. How much did you have to drink last night? Is that what you were wearing?"

I flinched and shivered in my crop top and shorts.

"Are your friends going to say you went with that guy of your own free will?"

"I didn't mean to get that drunk. He kept giving me drinks."

Dad shook his head. "Did he pour them down your throat? What did you think he wanted when he took you back to his room? To play cards? Think about how it looks."

"It looks like this." I yanked my shorts up so he could see the bruises on my thighs.

He looked away. "It looks like you put yourself in a bad situation and bad things happened. There's no point in filing charges — any decent defense lawyer will get that boy off. They're going to say you wanted it until you woke up the next morning."

Yes, I wanted him to kiss me, but I hadn't wanted what came next. I'd been very clear. No. And my dad didn't even care what really happened.

"You think I had it coming," I said.

He shook his head sadly. "No. Of course not. But I don't think this is a battle we'll win. I know how these lawyers will act. All that filing a case is going to do is drag what's left of your reputation through the mud. Believe it or not, I'm thinking of you. Let's just go home."

He made it sound like he was doing it for me, but even with a huge hangover and feeling sick from what happened, I knew it wasn't ever about me. It was about him. About what people would say. He came up with a story about me having my stomach pumped. Just a girl gone wild.

He didn't think I was a slut who deserved it — but he believed it. And belief is stronger than logical thought.

My dad tried to make it up to me. He made plans for us — talked about how we could both move forward. But I'd been making some plans of my own. And I wasn't done yet.

TWENTY-FIVE

Mr. Lester's secretary was an easy read. "I'm going to draw another card to see if we can get at the heart of what's going on." I tapped the nine of swords — it has an illustration of a woman in bed weeping into her hands, which is only fair, because she has nine sharp blades suspended over her head. It typically means anxiety or worry.

Basically this card is my life.

Ms. Brew admitted she had been feeling stressed lately, which I didn't have to be psychic to figure out. She had about a million coffee cups on her desk, and there were the wrappers for what looked like an entire pack of Nicorette gum in her trashcan. I flipped another card. Two of cups.

"And that one?" she asked.

"It can mean a change in an existing relationship. Is there anything going on at home?"

She fidgeted in her chair. Maybe it occurred to her that asking a student about her married life wasn't exactly going to meet the standard of conduct in the employee handbook. "Tom, my husband, wants to start a new business."

"And you're worried about the idea," I finished for her.

She sighed. "He works at a place with a good pension. This economy doesn't seem like a great time to launch—" She flushed.

I smiled. "It's fine. You don't have to tell me about it." I passed her the rest of the cards. "Shuffle these while you think about all the stuff that's stressing you out. You can close your eyes if it makes it easier. Then pick a card, and it will give us an idea of what happens next."

When she was done, I put the deck down in the center of her desk. I tapped the top card and then flipped it. "Three of wands. It means good things are coming, but you may need to wait." She picked up the card and inspected it more closely.

She nodded, satisfied, and put it back down. "Can you do a reading about my daughter and her new partner, Amy? They're thinking about adoption."

I picked up the deck. It was starting to feel like it weighed a thousand pounds. When this was over, I would burn them. Before I could lay out another deal, Mr. Lester rushed back in, and Ms. Brew and I stood.

"They found where Paige was being kept." He was practically panting with excitement. I made sure I didn't smile. This was it.

Ms. Brew's hand covered her heart. "Is the poor girl—" She couldn't bring herself to finish the sentence, in case the words alone had the power to shape what had happened.

"She wasn't there."

The sound of the blood rushing inside my ears blocked out what he said next. There was just a whooshing noise growing louder and louder.

"Sit down." Mr. Lester pushed me into the closest seat and shoved the back of my head toward my knees. I struggled at first, then realized he was trying to keep me from passing out. "Take a slow, deep breath."

His arm had me pinned to the chair. I tried to wriggle away from him.

"Stay where you are. Just keep breathing."

I stared down at the linoleum floor and made myself count the squares to distract my brain until my breathing evened out and I no longer saw black dots around the edges of my vision.

"You okay?" I nodded, and Mr. Lester let me sit up. "Monica, can you grab a glass of water for Skye?"

She looked like she was scared of me. She rushed out to the water cooler and came back a second later with a tiny paper cup.

"They didn't find Paige?" I finally managed to ask.

"No, they found the cabin you saw in your vision, but it was empty." Mr. Lester bent down so he was even with my face. "Hey, it's okay. It's not your responsibility to find her. What you told them was great. It's going to give them all kinds of new leads."

I wanted to grab his shirt collar and tell him I knew it wasn't my fault. It was Paige's. She was supposed to be there. *Where the hell was she?*

I'd gone into Mr. Lester's office this morning and told him I'd had another vision. He called in the detectives, and I told them what I'd seen. A lot of trees. Maybe a trail. There was a cabin. I knew that could be a thousand places in our town alone, let alone all of Michigan, so I had to narrow it down. I mentioned I saw an owl.

They were all clustered around me like I was telling them the best bedtime story ever, and when I mentioned the owl, they all looked at one another, trying to see if anyone else knew what that meant.

"Do owls have some kind of symbolism?" Detective Jay asked.

"In the Sioux tribe the owl was considered a messenger of evil." Mr. Lester played with his beard.

I wanted to scream in frustration. I couldn't be too specific, but I also wasn't interested in playing twenty questions while they tried to piece it together. Detective Chan looked out the window while Mr. Lester talked about calling someone he knew who was some kind of bird expert and who might know if there was a place owls liked to nest around here. Suddenly, Chan interrupted him.

"The park. Out by the highway. Doesn't their sign have an owl on it?"

Everyone went silent.

"Comstock Park," Jay added.

Jesus, finally.

"Isn't there a ranger cabin out there too? One they don't use anymore?"

The two detectives stood in unison. Chan pointed at me. "You stay here while we check this out, and don't anyone say anything until we get back. The last thing we need is the media crawling all over the place."

Lester and Ms. Brew nodded solemnly, and then we were stuck waiting. Three hours. I'd finally busted out my tarot cards to do a reading for Ms. Brew while Lester sent notes to my teachers giving vague reasons why I couldn't be in my classes.

Paige was supposed to have been tied up nice and tidy in the corner waiting to be found.

"Were there signs of a struggle?" I asked.

"No. They found some of her clothing and food. There were also some diary pages in her handwriting."

"She kept a diary?" My stomach twisted. What the hell had she been writing down?

"It looks like she wrote as a way to pass time. Detective Jay says the pages are heartbreaking. You can tell how scared she is, even though she's trying to be brave."

Ms. Brew grabbed a Kleenex from her desk and wiped her eyes.

"Once the police have collected evidence, they may have you touch the pages, see if you can get a vibe or something." He patted me on the shoulder. "We're getting closer."

There was a sour knot of bile pushing its way up my throat, keeping any words from coming out. I wanted to kill her. I should have known she was going to screw me when she gave in so easily. We had a plan. Now who was the one who couldn't follow directions?

Lester smiled. "The good news is that the diary shows that she's alive."

Not for much longer if I had anything to do with it.

TWENTY-SIX

I opened the apartment door slowly, but it was quiet. My mom must've been working. I shut and locked it behind me. I waited for a beat, half expecting someone might suddenly start pounding on it, but when nothing happened, I bolted to my bedroom. I shut that door too and then fished the burner phone out from under my mattress.

No answer.

I dialed again. *Pick up the phone. Pick it up*, I chanted inside my head.

Pick.

Up.

The.

Freaking.

Phone.

I hurled it against the wall and then dropped to my knees to make sure I hadn't broken it. It was the only way I had to reach Paige. I couldn't go out to the cabin and drag her back by her hair. I didn't have any idea where to find her anymore.

Was it possible something had happened to her? I ran through possibilities from Ryan to a random wild animal attack, but I kept circling back to the fact that a very select few items had been left behind. And while it wasn't impossible, the idea that Ryan had followed me out to the cabin to confront Paige seemed unlikely. The entire situation smacked of Paige.

I left school without going to the rest of my classes. Lester told me the police wanted to talk to me personally. He offered to take me, but I wanted to go alone. They were going to ask me if I'd ever been to the park, and I had to figure out whether I should keep lying or tell the truth. I needed privacy to think. I couldn't decide if each lie was helping me build a bridge to get out of this mess or burying me alive. I sat with my back against the bed and wrapped my arms around my knees.

I had to figure out what to do next. I mentally turned over each moment, trying to look at it from a different perspective, seeing if it would lead me in a new direction.

Paige had planned everything down to the tiniest detail. She did all her research on the library computers so that her laptop wouldn't have anything weird in the history. She figured out that the airport cameras were down in the long-term lot. She planned her route to make sure she wouldn't be caught on any traffic cams. She planted her blood, just enough, in the car. She stocked the cabin with what she would need. Both the detectives had talked about how they were sure I hadn't done anything, because the whole thing was too well organized. Nothing that girl did was by accident.

She'd thought it all through. She loved the mental gymnastics of it.

And when she realized that she would need a partner, someone who could be connected to the outside world while she was gone, there was no way she left that to chance.

She played me.

I slammed my fist down on my thigh. She brought the idea up like it was a lark at first, and somewhere along the way, I went from telling her it was crazy to debating the details. I'd been carefully selected.

How did she know how badly I needed the money? It was possible she assumed anyone who lived where I did could always use some extra cash.

I rubbed my temples. Paige had disappeared. She'd left a diary behind, and that would have been no accident. She wanted those pages found. Whatever was on them was meant to be seen.

Paige had enjoyed putting this all together. She was practically giddy when we talked about it. I could still remember meeting with her at the library a few weeks earlier. She had said we couldn't meet anymore. There was too much of a chance that people would see us together.

"We'll go old school. I'll leave you notes here, and you leave your responses for me in the same place," Paige whispered to me as she pulled one of the giant encyclopedias off the shelf. "We'll type all of

our correspondence. Use the library printer downstairs so it can't be traced to us. No handwriting if it can be avoided. We'll come up with names, aliases."

I touched the book nervously. "Isn't this over the top?"

"No. It's careful. From this point on, you should think of me as Pluto."

"Pluto?"

"Like the planet—the one that's not a planet anymore. Get it? It's missing!"

"It's still a planet, just a dwarf one," I said. "And it's still there. It's not like it disappeared."

She rolled her eyes, then burst out laughing. "Whatever, you want to make sure that thinking of me as someone else, as Pluto, comes as second nature. There is Paige, the girl who's missing, and Pluto, the guy who you're involved with. You need to mentally see us as two different people. You can pick whatever name you like."

"I don't know—"

"It can be whatever. The more random the better. We can change it if you want—it doesn't have to have some big meaning." She pulled the encyclopedia closer to her. "Now look, I doubt anyone has opened this book in years. I've got some throw-away phones to use when I go missing, but until then we'll use this for communication. We only use the phones for emergencies once I'm gone—those can be traced. The police can see where calls are made from based on what cell tower was used. The fewer times we use the phone, the better."

"I'm not agreeing to this," I said. The "yet" hung in the air between us.

Paige gave me a pageant smile. "All I'm asking is that you think about it. Feel free to leave any questions for me here, and I'll do my best to answer them, but I think it's a good idea if you don't know all the details. You don't have to worry. This is going to go off without a hitch. If you don't do it, you're going to kick yourself for missing the chance."

I nodded. Intrigued, but scared.

"But you have to make up your mind soon. I'm going to do this, with you or without you." She tapped me on the nose. "Picture it: when school is over, you'll have more than twelve grand. That's a new life."

I still hadn't said yes until the afternoon when Drew canceled her dorm plans. But I might have done it anyway. Paige hadn't been stupid. She picked me because she could smell the desperation.

And now I was more desperate than ever.

TWENTY-SEVEN

My foot bounced up and down while I waited in the police station lobby. My anxiety was like an out-of-control zoom lens on a camera. One second I would take everything in and be drowning in sensory overload, and the next my brain would drill down on a single detail and not be able to let go. The whipping back and forth between the two made me nauseated. I kept swallowing over and over as my mouth filled up with sour saliva.

The door to the back opened, and I saw Detective Chan step out leading Ryan.

Holy shit. My heart picked up more speed. It was going so fast it seemed ready to explode. I couldn't hear what they were saying. Ryan's hands were shoved deep into his pockets, and he kept giving these curt nods.

Finally, Detective Chan looked past Ryan, spotted me in the waiting room, and waved me forward. The nerves running from my brain to my legs seemed to have short-circuited because for a split second they didn't do as I commanded and I didn't think I'd be able to stand, but then I jerked up like a puppet who'd had her strings yanked.

I made myself walk toward Chan. Ryan and I passed each other midway through the room. I tried to tell what his expression meant as he went by. Was he warning me? Was he pissed? A quick look at Chan didn't tell me anything either. His face was a total blank. He'd be a killer poker player. A nervous giggle threatened to bubble up, so I made myself cough instead. Chan stood back and motioned toward the interview room.

Detective Jay was already waiting inside. He stood as I came in. I hoped he couldn't smell the sweat breaking out under my arms. I nodded rather than said hello because I wasn't sure I could manage speaking.

I took a long time getting myself settled, pulling the chair in and out slightly. I could feel the panic inside me pushing back, wanting out. Trickles of it sought any weak points in my defenses, slowly eating away my control.

". . . as you can imagine."

My head shot up. I'd missed what Chan had said. "Sorry, can you repeat that?"

The two of them exchanged a glance. "I said, we're very concerned for Paige's safety."

I nodded, then realized I was doing it too quickly, my head

jerking up and down, so made myself stop. "Me too. You mentioned having me touch her diary pages to see if could pick up anything."

"I'm afraid we can't let you see them quite yet. Right now we're not releasing the full content." Detective Jay's expression was neutral. "I'm sure you understand."

"Oh. Okay." I curled my toes inside my shoes in beats of five. Had she said something in those pages they didn't want me to see?

"We just had a couple questions for you," Detective Jay said. "Have you ever been out to Comstock Park?"

"You mean, like, recently?"

Jay smiled like it wasn't a stupid question. "Well, we're most interested in recently, but ever is good to know too."

Images of me walking through the park ran through my brain. I pictured them finding evidence I'd been there — a hair, a piece of paper from a pocket drifting to the ground. "I used to go out as a kid, for walks with my mom. And a few people used to have parties out there."

"By the river? Near the picnic setup?" Chan asked.

I nodded.

"How about the rest of the park? You take any hikes out there lately?" Chan pushed.

I shook my head. Had Ryan told them he'd met me at the theater and I'd been walking out behind the building? This was the moment of truth. I'd decided before I came that denial was my best plan.

"Have you had any other visions of Paige? Any sense of where she might be now?" Jay asked.

"No," I said.

"Can you try to get a reading from something?" Jay reached into his pocket. He pulled out a small bag. The air in my lungs locked into place.

There was no easy way to refuse. I held out my hand, and Jay poured the item out into it. I recognized it instantly. It wasn't anything of mine.

It was Ryan's bracelet. There was a piece of white medical tape over the name plate so I couldn't read the engraving. I stared down at it, my heart hammering away in my chest. If they hooked me up to a lie detector, I'd make it blow up.

I closed my fist around the bracelet and shut my eyes. It was easier if I didn't have to see them. My brain spun as I tried to figure out what to say. I could say I didn't have the sense it had anything to do with Paige, but they must already know it belonged to Ryan. I could admit I knew it was Ryan's. That would give me points for accuracy, but it was also possible he'd already told them he gave it to me. If I was him I would have given me up in a heartbeat, but I had a hunch he hadn't told them anything. He was playing for time, to get Paige back. He wouldn't tick her off if he could avoid it.

"I'm not getting anything." I opened my eyes. "Sorry."

Jay sighed. "It's okay. It was just a shot in the dark."

Chan stood, his chair squeaking on the floor. "Thanks for coming in this afternoon," he said. "Let us know if you've got any plans that would take you out of town."

I nodded. They suspected me of something. They were saying, in not so many words, that if I left, they'd consider it running.

"Would you like me to take you home?" Jay offered.

"No thanks." The last thing I wanted was time for more awkward conversation.

I walked slowly out of the building. There was always the chance that Paige had left the bracelet there by accident, but I didn't think that for a second. She'd left it to be found.

I walked down the steps just in time to see the bus turning onto the street. I started to run. I reached the stop just as it braked in a cloud of exhaust. I pulled myself inside, flashing my pass to the driver and dropping into a seat half way back.

That's when I saw Ryan. He was sitting across the street from the police station on a park bench.

Watching me.

TWENTY-EIGHT

"There you are!" Drew moved past me into the apartment, shoving a giant bottle of Diet Coke into my hands along with a bag of Doritos. "You haven't answered any of my texts. You left me with no choice but to show up here. At least I brought snacks."

My heart was still beating madly. I'd been half certain the detectives had come for me when I heard the pounding on the door, but it was just Drew babbling about how the school was buzzing with the news of Paige.

"A bunch of people are organizing a candlelight vigil tonight out at the park for Paige's safe return." Drew plopped onto my sofa. I moved my books so she had more space. "Do you want to go?"

The last thing I was going to do was provide the media with a photo op of me standing around praying for Paige. "I don't think I'm up for it," I mumbled.

Drew reached over and grabbed the bag of chips back from me and opened them. "How did your meeting with the police go?"

"Fine."

Drew folded one leg underneath her, settling in. "Seems the least they could do is tell you what's going on."

I wanted her to leave. I needed to think. I waved off the open bag of chips. The smell of nacho cheese made my stomach roll. "Sorry I didn't answer your messages; the entire day has been exhausting."

She ignored my subtle hint. Her foot nudged my leg. "It'll be okay."

"Maybe." I lowered my voice. "I think the police suspect I had something to do with it."

Drew's face wrinkled up. "Why would they think that?"

"Because of the stuff I've known." *And because they would be right.* I needed to talk to Paige, but whatever she was doing, she certainly wasn't answering the phone. I'd called roughly a million times. My eyes fell onto my bag on the floor. I willed the phone inside to ring, but it was silent.

"Hey."

I looked up.

Drew smiled. "I can see the wheels in your brain turning. I'm guessing you're already picturing yourself in prison."

"I would look like shit in an orange jumpsuit."

She laughed like I was joking. "They can't put you in jail when you haven't done anything. All you did was give a prediction. If anything, you've been helpful." Drew tossed another chip into her mouth, which was already full of carrot-colored mush. "You need to look at the bright side."

"There is no bright side."

"You're getting tons of attention; everybody wants you to do a reading for them now. Seriously, everybody."

"Attention is the last thing I want," I said.

"I know you hate feeling hassled, so I started a list of people who want you to read their cards," Drew said. "I told them not to bug you. The only way they get on the list is by talking to me." She pointed at her chest with her thumb and then leaned in. "Guess who is on there?"

"I have no idea."

"Ben Adler." Drew leaned back and smiled. "Only the very person you've had a crush on since eighth grade."

"It wasn't a crush," I insisted. "I just thought he was nice and, you know, kinda cute."

"Earth to Skye —" Drew thumped the side of her head. "That's the definition of a crush. Get this: he wants you to come to his house to give him a reading. Apparently his dog died a couple years ago, and he wants to know if you can put him in touch with her."

The idea of pretending to send messages over the Rainbow Bridge to Ben's long-lost Lab filled my stomach with a fresh dose of acid. "I don't know if I can."

"I told him a home reading was going to be sixty bucks."

I was so shocked I knocked over my water, sending a puddle all over the coffee table. I yanked the magazines out of the way before they got soaked. "Sixty dollars?"

"You're going over to his house — that's pretty good service. A reading at school is only thirty."

"I've never charged more than ten," I said. There were times when I did it just for free beer at a party. Even my mom only charged forty, and she was the professional. I'd never imagined being able to make that kind of money.

Drew passed me a wad of Kleenex to blot up the water. "Way too low. Especially with all that's going on."

"I wish you hadn't done that."

"Why? With me to organize things, we can make some serious cash in the next few weeks." She held her hand out for me to high-five.

"It has nothing to do with you," I pointed out. "You wouldn't even care if it wasn't Paige."

Drew stiffened. "Is that what this is about? What's your issue with her?"

"My issue is that you won't admit you have a thing for her."

"I don't have a *thing*. So I like her, what's the big deal?"

"She's not a nice person."

"You don't like anyone in that crowd." Drew shook her head. "And if you don't like Paige, why are you trying to help her now?"

I bit my tongue to keep myself from saying anything I shouldn't. I didn't even know why I was fighting with Drew. "I don't know why I even said that."

"I don't either," Drew fired back.

A ring blared from my bag. I was about to ignore it when I realized it was the burner phone. I jumped up, fishing for it madly amongst all the other crap I was carrying around. "I have to take this," I babbled to Drew, then jabbed the button just before it cut off.

"Hey, can you talk?" Paige's voice seemed incredibly loud.

My heart rabbited into overdrive when I heard her voice. "Hang on." I stepped closer to the kitchen, away from Drew.

"I can call later if now's a bad time," Paige said.

"Don't you dare fucking hang up," I whispered into the phone.

"Language, language," she said.

"Sure, Mr. Lester," I said loud enough for Drew to hear me. "Just a minute." I put the phone down on the counter and took a deep calming breath, before ducking back into the living room. "Listen, I have to talk to Mr. Lester. He got some information from the police."

Drew's eyebrows furrowed in confusion. "You want me to leave?"

"It needs to be private because of the investigation — it's, uh, still active."

Drew stared at me, then grabbed her bag. "You can just say you don't want me here. You know I would never say anything. You don't have to lie."

"Drew —"

"Whatever. See you tomorrow." The door shut behind her.

I wanted to go after her, but I didn't have time. I'd make it up to her once all of this was over. I ran back to the kitchen and picked up the phone, praying she was still there.

"Hellooo," she sang out.

My limbs felt loose with relief at finally hearing from her. I scurried back to my room and shut the door. I hunched over my phone. "This isn't a joke," I said. "Where the hell are you?"

"Look, I called to say I'm sorry—"

"Sorry?" I cut her off. "You realize I sent the cops on this wild goose chase, right?" I had so much built-up energy I felt as if I could have run up and down a thousand steps without breaking a sweat.

"It wasn't exactly a bust; they know I was kept there. Have you seen the diary pages?"

I clenched my fist.

"Listen, Paige—"

"Pluto! Seriously, how freaking hard is it to remember one single name?"

"Do not yell at me," I yelled back. I counted to ten. "Why weren't you at the cabin?"

"I needed some breathing space." Paige sighed. "I told you to play this my way, but you didn't believe me. Besides, I didn't tell you I'd be there. I told you to tell them about the cabin. You just *assumed* I'd be there. Have you been watching the news? I hoped they would show a shot of my parents, but so far there's only been the statement from Gregory, our family lawyer, saying that the family was praying for my safety and requesting that if anyone knew anything to please call the police."

"Yeah. I saw that," I said, my voice flat.

"He read the statement off a piece of paper. He didn't even look up into the camera. It was a missed opportunity, if you ask me. If my family really wants me home, they should have made an emotional plea themselves."

"Maybe they're too upset."

"Could be. My dad must be all broken up, because trust me, that guy never turns down an opportunity for some camera time."

Paige sounded elated. Like things were going brilliantly. If I could have reached through the phone, I would have choked her. "I'm not sure if you understand how serious this is."

"Have the police mentioned the failure to pay ransom to you yet? My dad and Gregory must be scrambling to keep that particular detail out of the press, but sooner or later, it'll leak. I made sure to have a big boo-hoo about all of that in my diary. It's going to cost him way more than what we asked for to rehabilitate his reputation when it hits the news."

I paced back and forth in front of the tiny space by my bed. "Are you enjoying this?"

She laughed. "God, yes! Doesn't everyone have this daydream? The one where you've died in some kind of tragic accident, the kind that still lets you leave behind a beautiful corpse and everyone has gathered at your funeral. They're all crying and declaring how they should have been so much nicer to you when you were alive and how their lives will be empty, shitty shells without you." She sounded almost manic.

"Are you ever coming back?" I hated how my voice sounded like I was begging.

Paige clucked. "Aw, do you miss me?"

I bit down so hard I thought I could hear my teeth creak as they ground together, threatening to crack.

"Don't worry. I don't plan to stay gone forever, but I do need enough time for people find out my dad didn't pay the ransom."

I forced myself to take a deep breath the way Lester had taught me. "Do you get what a big story this has become? I'm in the middle of all of it, and the pressure is huge." The press had been outside our apartment again this morning, this time several groups, and before heading out, my mom had primped for her now daily press conference. My efforts to make her stop were about as effective as trying to reason with waves coming to shore.

Everyone at school was talking about it. When I looked around, people were looking back. They were *watching* me. There were whispers in corners, and people ducking behind locker doors to hiss "that's her" to their friends as I walked past.

". . . *People* magazine!" Paige said, and I realized I'd stopped paying attention.

"Wait, what?"

Paige sighed impatiently. "I *said*, there's a rumor my story is going to be in *People*."

I couldn't imagine what to say to that.

"Sure, it's no *Vogue* or *InStyle*, but still, it's pretty cool. Attention like that could open doors. You never know what might happen."

I closed my eyes. She totally didn't get it. Once people had the bright light on you, they started to notice the cracks and imperfections. It was better to stay in the shadows — safer.

"This wasn't supposed to be about fame," I said.

"It's better than nothing," she fired back. "Listen, I had my own reasons for doing this, but now I'm in a situation where I'm figuring out what I can salvage. I know what you're thinking, that this is some vanity thing, but that's not true." Paige paused. "Well, it's not entirely that. I might be able to make something out of this mess. I promise if I make any money I'll share it with you. Lots of places pay big for interviews, you know. It could be lucrative, maybe even more than the ransom."

"This is going to blow up in our faces," I said, putting into words my biggest fear. I'd been caught in a lie once, and this would make the situation with my fake dad look like a walk in the park. "If you think the media loves a story about a missing rich girl, try and imagine what they will do if it comes out that you faked the whole thing. They'll eat you alive."

Paige was silent. Maybe she was picturing the headlines, the shaking head of some news anchor, repulsed as she told the story.

"I want out of this. I can't make you come back, but I don't have to participate." I hoped I sounded stern and sure of myself.

"Jesus, will you lighten up? That's why I called. I'm coming back. I just needed to give everyone one more day to figure out the stuff with the ransom. I need you to have one final vision."

The tension that had been wrapped around my chest like a coil of barbed wire suddenly went slack. I felt as if I could take a deep breath for the first time in days. The top of my scalp prickled. This would be over soon.

"Tell me where you are."

"I'm bunking down in one of the fruit stands that's closed up for the season."

There were tons of seasonal sheds that local farmers used during the summer to sell their produce to tourists on their way to their vacation homes. "Why would the kidnappers take you to a fruit stand?"

"Who knows why anyone does anything? I'll say they drove me there and tied me up. Give me extra credit for planning ahead."

I spit a sliver of fingernail out. She loved reminding me that she was always two steps ahead of me. "Okay. I'll have images of fruit and that it is some kind of store. Which one is it? Is it close to the lake?"

"Yeah, you can see the water from here."

"Okay, I'll include a hint of water too."

"You better have something else, to lead them," Paige said. "They need to find me pretty quick because I'm going to be stuck tied up. Mention a dancing banana. It's on the sign. My mom will recognize it right off the bat. We used to come out here when I was a kid. It's on County Road Forty, the one that hooks up to Traverse City. There's a horse farm across the street."

I scribbled the details down. "Okay, I got it. I'm going to go to the cops first thing in the morning before school."

Paige sighed. "I guess that's it, then."

"I guess," I said. "You are going to be there this time, right?"

I wanted her to promise, even though I knew by now I couldn't trust a word out of her mouth.

"Yes, this time I'll be there." She sounded tired of my questions. "You can't blame me for having a backup plan."

"I blame you for not telling me everything."

"For someone who likes to see herself as jaded, you're freakishly naïve. Darling Skye—I picked you because you are the type to not ask too many questions. You want to believe everything happens for a reason, but the real reason is because other people make those things happen. You keep waiting for luck to lead you, and you aren't going to get anywhere."

I stared at the phone. I had no idea what to say.

"If it makes you feel better, even though you can be a real bore, you've been a good partner. I wish I could have gotten you the money. You deserve it."

"Thanks," I mumbled and then was pissed at myself for thanking her for fucking up my life.

She laughed. "Once I'm back, we'll go out. I'll tell you everything. Trust me, there are things you will *not* believe."

"But—"

"See you tomorrow." She clicked off the phone.

After Paige hung up, I dropped my head between my knees until I got my breathing back under control. My guts cramped, and I bent farther over my knees. I couldn't pull in enough air. Panic was starting to set in.

I stumbled out into the living room. My mom stood in the open door, her purse under her arm and keys in her hand.

"I'm going out," I said.

"Skye, baby, we should talk. I heard about what happened today."

I cut her off. "Spare me how you're upset that I didn't tell you about my vision first. What you're really mad about is that you didn't have a chance to run to reporters before anyone else."

She pulled back, shocked, and I winced. Lately I was incapable of not offending everyone around me. "I'll be back later."

"Skye—"

"Later." I stepped past her quickly as if she might try and stop me, and headed out into the night.

TWENTY-NINE

I felt like I hadn't slept, but when I rolled over and looked at the clock, it was already six. I lay there working myself up for the day ahead. I kept reminding myself that I just had to push through, and by the day's end, it would be over. I'd smooth things over with Drew. If she could still organize the readings she talked about, there was a chance I could come up with the money I needed for New York. I tried to do the math to figure out how many readings I'd need to do to have enough for a security deposit, but my brain kept skipping around, unable to focus.

I was so tired the idea of getting up seemed as impossible as climbing Everest in flip-flops. I reached for my phone and texted Detective Jay, saying that I needed to meet with him. One step closer. All I needed to do was break the day into small, manage-able bites.

My nose twitched. Toast. I padded into the kitchen and stopped short. My mom was sitting at the table fully dressed, sipping out of one of our chipped mugs. Even her hair was done — not in a ponytail, but blown out.

"Coffee?"

"Um, sure." I felt underdressed in my T-shirt and boxers. I sniffed the milk before pouring some in my cup. "Listen, about last night," I started.

She waved off what I was about to say. "It's been stressful. Let's not talk about it."

"What are you doing up?" I asked.

"I'm going to the police department," she said.

My hand shook, and a dollop of coffee splashed down on the counter. "What?"

"I had a vision." She tidied the stack of catalogs in front of her, flipping through one at random. "About Paige. I was going to tell you last night, but then you went out. I called the police department first thing this morning. The detectives are going to meet me there." She chewed the rest of her toast; a tiny drop of melted Jif peanut butter dropped on the page. Mom licked her finger and wiped it off the smiling model's face.

I blinked. "What did you see?"

She leaned back in her chair and sighed. "I don't feel her any-more. I used to sense her out there, like a small vibration. I think she's gone."

"Gone? You mean, like, dead?" She nodded. Just when I thought things were already too complicated. There would be no way to talk her out of it.

"I had a vision too," I admitted.

"Tell me what you saw. I'll share it with the police when I tell them mine. Then you don't have to be involved." She leaned forward, cupped the side of my face. "I know you think this is all about me wanting media attention, but it's about keeping you out of it, the way you wanted."

"I already texted Detective Jay."

Her mouth pursed. "I wish you hadn't done that." She stood and straightened her skirt. "You better get dressed. You can ride with me."

THIRTY

I shifted in the chair. The interview room hadn't changed since the last time I was there. The detectives had separated my mom and me. They listened to my story and then went to talk to her.

On the drive over, the news on the radio had been full of the revelation that Judge Bonnet hadn't ponied up the ransom money. Paige had gotten her way. Sometime during the night, the police had released more snippets from the "diary." I had to hand it to her—she laid it on thick, talking about how she just wanted to come home safe and how betrayed she felt. Their family lawyer issued a statement that the Bonnets hadn't believed that the ransom request was from the actual abductors, just someone trying to con them. They came across as heartless, which was pretty much Paige's goal, so I suspected she was happy. Or would be when she finally heard. I felt bad for her mom and dad. They likely had no idea what they'd spawned.

I checked the time on my phone. Another minute had ticked past. If Paige hadn't already put on the zip ties, then she would soon. She'd be sitting on the dirt floor, waiting to be found. I couldn't escape the sensation that we were running out of time. If she had to wait too long, who knew what she might do. It wasn't like she was the most stable person in this equation.

Detectives Jay and Chan finally bustled back into the room. "Let's go over it again."

I scootched forward in my seat. "I don't have anything else to tell you." I bit back that I'd all but drawn them a map. All they had to do was go out and pick her up. Cue the media for her dramatic coming home photos. Jay glanced over to the two-way mirror.

I was suddenly positive that Paige was sitting in the other room. She'd found some way to blame the whole thing on me. Or maybe Ryan and me together. My mouth went dry. Who were the cops going to believe — me or a judge's daughter? My glance slid to the side to catch my reflection. I pictured Paige, her family around her in a protective circle, patting her shoulder, all watching me. Letting me squirm. Adrenaline flooded my system.

I started picking at my thumbnail and then made myself sit on my hand to stop. They would be watching me. I'd seen enough TV cop shows to know this room was wired for sound and video. Blotchy hives bloomed on my neck and chest.

Chan leaned forward on the balls of his feet. "What makes you so sure Paige is fine?" Detective Chan asked, picking up from where he'd left off earlier.

I made myself take a deep breath before I went off script. "I don't know," I said. "It's just a sense that I have. She's alone, but she's not harmed."

"What I don't understand is how you and your mom saw so many of the same things."

"What do you mean?"

"You both saw water. You mentioned a farm; your mom thought she saw some kind of field. But how do you explain that your mom's vision is different in one big way? You say she's fine; your mom isn't so sure." Detective Chan raised an eyebrow. "I didn't know the spirits were so unreliable."

Detective Jay cleared his throat, sending Chan the message to turn the sarcasm down.

"I can't explain what I do, or my mom. All I can tell you is what I feel. And all that really matters is finding Paige." I realized I was picking at the ragged edge of my thumbnail again and made myself stop.

"We've got a car headed out to check a few leads based on what the two of you said. If she's there, we'll find her," Jay said.

"Or we'll waste a bunch of time and resources chasing after messages from the great beyond," Chan said quietly.

Jay glared at him, and Chan shrugged. Detective Jay pushed up from the table. "Look, why don't you wait here? We'll know soon enough if she's out there. And if not, we'll want to talk to you more, see if we can think of any other ideas based on what you saw."

Chan mumbled something under his breath. I couldn't make it out, but I wasn't interested in asking him to repeat it. My insides were already pinched and tight without adding to my stress levels by knowing what he really thought of me. Jay brought me a glass of water and left the door open when he walked out. I peered down the hall into the lobby.

It was empty this early in the morning. I couldn't see her from this angle, but the receptionist had a super-long manicure, and her nails clacked on the keyboard. It reminded me of the sound of beetles scuttling around.

I stood and then sat again. Needing something to do, I tossed the cold water back quickly, like it was a shot of tequila. I looked at my phone again to check the time—well, that had killed all of thirty seconds.

What were the odds that my mom would have a vision about Paige on this day of all days? She didn't *know* anything. Water? We lived in Michigan. You couldn't go a mile without stumbling across a river, pond, lake, or puddle. Water could also mean a bathtub or a pool. It was a rural area, so farms and fields were also useless data. Her vision would only sound correct when they looked back on it once the truth was out.

The phone at the reception desk started erupting with calls. A few officers bustled in and out of the back, and I heard raised voices from somewhere down the hall. Something had happened. I heard Officer Chan's voice.

"Someone get the Thorn woman from interview room three and put her in with her daughter."

I stood up straight. They'd found Paige.

THIRTY-ONE

Mom plopped into the seat across from me and pulled her CoverGirl compact out to rub beige powder over her cheeks. Under her chin, I could see the tan line where her makeup wasn't blended to her skin.

Before I could open my mouth, Chan marched in, his eyes flashing. "You called the media?"

My mom nodded. I drew back at his anger, but she didn't seem shocked at all. When the press outside heard that Paige had been found, they were going to think my mom was the second coming. The fact she was alive and not dead wouldn't matter. My mom would claim that the death she saw was what would have happened if Paige hadn't been discovered in time.

Worse than just claiming it, she'd believe it. She'd stumbled into the psychic lottery — a lucky guess that paid off huge.

"What? I had a vision about Paige." Mom shut her compact with a click. "I have a responsibility to share that. I'm doing my best to get the girl home."

I stared at her. My heart cracked, and my throat tightened. My mom wanted this so bad. To discover that she was the chosen one and that her whole crappy life was for a bigger purpose.

Chan shook his head, his annoyance at my mom dripping from his expression. Jay joined him and shut the door.

"The girl is dead, isn't she?" Mom asked before the detectives even sat down.

Chan nodded. "Paige Bonnet was found murdered at a fruit stand on County Road Forty."

THIRTY-TWO

I stood up so quickly my chair fell to the ground with a clatter. "What do you mean, she's dead?" I looked back and forth, waiting for one of them to admit it was some kind of horrible, not-funny joke.

"Why don't you sit back down." Detective Jay picked up my chair for me and guided me into it.

She's dead. Paige is dead. Oh my god. I swallowed over and over to keep from vomiting.

"That poor girl." Mom shook her head. "Have you told the family?"

"No," Detective Jay said. "Not yet. The patrol just called it in. We're taping off the scene now."

"I'd be happy to speak to her parents if they'd like that."

"I think you're the last person they'll want to talk to," Detective Chan said. His face was blotchy and red.

Mom tugged her shirt down. "I'm not trying to upset anyone. I'm simply trying to help."

"You don't seem surprised that she's gone," Chan said.

Mom blinked. "I'm not. Have you forgotten that's why I came here today?" She sighed. "I hoped I was wrong, but when I didn't sense her at all . . . well, I suspected this would be the outcome."

Chan rolled up his sleeves. "What else can you tell us? What's the manner of death? Was she shot? Stabbed? Did she know the attacker?"

As he fired off options, images popped up in my head like some kind horror slide show. I pictured Paige lying there in a puddle of blood. Her hair sticking to the ground as the blood dried a dark maroon, turning tacky. Her eyes would be wide open, and her flesh would be cold. If she'd been tied up waiting for me to send the cops to her, she wouldn't have even been able to fight back. She'd have been a sitting duck.

Mom spread her hands wide. "I'm sorry. I told you everything I know already."

Chan spun to face me. "What about you?"

I opened my mouth, but nothing came out. *Should I ask for a lawyer?* Mom reached over and patted my hand.

"If you have any information, now is the time to start talking." Chan was so close to me I could smell coffee on his breath.

"I don't know anything," I whispered. Every time I blinked, Paige's terrified face flashed through my mind.

"Do you have any sense when this happened?" Detective Jay asked. His voice had grown cool and professional.

"She —" I started to say, and then closed my mouth. I'd almost said that she was fine when I talked to her last night. The words had been in my mouth trying to escape, ready to betray me. My heart was beating so fast it vibrated like a motor engine. I needed shut up. "S-s-she's really gone?"

Jay nodded. "We've got a forensic team on the way out there now. They'll establish manner of death and time. We've got some preliminary details, but we're not at liberty to share them now.

I bit my tongue to keep from asking any of the questions piling up in my head. I had to know how she died. I had to be able to picture it.

"They'll get evidence," Chan said. "Anything that was left behind. Hair, tire tracks, DNA —"

"Good," Mom said, cutting him off. "I understand that you're upset. We are too. I had a feeling, but I didn't *want* it to be true. There's no point in being angry with us. We want whoever did this to be caught just as badly as you do. If there's something we can do to help, we will."

"You've helped plenty," Chan said flatly.

Mom sighed. "I'm not sure there's any point in us staying." Her eyebrows arched. "Unless you're saying we can't leave."

Detective Jay stood. "Of course not. You're not suspects."

"Not officially," Chan added.

Jay rested his hand on Chan's shoulder. "We need to go to the crime scene. We'll want to talk to you again, but while we're gone, I'm going to ask you both to give a statement to another one of the officers."

"I'm not sure there's anything we can add."

"We'll still need a record. From the start. When you first had a vision about Paige. Every vision since then. Any detail you can remember. Once we've had a chance to see the scene, we'll be in touch with further questions."

Mom stood and hugged Jay. He went stiff in her arms. She pulled back and looked into his eyes. "This isn't your fault. I don't think there was anything that could have been done to shift what happened to Paige. All you can do now is find who did it. Get justice for her."

I shut my bedroom door behind me and slid to the floor. I could barely remember the rest of the morning. We each went over everything we'd ever said about Paige. The officer asked the same questions over and over in slightly different ways. Looking for inconsistences and mistakes. I hadn't been able to stop shaking. Usually it was my mom who was the drama queen, but we'd swapped places, and she was calm and collected, answering each question patiently until they let us go.

What the hell had happened?

My mind raced in circles, but there were only three options. One, that Paige had faked her death. Two, that a random person just happened to come across her at the fruit stand and killed her. Three, someone else knew about Paige's plan and killed her to keep her from returning.

There was a *body*. I shivered at the word. There were too

many things the police could check out—DNA, fingerprints, hair and skin samples. If Detective Jay said they'd found Paige's body, it was hers. There was no way for her to fake that.

I know people look for patterns. It's what makes faking psychic skills so easy. They see links between things that are random. The truth is, coincidences happen all the time. Not everything has a purpose. There *are* random crimes. People are murdered for being in the wrong place at the wrong time, but I was certain that wasn't what happened in this case. Paige ending up dead wasn't a case of bad luck. No one just stumbled across her way out there.

That left only option three. Someone knew where to find Paige, and they killed her. And if they knew enough about her plans to know where she would be, it meant there was a good chance they knew I was involved too. Maybe I hadn't been paranoid the day I'd been out there and thought I heard someone in the woods. She might not have hit herself to make things look real—someone might have been trying to teach her a lesson. And if I had heard them, they would have seen me for certain.

I pushed myself up from the floor. I couldn't afford to lie around feeling terrified. I had to make sure there was nothing to connect me to Paige in case the police searched the house. Detective Chan didn't trust me, and with a dead rich girl on his hands, they were going to check out every possible lead. I crossed the room and dug the pay-as-you-go phone out from under my mattress, as well as all the notes we'd passed back and forth in the encyclopedia, and piled them all into the middle of the bed. I stuffed everything into my bag and headed out. As soon as I was outside the apartment building, I stopped to pretend to tie my shoes.

The late afternoon sun was hot, and a trickle of sweat made its way from my hairline down my neck and snaked under my shirt. I couldn't shake the feeling that I was being watched. The hair on my arms prickled like antennae trying to pick up a signal.

I walked toward the street as if headed to the bus stop. Traffic rushed past. I waited until I saw two semis coming in my direction and counted in my head trying to time them. When the trucks crossed in front of me, I turned and bolted down a narrow dirt path that led down to the creek behind the bus stop.

My feet slid on the dirt and pebbles, almost landing me on my ass. I caught myself by grabbing on to a tree. The bark ripped the skin off my palm. I jogged down the path, darting a glance over my shoulder every few steps. It was probable that no one was following me, but I wasn't taking any chances. Especially while carrying a bag full of evidence that connected me to a murder.

Bile rose up in my throat while the word *murder* bounced around in my brain. I shook my head to clear my thoughts. I had to focus. I could panic later.

The trail cut behind a mini-mall with a hair salon, a pawnshop, and a dollar store that had gone out of business last year. I came up behind the 7-Eleven and paused, catching my breath.

I walked down the street and ducked into the alley between the recreation center and the grocery store. I pulled the SIM card out of the phone, rubbed the card with the hem of my T-shirt to get rid of any fingerprints, and dropped it down the grate into the storm sewer. Trying to ignore the shaking of my hands, I wiped down the rest of the phone, and then stomped on it until the screen cracked and broke. With one last look around, I chucked it into the dumpster. I fished the notes out and tore them into tiny strips, then set them on fire with the lighter stuffed in my pocket. I used my sneaker to smear the ashes left into the asphalt. No one was putting those back together again.

So long, Pluto.

A wave of relief washed through me when all of it was gone, and I felt lightheaded. I mentally went through everything we'd done. Paige had been careful, and I owed her for that. There were no calls between our personal phones, and we'd met in person only a couple of times. Nothing connected the two of us other than my predictions. That might not even be enough to give the police grounds for a search warrant. It was suspicious, but not damning. Ryan had given me the bracelet to give to her, but I didn't think he'd tell the police. The information damned him as much as me. If there was even the slightest chance he was involved, there was even more reason for him to stay quiet.

There was a split second when I imagined telling Paige how brilliant she'd been before I remembered she was dead. The knowledge sat thick and heavy in my gut. It wasn't grief exactly. Paige and I weren't friends.

The real question was, who killed her?

And did they know about me?

THIRTY-THREE

The next morning the scene outside school was surreal. I got off the bus and stood there taking it in. There were trucks parked on the street with satellite dishes on top, each emblazoned with a different network affiliate name. An alphabet soup of media. They must have driven here from all over, drawn by the story. A group of reporters stood around in crisply starched clothes, all checking their hair. Our tiny town had hit the big time.

I rubbed my face. My eyes were dry and scratchy. I cried so long last night that they were dried out.

Then there had been the dreams. Over and over, I woke up with the image of myself raising a knife above an already bleeding and dying Paige. My right arm was sore, most likely from gripping an imaginary murder weapon all night. It wasn't hard to understand—I felt guilty. If I'd told people where she was earlier, she wouldn't be dead. I hadn't killed her, but I hadn't stepped forward with everything I knew either.

Packs of reporters clustered across the street, trolling for people willing to give a reaction on the record. Suddenly everyone had been one of Paige's best friends. They positioned for camera time and cried on cue. The front fence had morphed into a creepy memorial complete with flowers, teddy bears, and notes woven into the links.

Paige's abduction had been the most exciting thing to happen at our school, and her murder took it to an entirely new level. People vibrated with excitement.

I gave the front door a wide berth. The last thing I wanted was to be caught on camera. The media didn't need my face; they had my mom. I'd tried to convince her that she shouldn't talk to any reporters, but I didn't stand a chance. She kept saying how horrible the whole thing was, but when I got home from getting rid of the burner phone, she'd already heard from two publicists who wanted to represent her.

Last night I'd lain in bed and tried to figure out if I should go to the cops and confess. This was murder, after all, but no matter which way I looked at it, I couldn't see how talking to the police would help. I had no idea who'd killed her, and if I came forward, there was the very real chance the police would blame me. The only plan I had was to keep my mouth shut and pray that whoever killed her didn't know I was involved. Or figured I wasn't worth the hassle if I was keeping quiet. It was a shitty plan, but it was the best I'd come up with so far.

I stepped into the flow of the hallway as everyone picked up speed before the last bell. People moved away from me like I was contaminated. It was one thing to have a touch of psychic ability. Being connected to murder was a different animal altogether. That wasn't cool. It was creepy. The crowd parted as Drew barreled toward me.

"I texted you a thousand times." She threw herself into my arms. "Are you okay?"

"Yeah, I'm okay." I bit my lower lip. "Listen, about the stuff I said when you came over yesterday—"

She waved off whatever I was about to say. "Don't. I was being an idiot. But that doesn't matter. What matters is that you're all right."

I nodded, my throat tightening. "I'm sad for Paige's family."

"I bet," a voice mumbled behind me.

Drew and I both whipped around. Lucy stood there throwing stuff in her locker.

"Is there a problem?" I asked.

Drew rubbed my upper arm while shooting Lucy a nasty look. "Everyone's just shocked at the news."

Lucy snorted. "What shocks me is that the police don't think it's weird you and your freak-show mom knew so much about Paige."

Drew sucked in a breath. Dougie, who was standing next to her, made a low whistling sound. Before I could think of a response, Mr. Lester's voice boomed out.

"Lucy Lam, that is *enough*," Mr. Lester barked. Everyone in the hall froze. Drew's eyes were wide, and her hand covered her mouth as if she were a witness to a drive-by shooting.

Lucy started to say something, but stormed away down the hall instead.

"Okay, people, move along," Mr. Lester said, just as the bell rang. "Drew, give me a minute with Skye." She looked at me to make sure I was okay, and I nodded.

Mr. Lester directed me into his office. Ms. Brew was nowhere to be seen. "Let me make you a cup of tea."

"I don't need anything." Lucy had basically accused me of murder in front of the entire student body. I swallowed hard to keep a sudden rush of tears back. The fact I felt like crying made me irate. I didn't want to give a shit what Lucy thought of me, but apparently I did. I hated this town, and I still wanted everyone to like me.

Mr. Lester fussed with his kettle. "It's no problem to whip up a cup; I'd already boiled water for myself. Besides, I've always believed tea makes everything a bit better." He passed me a mug. I wrapped my hands around the hot ceramic to keep them from shaking. I didn't want to drink it, but if it had been possible to crawl inside and let the hot water rush over me, I would have.

"This is a hard situation. We're bringing in extra grief counselors. But you should feel free to come directly to me."

He acted like he was a pro at handling these kinds of situations, when I knew nothing like this had ever happened at our school before. He was making up what to do the same as the rest of us. Relying on what we'd seen in movies and on TV shows to figure out how to respond.

"People think I did something to Paige," I said.

"No. That's not true," Mr. Lester rushed to say. "Everyone

knows that you and your mom were doing everything you could to bring Paige home safe."

I wondered if it was hard for Mr. Lester to continually see the best in everyone.

"Lucy doesn't believe that," I said.

Mr. Lester took a deep breath. "Lucy has her own issues that likely color how she's dealing with this news."

I sat up straighter. "What kind of issues?"

Mr. Lester tugged on his beard. "I can't say, but she and Paige had a complicated friendship. And at your age, people tend to feel invincible, so this kind of tragedy hits extra hard. I'm certain once everything has had a chance to calm down, things will look different." He patted my shoulder.

The tea sent up steamy clouds of bergamot and vanilla, and I breathed them in deeply. I took a sip. It was still too hot, and it burned my mouth, making me wince.

I let my eyes fill with tears. "I guess I'm more upset than I thought."

Mr. Lester passed me the box of tissues.

I blotted my face and sniffled. "Thanks."

He smiled. "No problem." He leaned forward. "Would you like to talk about how you're feeling?"

"Can I ask a favor?"

"Of course."

I lightly touched my temple. "I have a terrible headache. I didn't sleep well last night and then with everything today . . ." I sniffed again, attempting to look sad enough for him to feel bad, but not so sad that he felt we had to dissect my feelings.

"If you head down to the nurse, she'll give you some Tylenol."

"It's just, her office is right by the cafeteria," I said. "I don't want to see a bunch of people when I'm like this." I motioned to my face. "All of them wondering what's wrong with me." I rolled my eyes. "I know I'm being stupid."

Mr. Lester slapped his thighs and stood. "I think you're entitled to be a bit sensitive today. I'll pop down and pick up some pain relievers for you. Until then, you relax here."

"Thanks, Mr. L," I said.

He smiled and waved his finger in my face, the cedar smell of his cologne filling my nose. "No problem. But don't go telling everyone you got this rock star treatment, or people will think you're my favorite."

Great. Now I could add guilt on top of paranoia. I counted to sixty after he left. I stood and moved toward the filing cabinet. The top drawer was cracked open. My hand hovered over the handle, but I couldn't seem to bring myself to grab it. I was certain as soon as I did Mr. Lester would suddenly return, remembering that he had a bottle of Tylenol in his desk. The only times I allowed myself to go into his cabinet before were when I knew he had a meeting or was out of the building. Doing it when he was just down the hall seemed reckless. I could perfectly picture his face if he caught me going through the student files. Betrayal. Disappointment. Suspicion of what else I might be capable of doing.

Do it.

Sweat poured down my back. My hand shot out and yanked the drawer open. It came out so fast that the entire cabinet tilted.

I shoved my leg forward to keep it from falling over. My knee slammed into the metal side and pain radiated up into my thigh, throbbing in time with my heartbeat. I glanced quickly over my shoulder to make sure I was still alone. Then my fingers flew over the files, the order of the alphabet momentarily completely erased from my memory.

Finally, I spotted Lucy's file and pulled it out. I flipped through pages of test scores and grades. My finger trailed down the individual sheets of paper as I looked for something to jump out at me.

Bingo.

Around the holidays, she and Paige had been brought in to talk to Lester because of a fight they had in the locker room. I knew I had remembered something from Paige's file, but I'd never looked in Lucy's. There were more details of the fight in hers. It said that it hadn't been really violent: there had been screaming, some hair pulling, and Paige had pushed Lucy. Neither of them would say what the fight was about, but Lester had indicated he thought a boy was involved. Lester had written something about "competitive friendship" and "lack of communication skills." I squinted to make out his handwriting. There was something that, despite Lucy's past, he had no further concerns. *What did that mean?*

There was a note that Lester had followed up a week later and both of them had insisted they'd made up—good as new. I had my doubts about that. Neither of them struck me as the type to forgive and forget. I flipped forward to the end of the file and saw there was a manila envelope from Lucy's old school stuffed in the back. It was marked CONFIDENTIAL in a bright red stamp across the back flap, but it had been opened before. I pulled out the sheet inside and scanned it quickly.

Holy shit.

Lucy had been hiding a lot more than a hookup with her friend's boyfriend. She hadn't transferred here because our school had more AP classes; she'd been kicked out of her old school. I flipped the sheet over, looking for more information. All it said is that she was being expelled for "violence against another student and concerns for the emotional impact of Lucy remaining in the current toxic environment."

There was a note scribbled on the bottom of the sheet in pencil noting "no criminal charges filed."

My heart thudded in my chest. Did the police know about this? If there hadn't been charges, it was possible her record was sealed. If Lucy had a history of violence, and she and Paige had it out over Ryan, who knew what she might be capable of doing.

There was a sound in the hall, so I stuffed the paper back in the file and slammed it shut. I'd answered one question and raised a whole bunch of new ones.

THIRTY-FOUR

I needed to find out more about Lucy's past, and there was no way Mr. Lester would tell me. I waited until fourth period, then lurked outside the gym waiting for Lindsey. She finally came out of the locker room, her fine blond hair still wet from the shower. Her eyes were red and puffy.

I stepped into her path. "Hey, can I talk to you for a second?"

She stopped short and looked around. I'd checked her schedule before I left Lester's office. This was the only class she had all day without any of her usual crowd in it.

Lindsey hefted her gym bag higher onto her shoulder. "What do you want?"

I motioned to the open classroom behind me. "It'll just take a second." When she didn't move, I laid on the guilt. "I'm working with the police, and I need to ask you something about Paige. It's important."

She followed me into the empty chem lab. She put her bag down on one of the long tables and crossed her arms over her chest. "I've talked to the police three times. I don't *know* anything." Her lower lip shook.

There was a faint burnt-chemical smell in the air. Someone's experiment had gone wrong last period.

"But you guys shared a lot of secrets. Stuff you didn't even tell other people in your group." I cocked my head to the side. "She was the only one who knew why you really dropped the debate team."

The blood drained out of her face, turning her skin a pasty gray. "How do you know—" She shook her head. "It doesn't matter. I'm not telling you anything. Maybe you're working with the cops, or maybe you're just trying to dig up dirt so you and your mom can spread it around in the press. She might be a story to all of you, but she was my best friend."

"I don't need you to share any of her secrets. I need to know someone else's. Did she ever talk to you about Lucy and Ryan?" I held my breath, waiting for her to answer.

Lindsey's eyes widened. "How do you know about that? Paige didn't want anyone to hear that story."

"That's why they had the fight back around Christmas, isn't it?"

"That and the fact that Lucy was basically this huge leech. She was always trying to outdo Paige. Whatever Paige was into, then Lucy had to do it too, only bigger and better. It was like she wanted to be Paige or something. It was weird. Then she went after Paige's guy. Technically, Paige and Ryan were broken up at the time, but what kind of slut sleeps with a friend's ex? It was like because Paige had him, she had to."

"Why didn't Paige want anyone to know?"

Lindsey sighed. "I'm not sure. I told her we should take that bitch down, but Paige said no. They had it out, and then after that, Lucy kissed her ass. Paige was a bitch to her, but Lucy just took it." She shrugged. "I figured maybe the whole thing would just blow over."

"Did Paige ever talk about Lucy's past?"

Lindsey's eyebrows drew together in confusion. "Like what?"

Shit. So much for hoping Lindsey would be able to fill in all the gaps.

"I mean, there was something," Lindsey said. "She told me once after their fight that she wasn't worried about Lucy anymore because she knew something about her that Lucy would do anything to keep quiet."

"But she didn't tell you what it was? A hint — anything?" I strained forward.

Lindsey threw her hands up in the air in frustration. "I don't know. You're the one who's supposed to know everything. But if you want to find out, you should ask your friend Drew."

I bumped back into the table behind me. "Drew?"

"Yeah. Paige said she was the one who told her."

My scissors cut through the thick crepe paper. Drew had talked me into helping her and the art crowd make decorations for graduation. They were creating a large painted mural with words like *success, dreams, future,* and *celebration* woven into the edges and curves of an elaborate mandala design that would hang along the far wall of the gym for the ceremony. Not to be trusted with the level of detail required for the mural, I'd been assigned cutting out thousands of squares of brightly colored paper that would be strung together and used to decorate the stage. I didn't mind; the repetitive task gave me time to try and think.

All day my mind had been picking up the things that I knew and moving them around, trying to make sense of all of it. Like turning puzzle pieces to make them fit. Something had happened at Lucy's old school, something violent. Ryan and Lucy hooked up. What didn't make sense was why Paige would have forgiven her and made up. Why not tell everyone what Lucy had done? Paige was the victim. Lucy would have been the villain. Sleeping with your friend's boyfriend was total skank territory. Paige had only told people she could trust to keep it secret.

And that didn't make sense.

I took a peek over at Drew, who was sitting on the ground, focused on her task as she filled in a portion of the mural. How would she have known about Lucy's past? Drew had always had a bit of a girl crush on the popular crowd. And while she never had pursued her, I knew she liked Paige. I could see her enjoying having a chance to share something to finally connect her to Paige, but what I couldn't understand is why she hadn't told me. Not even after Paige went missing. She never mentioned it once. And that wasn't like her at all.

I made a stack of red squares and then started in on the yellow.

Drew plopped down next to me at the table. "You don't have to sit here by yourself, you know."

"It's fine." I searched her face, trying to figure out what else I didn't know.

Drew picked up another pair of scissors and began cutting alongside me. "Anyone else give you a hard time today?"

"No." It depended what you considered a hard time. Lucy clearly wasn't the only person who had decided that being psychic wasn't a cool party trick anymore. No one said anything — it was the way they looked at me as I moved through the halls and sat in class. Like I was a walking bad luck charm.

"You sure you're okay?" Drew asked.

"You've asked me that at least a hundred times." I focused on the paper I was cutting as if it held the secret of what I should do next.

Drew put down her scissors and turned so we were face-to-face. "I keep asking because I know you're not fine, no matter what you say. I'm worried."

"You don't have to worry about me." My eyes started to fill with tears.

"I know I don't *have* to do anything. I want to. I'm your best friend. You can try and tell me you're fine, but I can see you're not. You keep avoiding me." Her voice was a mix of irritation and worry. "You don't listen to what I'm saying half the time. It's like most of you isn't even here."

My hands started to shake, and I dropped the scissors on the table before she noticed. "Things are complicated." That was the understatement of the century. I swallowed over and over.

"Tell me what's going on." She rested her cool hand lightly on my arm.

I wanted to tell her. I'd told Drew almost everything in my life. We had years of slumber parties and whispered secrets between us. Even though we had grown apart over the past year, she was still the closest thing I had to a sister. She would understand how things had gotten out of control — that I never wanted this to happen. I just wanted to go with her to New York. I wanted to not let her down. We'd figure this out together.

"Hey." Drew's voice was soft, and I realized I was crying.

"I don't know where to s-s-start," I stuttered. I could feel all of it bubbling up inside me, ready to boil over. I looked around, trying to tell if anyone was paying attention. "Drew, I —"

"Drew! We need you." A junior held a paintbrush and a ruler. "Don't freak out, but I think we got the measurements wrong."

She looked at them, annoyed. "Just a sec." She nudged me. "Go ahead, I'm listening."

I shook my head to clear it. There was no way we could have this discussion here. I needed to get my shit together first. There was part of me that wondered what else she was keeping from me.

"Later," I said. "I've got to work tonight, but I'll text you tomorrow."

Drew sighed. "I'm holding you to that."

THIRTY-FIVE

That night I double-checked the stock in the cooler at the Burger Barn. My mind wasn't on closing, but if I forgot to call in a re-order and we ran out of ketchup or cheese the next day, my ass would be on the line. Saturday was our busiest day. Gerry didn't care about real-life emergencies — he cared about ready access to condiments. I checked the clock that hung over the pass-through. It was taking longer than I'd planned.

Tyrone wiped down the grill and then snapped his wet towel in satisfaction. "Damn, that is a pretty thing." He put his hands on his practically nonexistent skinny hips to admire his handiwork.

Carla leaned her head in. "Till's balanced, and I filled all the shakers. I'm outta here."

"See you tomorrow," Tyrone called after her. He filled a bucket with steaming hot water and a squirt from the giant container of pink industrial cleanser to mop the floors.

"I can do that," I said. I needed him to go.

He retied the scarf he used to hold back his dreads. "So, you gonna tell me what exactly you got going on?"

Earlier in the shift I'd gotten Tyrone to call Ryan and pretend that he'd heard from a friend he was looking for work and invite him to come down for a quick interview after closing. "I told you," I said. "It's just a joke I'm playing on someone."

"Uh-huh." His expression broadcast he thought I was full of shit.

"It's hard to explain."

"You sure you want to be here alone with some guy? You know there's a killer out there." Tyrone swiped the mop back and forth across the floor. I nodded. Tyrone looked me over, then passed me the mop and wiped his hands on his checkered pants. "Fair enough, but be careful."

"Everything's fine. I know the guy." I half expected my nose to grow, Pinocchio-like, with the number of lies I was spewing.

Tyrone fished his motorcycle key out of his pocket. "In my experience, it never hurts to be careful. It's when you're sure things are fine, that's when things can go bad real quick." He nodded knowingly. He peeled his stained chef jacket off and tossed it into the laundry bag. "Make sure you lock up when you leave, and don't tell Gerry I left you here alone. He'll kick my ass."

I nodded and willed him to move faster than his usual slow amble. As soon as the door clicked shut behind him, I spun the mop around the floor, giving it the barest pass. Gerry would probably complain tomorrow, but it was good enough. I stuffed the coins and bills from my tip pouch into my bag and then checked the clock again.

Where was he?

There was a loud knock on the back kitchen door, and I jumped. I stepped toward it, and then paused. I snatched one of the chef knives from the magnetic holder above the prep station and slid it under my bag on the counter. Better safe than sorry.

I pulled open the door just as Ryan was raising his hand to knock again. He dropped it to his side when he saw me. "You," he said, his voice flat.

"We need to talk." I stepped back so he could come in.

"Let me guess — this isn't about a job."

"I didn't think you'd come if you knew it was me."

"You're damn right." He pushed past me and walked around the kitchen as if he was inspecting the place. I stood next to the counter and my bag.

"This way no one sees us together. The cops might be following me, or you. I figure that keeping things quiet is in both of our interests. I have some questions."

He stopped his inspection and spun to face me. "I don't owe you shit." He held up a hand to stop me from speaking. "Last time we met, that didn't exactly go really well for me."

"You gave me the bracelet to give to her," I said.

219

He nodded. "She's the kinda girl that requires a sacrifice." Ryan looked me up and down. "Are you wearing a wire?"

"What?"

"Are you recording this? Trying to trap me into saying something?"

I pulled my shirt up so he could see my bare belly. "I'm not recording anything. Are you?"

He laughed and lifted his shirt, showing off his washboard abs.

"I want to talk because I'm trying to figure out what happened. You knew Paige wasn't abducted."

He sighed. "I didn't know. *I suspected.*"

"How?"

Ryan rolled his eyes. "Did you know Paige at all?" He walked back and forth again. "She dragged you into this, didn't she? She musta had something on you."

"No."

He smiled. "Ah, so she let you think it was your idea. That you were the lucky one. You must have been upset when things didn't turn out the way she promised."

It took a beat for what he was saying to hit home. "You think I did something to her?" I struggled to find the words to explain how absurd that was. "I'm not that kind of person."

Ryan shrugged. "Most people aren't the kind of people they like to think they are. You have no idea who I am either."

"Like the kind of person who cheats?" I fired back.

Ryan took a step forward, his face flushed, and I skittered back, bumping into my bag. The knife fell from the counter and bounced onto the tile floor. I pounced on it before he could grab it.

He held up both hands in surrender. "Whoa. Take it easy."

I looked down at the knife, surprised to see it in my hands. Ryan was nervous, his gaze switching back and forth from the blade to the back door, calculating if he could make a run for it. A rush of power ran through my body. I was in charge now. "Tell me what happened."

He backed up until he was against the grill. "Calm down. I never cheated on Paige. She broke up with me. Her dad promised her money for a graduation trip if she dumped me. How's that for bullshit?"

"Why would her dad do that?"

"Because he's an asshole?" Ryan ran his hand through his hair. "Look, he never liked me, and he's used to buying whatever he wants, including the good behavior of everyone around him. I tried to get back together with her, but she wanted that vacation more than me. Then a few weeks after we broke up, her friend Lucy asked to meet me. She said it had something to do with Paige. I met up with her at Comstock Park, and at first she was acting casual, talking about school and stuff. Next thing I knew, she was trying to kiss me, shoving her tongue down my throat, her hands on my ass."

"I'm supposed to believe you're that irresistible?" I made a show of looking him up and down.

A trickle of sweat ran down his forehead from his hairline. "No. I'm telling you it was weird. I'd only met Lucy once before at a party at Paige's place. Suddenly she was all over me."

"Let me guess—you held her off because you're such a standup guy."

"Look, I can be an asshole, but I'm not a cheater. Yeah, Lucy and I fooled around, but Paige had broken up with me."

"Did you tell Paige?"

He shook his head rapidly. "Hell no. She must have found out some other way. Paige is scary jealous, even if it isn't rational. No way Lucy was going to tell her—Paige would have wiped the school hallway with her face. I thought it would be kept quiet."

"Wow, you're a real class act."

"I never said I was." His eyes flickered back to my hands. "Look, can you put the knife down? You're freaking me out."

I'd forgotten I was still holding it. I put it on the counter, but close to me. "How did Paige react when she found out?"

"She was pissed. She keyed my car."

"Did you call the cops?"

His look broadcast that he thought I was being stupid. "Yeah, sure. I called the police and told them that it was me with my criminal record, and that the judge's daughter just keyed my car, so if they would be so kind, I'd appreciate them arresting her."

"Why was she so angry if you guys were broken up when it happened?"

He rolled his eyes. "That wouldn't matter to Paige. It didn't matter that she didn't want me anymore. The point was that I should still want her. She figured I belonged to her." He shrugged.

"Did you want her back? Even after the thing with Lucy?"

Ryan sighed. "Yeah. No. I don't know. Things with her weren't good." He took a deep breath. "The girl was crazy, but there was still something about her." He threw his hands up in the air. "I can't explain it."

"How well do you know Lucy?"

"Not well. We didn't exactly spend a lot of time talking." He smirked.

"You didn't kill Paige, did you?" I asked, already knowing the answer. He shook his head. "I didn't either," I said.

"Does it matter? She's gone."

"It matters to me." I jabbed myself in the heart with my finger.

He sighed. "Well, you're on your own. Call me cold, but it's time I focused on saving my own ass."

THIRTY-SIX

I locked up the Burger Barn after Ryan left, but I didn't want
to go home. I couldn't sleep; my brain was spinning in circles.
There weren't many options of where to go in our town after
eleven. I walked over to the twenty-four-hour Pancake Palace
and wedged myself into a booth.

The waitress dropped off a cup of coffee and left me alone
so she could go back to comparing manicures with the hostess.
I stacked the creamer containers into a pyramid, knocked them
down, and then stacked them all over again.

I clicked around on my phone, trying to find information.
I searched using Lucy's name and her former school. I scrolled
through various pages detailing her track success, her role in the
play *Oklahoma!*, and her run for junior class president. Nothing

useful. Of course if it were that easy, someone would have stumbled across it before now.

I pulled up her Facebook page. She didn't post often. Her most recent post creeped me out. It was a picture of Paige with the caption *good friends are never gone from our hearts*. I scrolled back and realized her page started at the beginning of the school year. I leaned back. That was weird. I wondered if she had an earlier page that she'd deleted.

I watched the couple one table over. The woman would pour a drop of maple syrup onto her finger and then he would lick it off. I wondered whether they'd hook up before he went into a diabetic coma. They were the only people in the place other than a truck driver wearing a MAKE AMERICA GREAT AGAIN hat sitting at the far back, shoveling forkfuls of scrambled eggs into his mouth.

I pushed the mug of coffee away from me as if it were contaminated. Was Lucy capable of killing Paige? That was pretty damn dark. I didn't like Lucy much, but I had a hard time picturing it. But I was almost a hundred percent certain it wasn't Ryan.

I pulled out my phone and did a quick search of the online student directory. Once I found Lucy's number, I sent her a text. *We need to talk.*

Her answer came back almost immediately. *Stay away from me.*

I typed back furiously. *I know about you and Ryan.*

I folded my legs underneath me, waiting for her to answer. Nothing. I waited another minute. *I'm not going away until you answer my questions.*

Two more minutes ticked by. When my phone finally rang, I jumped.

"Stay away from me," Lucy hissed into my ear.

"You and Ryan hooked up." There was a loud clatter of plates as the busboy dumped dishes into the giant Rubbermaid tub balanced on his hip.

"How do you know about that?"

"It doesn't matter. Paige must have been really ticked. I bet the cops would find that interesting."

"You don't know what you're talking about," Lucy said.

I clenched my free hand into a fist. "I want to know what happened between the two of you."

"I don't have to tell you anything."

I paused while the waitress filled up my cup with the stale coffee that had been sitting on the burner for hours. Once she moved away, I lowered my voice. "If you don't tell me, I'll tell the cops you were sleeping with Paige's boyfriend. Then I'll tell them to check out what happened at your old school." I crossed my fingers that she wouldn't know I was bluffing and had no idea of the full story.

The phone was silent. The only way I knew she hadn't hung up was that I could hear her breathing. I'd had too much coffee. My hands were shaking again.

"How dare you bring that up?" she spit.

There was a pause, and the pressure in my chest made me realize I was holding my breath.

"Did Paige threaten to tell everyone about your past?"

"Stay the hell away from me, or I'll make you wish you had."
Lucy clicked her phone off.

I needed to talk to Drew. I glanced at the giant clock on the wall; the hands were made out of a giant knife and fork. It was after midnight. No way I could show up at her house now. She wasn't supposed to be on the phone this late either. Screw it.

I rang her cell number, hung up after one ring, and then called back, letting it ring twice before hanging up. It had been our signal forever. If she was still up, she'd call me back if she could talk. I took a sip of the bitter coffee and then pushed it away.

My phone buzzed, skipping along the top of the table, and I snatched it up.

"When you said we'd talk later, I didn't think you meant this late," Drew said softly.

"I need to ask you something."

She paused as if she sensed something was off in my voice. "Sure."

"What did you tell Paige about Lucy?" Silence. "You still there?"

"I could get in a lot of trouble if it came out that I told anyone."

The smell of bacon and burnt toast was making me nauseated. "I'm already *in* trouble. I know something happened at Lucy's last school. And I know you thought it was important enough to tell Paige."

Drew sighed. "This is just between us — right? I overheard my mom talking about it with one of her friends at work. There was a girl at Lucy's old school who was a patient in the hospital, Shawna something. She was hurt pretty bad. Depending on who you believe, Lucy either pushed her down a flight of stairs on purpose or it happened by accident."

My mouth was dry. "Why would people think Lucy did it on purpose?"

"Lucy was totally obsessed with a girl in her school, Cara. Cara hated Shawna. The police thought Lucy might have pushed Shawna down the stairs to get in good with Cara, but they couldn't prove it. The official story was it was an accident."

I blinked. "That's messed up."

"Tell me about it. My mom was pissed. She thinks if Shawna had been white, the cops would have dug harder. The thing is my mom could get in real trouble if people knew she was talking about patients outside the office."

"But you told Paige," I pointed out.

"It seemed to me Lucy was obsessed with her too. I felt like someone should warn her."

And Drew liked the idea of having a secret with Paige, but I didn't mention that.

"Do you think Lucy had something to do with what happened to Paige?" Drew asked quietly.

"I don't know. Have you told anyone else?"

I heard her swallow. "No. My mom is going to be pissed if this comes out. She's not supposed to talk about patients — there are serious rules about privacy."

The waitress paused at my table again. "Anything else?" She wanted me out of there. I'd been sitting at her table for more than an hour. I shook my head, and she slid the check closer to me. "I'll be back in a minute in case you need change."

"I gotta go. I'll come by tomorrow, and we can talk."

"What are we going to do?"

"I don't know," I admitted.

THIRTY-SEVEN

I'd been up most of the night turning over what I knew. Paige had pulled together this abduction project and kept all those plates spinning. She would have covered every base. Or at least she thought she'd covered them all, but one had come crashing down along the way.

A little after two in the morning I'd sat straight up in my bed. I actually got out of bed and moved toward the door before I realized I wasn't going to be able to break into the library. I'd have to wait until they opened at eleven.

By morning, I'd started to second-guess myself. Many things seem brilliant in the dim glow of streetlights, but ridiculous once the sun comes up. I was standing at the entrance of the library bouncing on the balls of my feet and waiting for them to unlock the doors five minutes before they were due to open.

"I can always tell when it's exam season," the librarian trilled as she pulled open the heavy door. "It's one of the few times this place is standing room only."

I smiled absently as I moved past her. Exams were the least of my problems. I checked my phone. Still no word from Drew. I'd texted her first thing this morning. Knowing her, she'd let her phone battery die and didn't even know it.

I took the stairs two at a time to the reference room. I stood in the doorway. If I believed in ghosts, I'd have expected to see Paige there. Nothing but dust motes spun in the rays of sunshine coming through the window.

I stood in the center of the room. It was a long shot, but it was worth checking out. Paige had planned for everything. Now I had to hope she'd considered there might be someone out there who didn't want her to succeed.

I grabbed the *L* encyclopedia off the shelf and dropped it onto the table. The whole reason Paige had picked this way to communicate was because the odds of anyone looking here were slim. I looked to the heavens and crossed my fingers. This was it.

I turned the thin pages, and there, at the entry that detailed the Lindbergh kidnapping, was a single sheet of folded paper. I backed away.

Jesus. I had to get control of myself. This wasn't some message from beyond the grave. Paige left it for me before she took off. It was her backup plan. Even though I'd guessed she might have done this, it was still a shock to see it there. I picked up the sheet, half expecting it to burn my fingers, but it was an ordinary piece of copy paper folded into thirds. It was typed, like all of our notes.

If you find this note, something went wrong. I didn't tell you everything. The kidnapping was never my idea. It was my dad's. I didn't tell him about you — or about our plan for a ransom.

His goal was media attention for his campaign. He gets to be the noble brave father. He told me if I went through with it, he'd give me money for a car. One of these days he'll figure out that paying me off is going to be more expensive than he ever imagined.

My goal is payback. Payback for all the manipulation. It's time he learned I'm a lot smarter than he gives me credit for. He's got a big surprise coming.

I'm sure everything will go fine — if a girl can't trust her daddy, who can she put her faith in? But at the same time, I'm leaving this note just in case. You seem like a smart girl. You'll check here eventually. You're my safety net he doesn't know about. If something went wrong, he's the one. Get the bastard.

Pluto

THIRTY-EIGHT

I sat on the edge of the leather bench in the reference room. I'd read the note from Paige at least a hundred times over the past two hours. She'd left me more questions than answers. I felt lightheaded, and not just because I'd missed lunch.

Until I'd seen the paper, I'd been so sure that Lucy was somehow involved. I'd expected to find something about her in the encyclopedia. I never expected this.

Paige's dad had been behind her abduction the entire time. Now that I knew the truth, it made sense. Things had been too perfect. Paige was smart, but she would have needed help to do everything. The cops had even admitted they didn't really see me or Ryan as suspects because they didn't think a kid could pull off something this big. Instead of realizing they were right, I'd just been impressed with Paige, but it was never all her. Knowing where there were cameras, making sure the cabin was abandoned, getting supplies out there, all of it telegraphed that someone logical and methodical had been involved. Someone with resources. An adult.

Her dad had been front and center for all the media events since Paige went missing. His calls for Paige's safety had been political ads — showing that he stood for truth, justice, and the American way. I'd known he liked the attention, but it never occurred to me that the entire abduction was about getting that attention. Judge Bonnet's reputation was for being tough, but having a daughter in peril made him seem more human, vulnerable. It made people feel sorry for him.

Maybe even want to vote for him.

Paige's so-called diary pages had been endorsements at first. How he was this great dad and how she knew he'd do whatever needed to bring her home. For all I knew, he'd written the pages, or at the very least given her direction on what she should write. Then she changed the rules of the game when she asked for the ransom. He hadn't seen that coming.

My mind scrambled back. The time I'd gone out to see her and thought I'd heard someone. Had he been there? If he'd been the one to set things up, he would have known where to find her. He might have gone out there to make her get in line. An image of her bruised face flashed in front of me, and I swallowed down a wave of bile.

Had he done that to her? My bet was that she was supposed to stay in Comstock Park for a set amount of time and then find her way back, having escaped. But I knew how stubborn she could be.

Of course if I was right, he had done much more than give her a black eye for changing the strategy.

The money didn't really matter. The real wound was that she hadn't done what he wanted. When she wasn't discovered at the cabin, he must have called her. Maybe he promised her the cash if she came back. Then she told him where she was. It was possible she thought they could talk it out. That since she'd made her point, taught him a lesson, she was safe to come back. But she'd been wrong. What's more sympathetic than a man who has had his daughter kidnapped?

A man with a dead daughter.

I flopped back on the bench, and the springs squealed in protest.

I chewed on the inside of my cheek. But it wasn't just sympathy. Paige was a liability. She had a tendency to get attention for all the wrong things. People figure if you can't keep your own kid in line — how are you going to run the government?

At some level, Paige must have suspected that her dad was capable of turning on her, or she wouldn't have left the note for me.

I glanced at the paper again. Paige said she hadn't told her dad about me, but she wrote this before she took off for the cabin. If they had a confrontation, or if he threatened her, she may have told him she wasn't in this alone. If the judge knew that I knew, or that I even suspected the truth, that made me a pretty big loose end.

I could go to the police and tell them everything. Detective Chan would be smug. He'd known all the time that something was weird about the situation. He'd never believed my psychic act. But would they believe me now? The only proof I had was a single sheet of typewritten paper. I could have typed it myself. I turned it over in my hands. I'd gotten rid of everything else that connected Paige and me right after she died. It was possible the police would think I was delusional.

Or involved in her murder and trying to cover my own tracks.

I felt as if I'd downed a dozen cups of coffee and chased them with a six-pack of Red Bull. I was trapped. I couldn't tell anyone, and I couldn't be sure I'd be safe if I kept my mouth shut either.

THIRTY-NINE

Everything in Drew's subdivision looked the same. The houses were all built by the same developer in the late eighties. Each one a carbon copy of the other, with only tiny details, like curtain color or a wreath on the door, to tell them apart. I hated my apartment complex, but at least it had personality. To find her place, I always counted the houses from the bus stop. I stopped at the front door and took a deep breath before knocking.

Drew opened the door, then stepped back as if shocked to see me.

"Hey." The silence stretched out between us. "I tried texting you."

"I know." Drew looked over her shoulder and joined me on the front step, closing the door mostly behind her.

"Let's go up to your room—we should talk."

"My mom's making dinner," Drew said.

I didn't see what that had to do with anything, but we stayed on the stoop. "I know you've been worried about me, and there's been a lot going on—"

"The police came by this morning."

That shut me up. Her right eye twitched.

"They wanted to know if I knew about your financial situation." Her voice rose. "They wondered if I was worried since we were supposed to move in a few months and you didn't have the cash."

"They've looked at my bank accounts?" The temperature of the blood in my veins instantly dropped twenty degrees.

"That's not what's important," Drew spit. "What the hell, Skye?"

I focused on her. "I was going to tell you," I said softly.

She shook her head. "I gave up my dorm space. Do you get what that means?"

"I—"

She cut me off. "I've got nowhere to live. I move in three months. You looked me right in the face and lied." Her mouth twisted as she said *lied*, as if the word tasted nasty in her mouth.

My spine stiffened. "You've lied too. You never told me that you talked to Paige about Lucy."

She jolted and shot a quick glance over her shoulder. "Lower your voice. I didn't tell you, because it wasn't any of your business."

"It wasn't yours either. You just wanted Paige's attention.

We're graduating in weeks, and you still care about impressing the popular crowd. Paige was never going to like you. She's not even gay, but you still wanted her to notice you." I shook my head, trying to clear the storm of thoughts clouding up my brain. "Look, it doesn't matter—"

"Don't try and make this about me. Your lie was completely different. Face it, you never really wanted to move."

I threw my hands up in the air. "What are you talking about? This is all we've talked about for years."

"But you didn't do anything to make it happen, did you?" Drew shook her head. "You didn't actually try to save any money."

A hot ball of anger grew in my belly. "It's not that easy. You've never had to help pay the bills. It's different for me—I had other responsibilities."

Drew stared me down. "Bullshit."

"What?" I spluttered.

"I call bullshit. I never said it was easy to save money, but you had *years*. Deep down, you were scared to go, and you gave yourself a way out. You can think you are so much more street savvy than me, but you're scared. You can make up excuses if it makes you feel better, but you never really planned to leave. You lied to me and maybe to yourself, but don't keep doing it."

That wasn't true. I had planned to go. I started to shake. "I need to explain."

"You can't come in. My mom doesn't want me hanging out with you." Drew's voice was low.

"What?"

"She's been watching the news about Paige, and she doesn't like how you and your mom are exploiting her death. Then with the police showing up, she really lost her shit."

I stepped back. "I didn't have anything to do with Paige's death. You can't actually think I killed her."

"No, of course not." Drew looked away, then shrugged. "Honestly, I don't know what to think."

Her words hit me like a punch to the gut. "What does that mean?"

"The ransom money for Paige would have solved a lot of your problems." Drew's voice was tight and tiny.

"I can't believe you're saying that. You know me."

"No. I think I know you and then you do something like this." She threw her arms in the air, nearly knocking down the wreath of spring flowers her mom had on the door. "You say we're best friends, but then you keep secrets. You tell me half stories."

"I don't tell you everything, because you don't get it. You get a new winter coat every year. You never wonder if the electricity will still be on when you get home. When you say there's nothing to eat in your house, what you mean is that you don't have anything *good* to eat."

"It's not my fault my family has money." Drew stamped her foot.

"It's not my fault mine doesn't," I fired back.

"Let's face it. We haven't been close in a year. You resented me for applying to colleges, for making plans." Her lower lip shook.

I rubbed my eyes. "I never resented you, but our lives are going in different directions. We've been pretending things would be the same. Both of us have been lying to each other."

"We might have changed, but I still thought we were friends. Or maybe you just didn't want to be my friend anymore, and instead of being honest, you lied."

I blinked, trying to figure out how this conversation had gone downhill so quickly. I could feel my throat tightening as tears threatened. "Sometimes I want so badly for things to be different that I don't want to admit the truth, even to you." I swallowed over and over.

"Maybe you should just go."

I opened my mouth to argue, but I couldn't think of a thing to say, so I spun on my heel and marched off. My legs were stiff, and my joints didn't seem to work right, so my walk was jerky, like a windup toy.

A headache thumped behind my eyes. It was just as well I'd talked to Drew. Now I knew where things stood. I was on my own. I always had been; I just hadn't wanted to admit it.

FORTY

When I opened the apartment door, the first thing I saw was the police. There was an officer in the kitchen rummaging through a cupboard and another going through our front hall closet. Every atom in my body turned to sharp ice crystals freezing me in place.

"What's going on?" I managed to push out.

Mom called out from the living room, "There you are, Skye! Come on in."

My feet felt rooted to the carpet, but I shuffled forward. Detective Jay was sitting across from my mom with the tarot deck on the coffee table between them. My bedroom door was open, and Detective Chan was inside.

Mom looked up. "You'll never guess what the police found."

I looked back and forth between Mom and Jay. "Wha—" I had to clear my throat before I could continue. "What did they find?"

Mom held up something tiny and black, her face splitting into a smile. "My glove! That one I was sure was lost forever."

No way there were three police officers in our house to help my mom track down missing accessories.

"This is standard procedure," Detective Jay said, guessing the question I hadn't asked. He cocked his head at an angle. "You don't have any reason to be nervous. Unless there's something you're not telling us."

There was an awkward pause and then I shook my head. This wasn't standard procedure. They didn't believe me, but they didn't have any proof either. They were trying to rattle me.

Mom waved a finger in my face. "You afraid they're going to find a hidden stash of booze in your room?"

"No."

Mom winked at Detective Jay. "She says that now, but last summer I caught her and her friend red-handed with a bottle of Grey Goose vodka and a bunch of regrets. Do you have kids?"

"No, ma'am. Not yet, anyway." He started to turn toward me, but Mom took his elbow.

"Let's see what you have in store." She flipped a few cards over on the table. "Interesting. Queen of cups."

Detective Jay inspected the card. "Is that good?"

"It means you'll be a dad at some point."

"It can also mean new insights," I pointed out.

"I guess I'd be okay with either of those," Detective Jay said.

"You say that now, but wait until they're teens." Mom laughed. "Insights are easier."

"Your psychic business has taken off, huh?" Detective Jay said, flipping the card between his fingers. I watched the queen wink at me as she spun in and out of view.

Mom nodded and raised her chin in the air. "I even got a couple TV interviews set up."

"You didn't tell me that," I said. If Judge Bonnet was willing to take out his own kid, getting rid of my mom or me wouldn't even cause him a second of discomfort. My mom was so focused on taking advantage of her big break, she wasn't aware of how much danger she was in. I couldn't let her do those interviews. She might as well put a giant target on her back. A new wave of panic began to rise. She had no idea. "Maybe you shouldn't," I hedged.

"There's nothing I can do for Paige anymore, but I can help other people." Mom folded her hands in her lap. She was trying to look professional, but I could see the excitement in her posture.

"There may be nothing you can do, but this case is far from closed," Detective Chan said, leaning against the doorjamb. "I did have a couple of questions for you, Skye."

"You've been through my bank accounts," I said.

He nodded. "We're checking everything out."

My mom sighed. "You can't honestly think Skye is behind this."

"I don't want to believe that, but I do have questions. Skye never mentioned her financial situation."

"Did you ask?" Mom inquired before I could answer. "Was she supposed to show up and say, 'I had this prediction, and oh, by the way, here's a recent bank statement for your review'?"

"No, of course not. But as you can imagine, since there was a ransom request, we're going to look at who might benefit from an infusion of cash."

Mom laughed. "Who wouldn't benefit from extra money? You could line up suspects on every floor of this apartment building if that's your criteria. Heck, this whole side of town." She lowered her voice. "And between you and me, half the people in those fancy places across the river are in debt up to their eyebrows. They're the ones with more to hide. If you're looking for people desperate for money, I'd look at those who would be most ashamed to be without it."

Detective Jay took in the room, with its ragged furniture and worn carpet, then looked back into my eyes. "We asked around. People at your school were under the impression that you had the funds to move to New York in a couple of months with your friend. They said you were very clear about that, but that wasn't true, was it?"

"It's obvious you never had kids," Mom said, waving away his words. "You think it's easy to be the kid who doesn't have the latest iPhone, the designer jeans, or the big after-graduation plans?"

Detective Jay looked uncomfortable under my mom's barrage. "Of course not, but you understand we have to check this out. I want to help, but I need you to be honest with me."

Suddenly the bag on my shoulder felt a thousand pounds

heavier. The last note from Paige was in there. I'd taken it to show Drew before everything went to hell. If he asked to search my bag, he'd find it. My brain scrambled as I tried to figure out what I would say if he asked. My lungs felt as if they'd shrunk five sizes and were incapable of bringing in enough air to keep me alive.

"I was embarrassed, so I let people think I was moving to New York."

One of the officers came into the living room. "We're done in the kitchen."

Detective Jay sighed as he pushed up from the chair and motioned for Chan to join him. "I think we're done here. I don't want to take up any more of your time." He shook my mom's hand and mine.

"Maybe now you can focus on who really did this," Mom said. "Get justice for that girl and her family."

"Don't you two worry. We're going to catch who did this." Detective Chan held my gaze for a beat too long and then he and the officers they'd brought with them shuffled to the door.

"You folks have a good day," Detective Jay added.

I crossed my fingers that he would leave before any of them realized that they still hadn't looked in my bag.

"Take care," Mom called out.

I shut the door behind them and clicked the deadbolt.

Mom absently flipped cards on the table, lining them up in different pairs. "Huh. Interesting."

I stepped toward her so I could see the card. Seven of swords. Deception and betrayal.

FORTY-ONE

The hotel ballroom was done in deep navy blue and silver with a giant crystal chandelier. The Bonnet family was at the front on a raised platform. They'd set up an easel that held a giant photograph of Paige. It was her senior picture, her hair blown out to glossy perfection and the soft light giving her the appearance of a halo. The TV camera focused in on her picture for a beat before backing up to show the full scene.

Mr. and Mrs. Bonnet stood center stage, stiff and formal like soldiers on parade. Paige's sister, Evelyn, was there too, standing to the side, her hands clasped in front of her and her head bowed as if she was praying.

"Our family is devastated at the death of our daughter." The judge stopped to look down before continuing. "She was a bright and vivacious young woman who was called too soon from this earth."

He didn't use any notes, but his speech was too polished to be off the cuff. He must have practiced. The idea of him doing the talk over and over again in front of his bathroom mirror, getting the timing for when he would let his voice crack just perfectly, gave me the creeps. Paige had told me not to buy into his fake persona, and I certainly didn't anymore. He looked the part of a brokenhearted father, but now I could see the ugly underneath.

"We're working with the police to find the person, or persons, responsible for this tragedy." The judge paused as if overcome. He hadn't mentioned Paige's name once. She was already less of an individual. An abstract tragedy. "We appreciate anything the public can do to assist, but also seek to remind people that this is a blow to our family and shouldn't be used by others for gain." The judge stared into the camera lens, as if he could see into my living room, and I fought the urge to pull out of his line of vision.

"I've built a reputation in my career for focusing on law and order. Now it's become personal. I don't want any family, any individual, to suffer the type of loss that my family has experienced. I am sending a message to whoever was involved. If you interfere with me or my family, I will make you pay." The judge paused to ensure we all understood his determination, then leaned in to the microphones. His closed fist tapped the podium with every statement.

I chewed on my thumbnail while I watched him. I had no doubt that message was meant for me.

"I will be recommitting myself to serving this community" — *thump* went his fist — "this state" — *thump* — "and this nation" — extra-loud *thump*. "Those who would feel themselves to be above the law, who barter in fear and intimidation, should consider themselves to be on notice. There will be no place to hide. I'll dedicate my life to serving the memory of my daughter."

His pathetic speech was nothing more than a campaign ad. All that was missing was a rippling flag in the background and an eagle swooping across the stage.

After a pause to make sure everyone had time to digest his words, the judge pointed at a reporter in the front row who stood to ask her question.

"Yes, does this mean you're formally announcing that you are entering the Senate race, Your Honor?"

He turned ever so slightly so his profile was to the camera. "I don't think now is the time and place to make a political announcement."

I gagged on the bile coming up my throat, knowing I would have bought this line of BS from him if I didn't know the truth. He pointed to another person in the crowd.

"Have the police identified any suspects?"

Judge Bonnet shook his head sadly. "I'm not at liberty to comment on the investigation, but I believe there are no imminent arrests planned."

"Has your family approached the psychic, Susan Thorn, to see if she can provide any further information?"

My heart skipped a beat. The vein above the judge's eyebrow pulsed when my mom's name was mentioned. "Our family is putting our trust in the police." He looked past her to see if there were any other questions.

The nerves down my spine prickled, like spider legs dancing down the thread of a web. What if he went after my mom? Despite all her bluster, she hadn't really predicted anything, but Judge Bonnet might not know that. Heck, even *she* didn't know that. He might think she knew something, and if he did, he'd want to stop her from knowing anything else. I burrowed deeper into the stack of cushions on the sofa, pulling them up and over me.

Judge Bonnet stood center stage with his arms wrapped around his wife and daughter as the press conference came to an end. He planned to stand on Paige's dead body as a way to leverage himself into office. Her limp form under his wingtips, her soft, decaying flesh giving way as he scrambled up the election ladder. Who would want to run against a grieving father?

I picked at a loose thread on the pillow. I was the only one who knew he'd done it. Without me, he'd get away with it.

FORTY-TWO

I couldn't just call the police and tell them to check out the judge. I needed to give them a reason. Trying to figure out a psychic vision that would lead the police to Judge Bonnet was tough. The best readings are vague. You guide a person part of the way with a half-formed idea and let them take it the rest of the way to the finish line. You mention that you see a man, maybe older, and then allow them to ask if it is their long-departed grandfather, or dad, or brother. I didn't want to run the risk of sending the police after just anyone, but I worried that if I was too specific, it would raise their suspicions further. It was a tricky balance.

I tried out different scenarios in my head until I decided it would be best to keep it simple. I'd say I kept seeing Paige and her dad and that the image gave me a sense of dread. I'd insist that I didn't know what it meant, but that I was certain it was somehow important to what had happened to Paige. Maybe it would force them to look at Judge Bonnet more carefully. He *must* have made a mistake somewhere. All I needed was for them to find it and start unraveling his story.

Detective Jay met me in the waiting room. I stood and moved toward the back where the interview room was located, but he stepped front of me. "Let's get a cup of coffee instead," he said. He winked at the receptionist, who was ignoring us while sorting a huge stack of files. "The stuff here isn't bad, but going out gives me an excuse to stretch my legs."

I paused. Coffee seemed . . . social. "I don't have a lot of time." I rocked back and forth on my heels. "I'm supposed to be in school. I shouldn't be too late."

"C'mon, I could use some fresh air. And you've got, what, just a week or so left until school's out? You won't miss much." Detective Jay headed for the door, leaving me no option but to follow him outside into the spring sunshine. A line of brightly colored red and yellow tulips bobbed in the wind in front of the building. He jerked his head across the street. "I know some people think Starbucks is the corporate overlord, but they do a pretty good latte. There's another place, but it's a couple blocks down."

"No, this is fine," I said. Closer was better.

He insisted on paying and told me to grab a table while he waited for our drinks. He walked over carefully with the cups in his hand and couple of small bags pinched between his fingers. "I got some banana bread. Don't tell Chan. He's got this thing about us cutting down on sweets, but banana bread is practically fruit, right?"

I raised a single eyebrow. "Sure."

He laughed and nudged the chai tea I'd asked for over to me. "You must be about ready for graduation."

I sipped my tea, inhaling the spicy scents of cardamom and cinnamon. Suddenly he was my new best friend and hadn't shown up at my house to rifle through my panty drawer looking for evidence. "Uh-huh."

"Since you're staying local, you still thinking about college?" His eyes watched me over his cup, blowing on it to cool it down.

"Nope." *Why didn't he want to know why I'd called?* My stomach was too tight to take even a sip of my own drink, but I picked up the cup and pretended.

"Did you ever think about checking out the community college up in Traverse City? They've got some good programs, some practical stuff too that doesn't take too long. Hairdressing and dental assistant, stuff like that, in addition to a bunch of university transfer options."

I put my tea down on the table, still sticky from the people who had been there before us. "I appreciate the career advice, but I called you because I had another vision."

Detective Jay sighed. "Yeah. About that. I should tell you before we go further, I didn't tell Detective Chan you were coming by, and I didn't officially log your call. This conversation is just between us, off the record."

"Why?" Another ripple of unease ran down my spine like a lit fuse, setting each nerve on fire.

He leaned back in his chair and it creaked in protest. "Did you know I grew up on the east side?"

"No." I pushed the slab of oily banana bread he'd bought me back to his side of the table.

He broke off a corner of the pastry and tossed it up, catching it in his mouth. "Yep. My dad died when I was pretty young, so my mom raised me and my three sisters on her own. Wasn't easy. There were times when I wasn't sure I was going to make it through school."

Was I supposed to express sympathy? Salute him as a brother in arms in the war on poverty? I fidgeted in my chair. "You know what they say — high school isn't forever."

He chuckled. "Thank god, huh?"

I pushed back slightly from the table. "I'm not sure what you're trying to say."

He sighed. "Chan's still new to this field. He figures if something doesn't add up, it equals guilt. But I'm trying to express that I get it."

"Get what?" I realized I was shredding the napkin he'd given me. There were tiny brown paper scraps all over the table and my lap. I swept them off onto the floor.

"I get that people might tell the police something untrue for all sorts of reasons that have nothing to do with guilt. I understand that it's hard. Hard to face graduation when it seems like everyone else is moving forward and you feel stuck in place."

"I'm not stuck." People at the tables nearby turned to stare, which made me realize I was almost yelling. I lowered my voice.

A woman pulled her baby carriage closer to her table. "I've got plans. Just because I don't have the money for New York doesn't mean I'm giving up."

"There's nothing wrong with wanting more than what you got. It's what drives us." His eyes softened. "But that doesn't mean you can say or do whatever you want."

My chest tightened. It felt like I couldn't get a deep breath. "What are you talking about?"

"I know you're not a psychic."

I blinked. How the hell had he figured it out? My breath came in shallow pants that I fought to get under control. I'd assumed if either of the cops was going to discover the truth, it was going to be Chan. I took another drink of tea to buy time and to keep myself from bolting toward the door in panic.

"You're not the first person to get caught in a lie and next thing you know it gets away from you, but you have to stop. You can't keep digging yourself in deeper."

I nodded, still unable to say anything. It didn't matter how he'd figured it out; he knew.

"Your mom only wants the best for you."

My heart locked up in my chest everything, coming to an abrupt stop. "Wait. My mom was the one who told you I wasn't a psychic?"

He nodded and brushed the banana crumbs from the napkin into his open palm and then ate those as well. "It must be hard, knowing your mom has that ability and you don't. There's nothing wrong with wanting to feel special."

Detective Jay glanced around the café. "I can understand why you made your mom's initial predictions sound like they were yours. Maybe you thought it didn't matter who had them as long as you tried to get Paige home safe. Or you thought if people thought you had this ability, you would look cool."

"My mom told you," I repeated. I wouldn't have been surprised if Lucy or Ryan, or even Drew had been the one to spill my secret, but that it had been my mom shocked me.

He nodded. "She came to see me after we searched your place. We met outside the station. She didn't call you out publicly; she didn't want to embarrass you or get you in trouble. I'm the only person she's spoken with about this."

The thoughts in my head tumbled around like laundry in a washer.

"Detective Chan thinks the predictions have just been lucky guesses," he said. I didn't point out that Paige hadn't ended up very lucky.

Detective Jay wiped his mouth with a napkin. "Lou's a great detective, but he's not comfortable with this kind of thing."

"Psychic phenomena," I said. The words made him fidget. Jay wasn't as comfortable as he thought either.

"He likes to rely on facts. Things he can see, touch, taste, feel. That's partly what makes him uneasy with this situation. Sure, your mom made some things that could be seen as random guesses, but that's to be expected. She got the cause of death wrong, and the thing about Disney never panned out, for example."

"I didn't know any of this," I said. The milky tea coated my mouth, a sugary sweet slick of fat on my tongue that I couldn't get rid of.

He smiled at me, like the face you make when elderly people are struggling to make change in the grocery checkout and holding up the line. The face that says you're trying to be patient, but you also think the other person is the tiniest bit pathetic. "If it makes you feel better, I think you were only trying to help."

"I can't believe my mom told you I was a fake."

"She didn't say it like that. She wanted me to know that you weren't involved."

"But you still think I might be."

Detective Jay leaned back. "I'm a pretty good judge of character. I don't think you've been a hundred percent honest with me, but no, I don't think you had anything to do with Paige's death. It would be better if you and your mom had more than each other as an alibi for the night Paige was killed, but police work isn't usually that tidy."

For a split second, it seemed like the entire café went silent. The whooshing of the milk steamer, the clamor of people in line asking for Venti cups and extra shots of syrup, the clank of the bucket-sized coffee carafes being loaded, and the metal *ting* of the creamer thermoses on the marble countertop — all disappeared.

"Alibi?"

He nodded. "She confirmed you two were together that night."

I pushed my chair back. Why would she lie about that as well? She knew I was out that night.

She thought I was guilty. That's why she told him the visions were hers. She wanted to get his attention off of me. "I guess there's nothing left to say," I said.

Detective Jay stood quickly reaching for my elbow. "Hey, I didn't want to upset you." He held me in place, staring into my eyes.

"You didn't," I said. My lie floated in the air between us, bloated and grimy.

"I wanted to talk to you because it's important to me that you understand that I get why you did it. I don't blame you and I'm not mad, but you have to stop. This is a murder investigation."

The walls of the café, complete with floor-to-ceiling shelves, seemed to be closing in on me. I was going to be buried under bags of dark roast and overpriced coffee grinders.

"Fine." I pulled back. I was ready to thank him for this touching intervention, tell him anything, just so we could end the conversation.

He let go of my arm. Perhaps they'd taught him in the police academy that holding a teen girl against her will in front of a bunch of witnesses was poor form. "I'm here if you want to talk."

"I'll keep it in mind." I gestured toward the door. "I need to get going. Really. I've got school." I hated feeling like I needed his permission.

He deflated back into his seat. "Okay." He waited until I had the door pushed halfway open before calling out, "You don't need to tell stories to be special, you know. You're a pretty neat kid just the way you are."

Everyone in line, or seated at the tables, looked up to catch this heartwarming after-school-special moment. I closed my eyes briefly, wishing that if I could have a magical ability, it would be teleportation, so I could vanish from this spot in a puff of smoke.

"Thanks," I said, then practically dove out the door.

FORTY-THREE

After I left Detective Jay, I walked quickly to school but stopped outside the front door. I should have gone in. I was already late. I'd missed more classes in the past couple of weeks than I had in the entire four years before all of this started. But each step looked a mile high; the door appeared to weigh a thousand pounds. I didn't have the strength to make it inside. Drew most likely would still be giving me the cold shoulder. Everyone else would be watching me, waiting to see what might happen. I tried taking the first step, but then stopped. I couldn't do it.

I spun and kept walking until I was outside the Catholic church. The door creaked open and the smell of the place — furniture polish, dusty books, and incense — enveloped me. It smelled like the place where magic potions were made. I crept in and absently rubbed the foot of the stone statue of the Virgin Mary that stood in the back of the lobby.

I slid into a polished pew and stared at the crucifix hanging at the front trying to calm my thoughts.

I shifted on the wooden seat. My eyes traveled around the walls of the church. There were paintings of various miraculous moments, a pregnant virgin, loaves and fishes to feed thousands, Christ floating up to heaven with his arms spread wide. No one saw anything exceptional in those miracles. They were accepted. Normal.

I'd always denied that my mom had any kind of special powers or ability. I made fun of the mere idea.

There were times when my mom *had* seemed to know things. The day my grandpa died, my mom had mentioned that morning that she dreamt about him visiting her. And there was the time she kept me home from school because she felt like something bad would happen, and that day a bunch of kids in my class got food poisoning from dodgy birthday cupcakes. I'd chalked those up to luck, but what if she *was* psychic? Maybe the person who wasn't willing to see reality was me.

The TV was on as I came into the apartment hours later, one of those ballroom dancing shows. The air smelled like a field after a rain, so my mom must have busted out the Febreze. She swept around the living room. It looked like she was doing the tango. She didn't stop when she spotted me and instead kept time with the music, her arms held out in front of her, embracing a ghostly dance partner.

"The school called," she called out over her shoulder. "They said you didn't show up today."

I should have known the secretary would call. "Sorry," I said. "Needed a break."

Mom stopped dancing and wiped the sweat from her brow. "Fine with me. I told them I'd forgotten to call you in sick."

"Thanks." I leaned against the wall.

She smiled. "No problem. I remember how hard it is to sit in class, especially when the weather gets nice."

"I went to the police department this morning."

She caught my expression and stopped dancing. "Ah." Mom clicked off the TV and sat on the couch.

I crossed the room and sat next to her. It was easier to talk when I wasn't looking directly at her. I pulled the afghan onto my lap, even though it was too hot for a blanket. I buried my fingers into the scratchy acrylic yarn. "Detective Jay said he knew I was a fake. That you told him that."

"You want something to drink?" Mom went out to the kitchen and poured herself a glass of white wine from the box in the fridge. She popped her head around the corner. "You want a glass?" She smiled at me. "After all, it's after five somewhere in the world."

"Of wine?" I asked, surprised. She'd never me offered me a drink before, and it seemed like a trick question.

She laughed. "You're eighteen. I'm not so old that I think this is the first drop of alcohol you've had in your life." She put her hands over her ears. "Not that I want you to tell me."

It wasn't my first drink, but she was wrong if she thought I was getting drunk at parties. Other than the time Drew snuck the vodka out of her parents' liquor cabinet, we hadn't done much. My mom often confused her wild teen years with mine. Drew and I had been more into Netflix and craft projects than boozy parties.

Mom passed me a glass. "Here's to good times ahead," she said, and we clinked.

I took a cautious sip. The wine was ice cold. It must have been near the back of our fridge, where things had a tendency to freeze. "Why did you tell him all the visions were yours?"

She shrugged and then fished out her bra strap to yank it back up. "They suspected you might be involved. Telling them all the visions were mine seemed the easiest way to get their focus off you."

I took a deep breath. She thought I was guilty. "If you thought I was faking, don't you wonder how I knew what I did?"

Mom put her glass down on the coffee table on top of an outdated *People* magazine she'd nicked from the beauty salon. "You have abilities."

I stared down at my knees. "I didn't have a vision. Not then, not ever."

She sighed. "You won't want to hear this, but your skepticism keeps you from seeing the truth. You have the ability, but you get in your own way."

I opened my mouth to argue, but she cut me off.

"You *were* involved with what happened to Paige."

If I hadn't been sitting down, I would have fallen. For a few beats, the only sound in the room was the ticking of the clock in the kitchen. "What do you mean?"

Mom picked up her glass and drank half of the wine in one long swallow. "I had a vision of the two of you. It didn't make a lot of sense at first, but I think Paige wanted to disappear and you helped her somehow."

I was lightheaded, and a thin sheen of sweat broke out all over my body. There was no way she could know. "That's why you told him we were together the night she died."

She nodded tersely. She took me by the chin and turned my head so our faces were inches apart. "I will do whatever I need to do to keep you safe. You are my child. I won't take even the slightest chance that the police will blame you." She leaned forward so our foreheads touched for a second. "You're a part of me. We don't always get along, but never doubt that I would do anything for you."

"Even if you thought I killed Paige?"

She closed her eyes as if the words coming out my mouth hurt her, then she kissed me on the cheek. "I don't need psychic abilities to know you didn't kill Paige."

I sagged back on the sofa. My entire body ached as if I'd run a marathon. I hadn't realized how I'd been tensing my muscles. "I know who did it. It was her dad."

Mom blinked for a moment and then stood. "This calls for more wine." She topped up both of our glasses and came back. "Tell me everything."

FORTY-FOUR

I lay in bed, the covers pinning me in place. I hadn't been tucked in since I was a small kid, but my mom had insisted. She came into my room, jabbed the blanket under the mattress, and then sat at the edge of the bed. She kept telling me how it was all going to be okay, trying to convince me, or herself. Eventually, she turned off the light and left me there.

I felt hollow, like after you've had the flu and everything inside you has been hurled violently out. The rest of the afternoon and evening had been unreal. We sat in the darkening room, our feet tucked under us, making a plan. The wine made my head swim, since I wasn't used to drinking, but I was still able to lay out, step by step, how the situation started and then unraveled. At times I got confused on what happened when, but I kept circling back until Mom knew everything. How Paige had approached me with the idea. I told her about Paige changing the plan when her dad didn't pay the ransom. Finally, I told her about the note and the realization that her dad had been involved.

I'd expected my mom to gasp in shock or throw her hands up in the air, one of her typical overly dramatic reactions, but she stayed silent. I could see her mentally taking notes. If anything, she became calmer the wilder my story became.

"Does he know about you?" she asked when I finished.

"I don't think so," I said. Mom stared toward the sliding glass door that led to our tiny patio, but I could tell she wasn't really seeing the headlights going past on the road outside.

"You can't tell anyone," she said. "He'll say you did it for the money."

"But he never paid the ransom."

Mom looked at me with a hint of scorn. "Do you think that will matter? He'll say he did pay and you killed her so you wouldn't have to split the cash, or he'll say that you killed her in revenge because she never had the money. His kind always comes out on top." Her voice was bitter. "He'll be believed because people like him always get the benefit of the doubt. But us? We're expected to be losers. You come forward with what you know, and trust me, you'll be the one to pay."

I'd never heard her talk like that. Her anger was pulsing in every word she'd said.

"I can't just walk away. He *killed* her."

"He's a judge. You're a teenager. Who do you think people will believe? Your best bet is to graduate and then get out of this town. Get to where he can't hurt you. You're eighteen. You'd be tried as an adult. You'd have already admitted to lying to the police about her disappearance."

"One lie doesn't mean I'm lying about everything," I said.

She clucked her tongue. "Do you hear yourself? You're supposed to be the skeptic out of the two of us."

My head fell back on the sofa. "I don't know what to do. I thought I could give the police a vision that would make them investigate him. He must have left evidence somewhere. But now that they think I'm a fake, they won't believe me."

We sat in silence. The wine was long gone. What unnerved me was the fact that I'd so badly misjudged everything. Paige, Drew, Lucy, my mom. I prided myself on my ability to read people, to peel back their layers and know their motivations, but I'd missed so much. I hadn't even been aware of my own motivations. Drew was right. I had talked about moving away, but I hadn't saved. I could have gotten a second job, I might not have had all the money I needed, but I gave up on myself years ago. I'd been scared to go away. It was easier to stay and complain than go and figure out that maybe I didn't have what it took to make myself over. If I couldn't even know why *I* did things, it made me wonder what else I hadn't seen. Or what I was still missing. I couldn't shake the feeling that there was a detail that was just outside of my view. But the harder I tried to figure out what it was, the more difficult it became to focus.

My mind ran over and over every interaction I'd had with

Paige. Everything that came out after she died. What I knew and when I knew it. Something was out of place, but I couldn't spot it.

My mom broke the silence. "You can't go to the police. "

"I know." I sagged.

She smiled. "But I can."

FORTY-FIVE

When I slipped through the metal detector, I half expected the alarms to blare as if I were smuggling in a gun, but my plan of attack came with less hardware. The armed guard rummaged through my bag, but then handed it back and waved me through.

The lobby of the courthouse was designed to impress. The ceiling soared up two stories with a wall of glass to counterbalance the stone walls on the opposite side. It wasn't an inviting place. There was a huge metal statue of Justice. She was blindfolded, which was supposed to show she was impartial, but it struck me that it looked more like she had been tied up, like a hostage.

My mom had left for the police station first thing in the morning to give the detectives the vision I'd thought of the night before. I argued that I should go along, but she was firm. She wanted me to stay home and wait. She said she didn't know if she could pull off faking it if I was watching her. She called me in sick again to school so at least I didn't have to sit in class.

My mom was confident that this would work, but I was less convinced. The cops might or might not have listened to her, but once she told them, Judge Bonnet would hear about it, and he'd see her as a threat if he didn't already. The judge had a nasty way of dealing with things he found threatening. Last night my mom had brushed off my concerns, saying that he wouldn't dare do anything to us, that it would look too suspicious. But I couldn't shake the feeling that he was the kind of person who had the cash and resources to make something look like an accident. Unless the police arrested him, we'd always be looking over our shoulders, wondering when he was coming after us.

We wouldn't be in this situation if it weren't for me. I was the one who got greedy and agreed to Paige's plan. I needed to be the one to fix it.

An elderly security guard sat behind a desk. He was listening to baseball on a small transistor radio. I didn't even know tiny radios like that existed anymore. It looked like he'd brought it back from World War II. He held up a single gnarled finger for a moment so he could hear the announcer and then shook his head.

"Cubbies are playing the Tigers," he explained. "You looking for a particular trial?" He pulled out a sheet of paper that had a spreadsheet in tiny print listing names next to courtroom numbers.

"Um. I'm looking for Judge Bonnet's office. His wife said he's here." The guard looked at me. "I went to school with his daughter," I explained.

He shook his head. "Damn shame, that."

"Yep." I forced my face into what I hoped would pass for a sad frown.

The guard pointed me down the hall to the offices. As I made the walk, the walls seemed to close in, and I kept reminding myself to remember to breathe. This was no place for a panic attack. He wasn't going to do anything to me in a place crawling with police, security, and lawyers. I paused outside the door that had Judge Bonnet's name engraved on a metal plaque.

I can do this.

The way you make yourself into the kind of person you want to be is by taking action. I pushed the door open and stepped forward. The secretary inside was practically buried under stacks of files that were piled on her desk in unsteady columns.

"I'm here to speak to Judge Bonnet," I said.

Her face wrinkled up. "He's not taking appointments today. If you give me your name and number, I can try to book you in as soon as possible, but he'll be off the rest of this week."

"He'll want to see me," I said.

She raised one perfectly tweezed eyebrow. "I doubt that. He's not a huge fan of things that aren't on his schedule."

"Tell him Skye Thorn is here to see him."

She shrugged, but lifted her phone to relay the message. Her mouth popped into a tiny *O* of surprise, and she mumbled a response. She hung up, and as she stood, she tugged her fitted black pencil skirt into place. She opened the door that led to his space. "The judge says he'll see you. He's asked me to go down to the cafeteria and get you something to eat. They have good blueberry muffins. Would one of those do?" Her annoyance at being made an errand girl was obvious.

The last thing I wanted was something to eat, but I was willing to bet what the judge didn't want was a chance that anyone would overhear even a word of our conversation. "Blueberry sounds great," I said, stepping past her into his private office.

They call them judge's chambers, which has almost a regal sound, but his office was boring. The walls were covered with shelves lined with books, and there was too much large wooden furniture for the space. He motioned for me to shut the door behind me. We stood there staring at each other. Now that I was here, I wasn't entirely sure how to start. It didn't help that every ounce of spit had dried up in my mouth, leaving my tongue stuck in place.

"I assume you're here for a reason," Judge Bonnet said finally when he heard the outer office door close.

I nodded. "Paige wants you to confess."

He rolled his eyes. "I suppose you have some kind of connection with her in the great beyond?"

"Yes." I was proud my voice stayed calm and even.

He snorted like it was a joke, but he grew paler. "And you expect me to believe that?"

"No. I suspect you won't." I kept my hands in my pockets so he couldn't see they were shaking. "It doesn't matter if you believe me or not."

"Then what are you doing here?"

"Paige knows what you've done. *You* know what you've done."

"What are you talking about?"

When he leaned forward, I stiffened my spine and stood straighter. He couldn't know I was scared. "I know the entire kidnapping idea was yours. I know everything."

His Adam's apple bopped up and down, and a slick smear of sweat broke out across his forehead.

"Then she asked for a ransom, and you couldn't have that. Or maybe you worried that she wouldn't stop asking for money."

"I loved Paige," he said.

"Then why did you call her a whore when she came back from Florida last year?" I said, throwing out one of the details Paige had told me when we first met.

He flinched. "She knows I didn't mean that. I was angry." He shook his head. "She must have told you those things before she died."

"Really? Do you think anyone would believe Paige and I were friends who traded secrets? Your daughter wants you to know that if you don't come clean with what you did, it will come out. She made sure of that. You won't win that Senate race. And it won't just be politics — you'll lose everything."

He wiped his forehead. "You can't put some kind of voodoo hex on me."

I laughed. "Of course not. This isn't about me. I just came to tell you so that you can confess."

"I'm not confessing," he said. "You and your mother can't prove anything. You're a bunch of" — he scrambled to think of the right word — "hucksters. I don't know how you're doing this, but I don't trust either of you."

I turned my head to the side. "You know what I find interesting? It's that you aren't protesting that you're innocent. Only that we can't prove it."

He stood straighter and gestured to the door. "I think you should leave."

I wrinkled up my nose like I smelled something foul. "You killed your daughter to avoid paying a measly ransom. How do you sleep at night?"

The vein in his forehead throbbed like a snake under his skin. "You need to leave now, or I'll call security."

My legs shook, but I held my ground. "My mom is at the police station. The police are going to check out your story, you know. They're going to crawl through everything. You better hope you dotted every *i* and crossed every *t*."

He leaned forward, his face in a snarl, and I backed up a step. "You think you scare me? I don't have to answer to you about what I did or didn't do. I'm smarter than you can even comprehend. The police couldn't find their own ass without me providing a map. They aren't going to find a thing I don't want them to find. They will *never* know my part in this.

"Are you so stupid that you think I did something this large without making sure every single detail was covered? You think I got to this point by being *careless?* You say whatever you want, but you have no proof. I will sue you and your low-rent mother. I will take every last fucking dime from your measly lives." Spittle flew from his mouth, hitting my face as he spoke. "I will make that shithole you live in now look like a palace. So if you and your mom have a brain cell between you, you'll leave me alone."

"Paige will never forgive you," I said.

"Look, I don't know if you're in touch with Paige or not, but she can't do a thing. She's dead."

"Fine, I'm going." I threw the heavy door open and stepped out into the secretary's still-empty space.

"You came here to warn me?" the judge called out from his office. "Maybe you better take a warning from me instead. Stay out of this. And if you really are getting messages from Paige, you best tell her to shut up too. No one wants to hear what she has to say anymore."

I bolted down the hall. Once I rounded the corner, I stopped and leaned against the wall. I bent over, sucking in air, my entire body vibrating with fear. This guy wasn't going to give in easily, and I sensed he didn't make a lot of mistakes.

But he'd made one.

My hands were shaking so hard I could barely pull my phone from my pocket. I flipped it over in my hand and turned off the record function. The fact Ryan had asked me if I was wearing a wire last time I talked to him gave me the idea. I wasn't going to have any more conversations I couldn't prove.

My mom was at the police station making her prediction. The cops might ignore it, but they weren't going to be able to ignore what he'd said. I didn't need Paige to speak from beyond the grave; the judge had done it for her.

FORTY-SIX

No more press conferences at fancy hotels. The judge's family didn't surround him this time; the guy next to him was his lawyer. When the only person you can get to stand by you is being paid to be there, it's not a good sign.

The lawyer stood in front of the bank of microphones. "Judge Bonnet will be making a short statement. We will not" —he paused to look out at the crowd of reporters as if they were naughty children— "*not*, be taking any questions. As you may be aware, Judge Bonnet surrendered himself to the police yesterday after some new information about Paige's abduction came to light and he was formally charged in the abduction and death of his daughter. He is currently free on bail. He vehemently denies any involvement in her death, and we look forward to having the opportunity to prove this in a court of law. We are cooperating fully with the investigation."

The lawyer stood to the side and motioned for Judge Bonnet to take his place. His hands quivered slightly as he gripped the side of the lectern. "I did not kill my daughter Paige. I did not hurt her in any way, nor would I. Like many fathers and daughters, Paige and I didn't always get along. I was frustrated when I felt she wasn't living up to her potential, and I suspect she felt that I didn't understand her. However —" His voice cracked, and he looked down for a beat to gather himself. "However, I loved my daughter very much. She was an amazing and complex young woman." He took several deep breaths as if he were about to dive into the deep end.

"While I was not involved in her murder, I'm ashamed to admit that I *was* involved in her abduction. With Paige's full co-operation, I came up with a plan to have her . . . disappear for a period of time so that it would seem she'd been kidnapped. I did this with the intent of gaining media attention for my run for political office. I am not proud of this decision, and am unable to understand how I came to a point where I felt this was, in any way, an appropriate choice." He stopped to look up at the crowd of reporters. "I didn't believe that Paige would be at any risk, and no one in my campaign staff was aware of my actions. The Republican party should not be held accountable for my mistakes, and I apologize to them and my supporters for this grave loss of judgment on my part.

"While I am willing to take full responsibility for the plan I constructed with Paige, I want to stress again that I was in no way involved with her murder. I'm willing to take whatever punishment is required for filing a false police report and will cover the costs of the investigation, but I did *not* kill my daughter. The police's insistence of focusing their investigation on me means that a murderer is still out there — free."

The judge blinked. He seemed to waiting for the reporters to take up his cry and demand the police do something, but they stared blankly at him with their microphones extended.

The lawyer moved to stand next to the judge and touched him lightly on the elbow to move him aside. "That's all we have for today. We ask that the media don't rush to judgment, even if the police have. We are confident that once all the details come out in court, a very different picture will emerge. We are offering a reward for any information that leads to Paige's true killer. And we remind you that in our system of justice, the accused is to be presumed innocent until proven guilty. Thank you."

I sank into the sofa cushions. It made me sick that he had the gall to stand there and talk about how he'd loved Paige. The only thing he was sorry about was that he'd gotten caught.

FORTY-SEVEN

The Burger Barn was slow. The rush was over, and there were only a couple of tables left. Early in my shift, a little kid had thrown his sundae at me because he didn't like "nilla" ice cream, so I had a smear of crusty dried hot fudge down the front of my uniform. I prayed no one else would come in so I could go home early. My feet hurt, and I had exams starting in the morning. With all the school I'd missed lately, I needed the study time.

The bell above the door tinkled, and I jolted when I saw it was Mr. Lester. He smiled and took one of the stools at the counter.

I held up a menu, but he shook his head. "Just a sparkling water."

Did he know where he was? Grease we had. Fat we had. Food products full of sugar and questionable chemicals aplenty. Sparkling water was not a Burger Barn staple.

"We have Sprite," I offered.

His nose wrinkled. "Green tea?"

"Lipton," I countered. I rummaged through the tin by the coffee station and dug out a creased foil package. "You're in luck —it looks like there's one mint left."

"Sold."

I pulled out a mug, filled the tiny metal teapot with water, and passed both of them over to him.

"You ready for exams?" He dunked the tea bag into the tepid water.

I shrugged. "Mostly. I'll cram a bit tonight. Then I've still got a paper to finish for English. We're doing a presentation instead of a test."

He nodded. "Must feel nice to be almost done."

I nodded and smiled because that was expected. I didn't honestly know what I felt anymore.

"I wanted to give you something." He slid an envelope across the counter.

I picked it up. "What is it?"

"It's a letter of reference." He took a sip and then put the mug right back down. "I know you don't have any college plans, but you never know. Plans change."

I swallowed hard. "Thanks."

"There's one in there from Detective Jay too. I kept copies of both in your file, so if you lose them, just let me know."

"I probably won't need them," I said. "This place doesn't require a lot of formal references."

Mr. Lester looked around. "Nah. I imagine not. But you won't stay here. You'll be on to bigger and better things."

"How do you know?" Maybe I hoped he was psychic.

He smiled. "Just do. Things often have a way of working themselves out the way they're meant to." He pushed away from the counter. "One other thing I happen to know is that there is someone outside who wants to talk to you."

I looked past him out the big plate-glass window. Drew stood by her VW Bug in the parking lot. "Can't help yourself, huh?" I asked.

He shrugged. "The peacemaker role comes as part of the job."

I stood at the counter fidgeting with one of the ketchup bottles, my fingernail making half-moon impressions in the paper label.

"Friends come and go," Mr. Lester said. "But I have to tell you, keeping the bridge open so they can return is never a bad idea." He gave me a half salute and headed out, tucking a few dollars under the saucer of his mug.

Part of me had hoped I'd be able to simply ignore Drew until she moved away. I sighed and peeled off my apron. "Tyrone, mind if I knock off early?" I yelled to the back.

He popped his head out. "You never do much work around here anyway; you might as well go."

I stepped outside into the cool evening air. I hated that she was seeing me in my stained uniform with sensible old-lady waitress shoes. I had a vision she'd come back from New York months from now and I'd have to replay this whole scene over. She'd keep getting more chic and fashionable, and I'd stay exactly the same.

Drew and I stood in the parking lot. There was a long quiet pause. If she thought I was going to talk first, she was nuts.

"You must be feeling better," Drew finally said.

At first I wasn't sure what she meant and then I realized she was talking about missing classes again yesterday. "I wasn't really sick the past couple of days," I admitted.

I heard her take a deep breath. "I heard the news about Paige's dad getting arrested," she said finally. "Everyone at school is talking about it."

I inspected my fingernails. They looked horrible.

"I wanted to say I'm sorry," Drew said in a rush. "I never should have said the stuff I did at my house. I feel terrible."

"Uh-huh."

"I hate that things are like this between us." Drew bit her lip.

"Me too." I searched my feelings, but all my anger at Drew was gone. There wasn't even sadness really, just regret.

Drew took a deep breath. "You still thinking about New York?"

"I'm not going," I said. "You were right. I could have saved the money, at least more than I did."

"Maybe if you save up for a year, we could get a place together then."

"Yeah, maybe." I kicked at a loose stone with my shoe. "To be honest, I think I need to figure out what I want to do before I make any big plans."

Drew nodded. "You could still come visit. We could go to the top of the Empire State Building and take that cruise out to see the Statue of Liberty."

I smiled. "That would be pretty awesome," I said. "You can show me around, give me the local's view so I can skip the touristy stuff."

Drew tapped her foot on the ground. "You want to come over to my place tonight? We're going to order pizza."

I wondered what her mom thought of that idea. "I would, but I need a shower." I tugged on my uniform. "Then I really need to study."

"We could study together after school this week," Drew offered. "Ice cream and cramming."

"Sure. Sounds good."

Drew relaxed and smiled. "I'd really like that."

"Me too." We stood there awkwardly. It was like a first date, where you're trying to figure out if you'll kiss or not. It was never going to be the same between us, but maybe it could still be all right.

FORTY-EIGHT

I trailed after the hostess through the maze of tables. One of the large glossy shopping bags I was carrying whacked into the back of an elderly woman who turned around to glare. As I passed her, I noted that rich people smelled different. Crisp and clean, like laundry on the line or fresh apples.

"Sorry," I whispered. It seemed like the kind of restaurant that called for lowered voices. I'd seen places like this on TV, but before this moment, the fanciest restaurant I'd ever eaten in was an Applebee's.

"Here you go." The bracelets on the hostess's arm clinked musically as she pulled out a chair and held it. I slowly lowered my butt to the cushioned seat, and she pushed it in before quickly rushing to help my mom. She handed each of us a huge embossed leather menu.

I waited until she walked away. "This place is expensive," I said, stating the obvious. "We don't have to do anything fancy," I said. "You already got me the dress and stuff for graduation."

Mom smiled at me over the top of the menu. "This is a celebration. You don't graduate every day."

"I haven't graduated yet," I pointed out.

"I'm pretty sure you'll make it through the final week." She winked. When the waitress came by, Mom ordered a glass of champagne for herself and a sparkling apple juice for me.

My finger trailed down the list of items on the menu. There were almost too many—my brain was swimming in choices. "I'm not sure what to get."

She smiled. "Don't be nervous. We got this. I'm going to get the salmon," Mom said snapping the menu shut. "I like how they say it's on a *bed of roasted vegetables*, like it's sleeping." She giggled. "All tucked in with a blanket of ginger sauce."

"I might get the pasta." My glance kept falling on the cost of each item.

Mom poked my menu. "Don't you want the steak? You can be a vegetarian when the options aren't so good."

"Are you sure?" The filet was the most expensive thing on the menu.

"Now, I know it's not on a bed of anything, but it still sounds pretty fancy. We're celebrating. Go for it." She wiggled in her seat like she was dancing.

We put in our orders and then Mom raised her glass. "To us," she said.

I clinked mine to hers. There wasn't a drop of booze in the sparkling cider, but it still felt as if the bubbles were going to my head. The waitress had left a tiny tray with olives, fancy nuts, and dried fruit that I picked at.

"I have some good news too. A bit extra to celebrate," Mom said. She squirmed in her seat, and I realized she was ready to explode with excitement. She'd never been able to keep a secret; her inner ten-year-old was a big blabber.

"What is it?" I poked her shin under the table with my sandal. "Tell me."

Mom tucked her hair behind her ears and sat up straighter. "As of this morning, ten thirty to be precise, I am pleased to announce that I signed a book deal."

I nearly aspirated the olive that had been in my mouth. I coughed the half-chewed chunks into my hand and wiped them onto the linen napkin. "What?"

She smirked, smug that she'd surprised me with her announcement. "You heard me. I signed a book deal. The publisher wants to call it *A Psychic Solution*. How cool is that? The agent woman set the whole thing up. I haven't even written a word of it yet, and they're still giving me half the money upfront." She lowered her voice. "It's almost as much as I make in a year at the Stop and Shop."

"Mom, that's awesome. You're going to be an author."

"Pretty fancy for a girl who didn't even finish high school."

She buffed her nails on her shoulder and laughed. Her face was flushed.

"I guess you better get used to eating in places like this," I said.

She picked at the bread they'd brought. "Maybe." She lowered her voice. "To be honest, I think most of the time I'd prefer Chick-fil-A."

"You shouldn't eat there," I started to say.

"I know, they're racist. You tell me all the time."

"Homophobic," I said. "That's just as bad."

"Could be, but they do make a good sandwich." She looked to the table next to us to see which knife the woman used to butter her bread and copied her.

"I'm really proud of you, Mom." I realized I was. It was like she was transforming into someone completely new, or was it possible that I was finally seeing her for who she could be if she only had a chance?

She lifted her glass again. "Here's to the Thorn girls moving onward and upward." We toasted that and then came up with increasingly silly toasts until the waitress brought out our plates. She placed them down carefully as if they were works of art instead of food. I had the urge to applaud.

I felt a bit guilty about eating a cow, but vowed I'd go back to lentils tomorrow. It was like what we were eating came from a different planet from the food that filled our fridge. I'd be stupid to pass up this opportunity.

Our plates were whisked away, and our waitress brought a

stiff parchment sheet decorated with calligraphy script. "Our dessert selections," she declared.

"I'm stuffed," I said. "If I eat one more thing, my pants are going to split."

"They have cheesecake with blueberries," Mom said, consulting the sheet.

"Well . . . maybe we could share," I said.

Mom laughed and requested two forks. "I have something for you." She reached into her bag and pulled out a tiny box that she'd tied with a red ribbon. She saw my raised eyebrows. "Consider it an early graduation gift."

I carefully untied the bow and opened the box. Inside there was a magazine picture folded up into tiny eighths so it would fit inside. I opened it and realized it was a shot of the New York skyline. I looked up, uncertain.

"I was going to put in a check, but you can't cash it until I get the book money, which won't be for a couple months." She smiled. "This was the best idea I could come up with for the meantime."

"What do you mean?"

Her smile grew wider. "I'm going to give you the money to go to New York. Enough to cover your half of an apartment for two or three months. That should give you time to settle in, find a job, and figure out what you'd like to do."

I traced the lines where the picture was folded. "Mom, are you sure?"

She reached over and touched the back of my hand. "I know I

haven't always done a great job at this mom thing, but I was only a kid when you were born. It took me a while to figure things out. Now I can do this for you, and I really want to."

My lower lip shook. I pushed the box back toward her. "It's your money."

"I want you to have all the chances I never had. You go off to the big city and knock 'em dead, kiddo." She tossed back the last of her champagne. "And when you want, you can come visit me to talk over your options." She paused. "But you won't be visiting me here."

I wiped my eyes to get rid of the tears that were threatening to fall. "You're leaving too?"

"No reason not to. I can write that book anywhere." She glanced over at me as if disclosing a secret. "You were right when you said I stayed here because it was safe. I was too scared to change things, but I'm not anymore. I think we'll both do better with a fresh start."

"Florida?" I guessed. My mom had always talked about the Sunshine State as if it were the Promised Land.

"Miami. I even checked out possible apartments on the Web."

I sat across from her, shocked. An idea flitted through my head like a hummingbird. "Starting over in a new place isn't going to be easy," I pointed out. "You won't know anyone, and it will take a while to figure out where you're going, what grocery store you like, all that kind of stuff."

Her lips pinched. "Yeah." She took a deep breath.

I nodded. "It might be better if you went with someone."

She shrugged like it wasn't a big deal. "I got nobody."

"You got me," I said. Maybe Miami was exactly what I needed, a new place, a fresh start.

Mom's eyes welled up as we stared at each other across the table. "Are you saying you want to come too?"

Her reaction made a tiny explosion of happiness in my chest like fireworks. "I only picked New York because of Drew. Miami could be pretty cool."

Mom put down her fork. "Are you sure? I'd love to have you, but I don't want you to feel like you have to take care of me. That's not your job."

"We'll take care of each other. I'd like to go." As the words left my mouth I realized they were true. I held out a warning finger. "No borrowing my bathing suit if yours is wet."

Mom's smile nearly split her face in two. "Deal. I'm predicting there's nothing but up for the Thorn family."

I laughed. "Is that an official prediction?"

"You can take that one to the bank."

FORTY-NINE

The number of people feeling overly emotional as we stood in the back of the gym the following Saturday waiting for the music to start surprised me. A bunch of them were hugging and vowing that they'd always be the very best of friends. They hung on to each other as if we were about to go in and face a firing squad, rather than a graduation ceremony. Despite the fact I'd been counting down the days I had left in school since grade eight, suddenly I started to feel connected to all of them too. I'd miss them in a weird way.

Drew rushed over as soon as she saw me. "You look really nice."

As if anyone was going to look attractive in a neon blue fire-retardant gown. "Thanks," I said.

"Let's get a picture." We threw our arms around each other,

and she held her phone out to grab a selfie of the two of us. We'd taken more pictures together in the past week than we had in years. It was like both of us wanted to document that there had been a time when we'd been the very best of friends. Drew had found a roommate service in New York and was talking to a bunch of people online. She was going to be okay. We both were.

"Are you going to come over after this?"

"Not sure. There's still a lot to do." Mom and I were leaving first thing tomorrow morning for Florida, and I still had packing to do. I had no interest in celebrating the past. What I cared about was ahead of me. It was a good feeling.

We'd sold or given away our furniture. We'd been bunking down in sleeping bags for the past couple of nights. We were only taking what we could fit in the car.

Ms. Clark, our biology teacher, was trying to get everyone else into the tidy alphabetical line that we'd practiced. She had sweat stains under each arm and sounded like we were getting on her last nerve. She clapped her hands and tried to herd us into order. I checked to make sure no one was looking right at me and picked my thong out of my rear. It was hot and sticky, and I wished I'd worn shorts instead of a dress.

"People, you need to be in line *now*. Please make sure you are in the right place. Remember, the alphabet is going backward for this." Ms. Clark checked her watch again. "We're starting," she said for the third or fourth time.

Almost nobody paid her the slightest attention. What was she going to do, give us detention?

"You'll call me when you guys get to Florida?" Drew asked.

"Of course." I poked her in the ribs. "You still going to come visit?"

"When I want a break from all the snow in NYC, you won't be able to keep me away."

The band burst into Pomp and Circumstance, and that got everyone moving. Drew hugged me before darting away. We shuffled into place with only a bit of jockeying to figure out where we were supposed to be and began marching in. I glanced around as soon as I was in the gym and spotted my mom. It wasn't hard. She was waving madly from the bleachers like she was trying to direct aircraft. I smiled and waved back. This was it.

"Commencement means beginning," Martina Lopez, our class valedictorian, said. I rolled my eyes. I'd hoped for more originality from someone who was a straight-A student and could swear in four languages. I closed my eyes and let myself drift while she talked.

"Our future is no longer a distant thing, something to talk about, to dream about — the future is here. We walked into this room as students, and we walk out as citizens of the world, ready to take on our destiny."

I wondered what her destiny would be. She was scary smart; she could do anything. I'd given Martina a tarot reading once, but I couldn't remember what she'd wanted to know anymore.

"At a time when we have everything before us, we should take time to remember those we've lost. Many of us struggled with the recent death of our classmate and friend Paige Bonnet. But she would be the first to tell us not to be sad, but instead to use what happened to her to motivate us to reach for our dreams."

I shifted in my seat and refused to turn around. Our class had decided to leave her seat empty for the ceremony as a tribute. I had the irrational feeling that if I turned, I would see her sitting there, staring back at me. Blood dripping in bright red drops onto the gym floor.

". . . Paige is a reminder that we never know how much time we have left."

Please don't say *carpe diem*, I thought.

"We need to seize all opportunities before us. Carpe diem!"

I stared down at my lap and realized I was picking at my cuticles. There was a tiny dot of blood on my gown. It looked almost black. Like the pupil of an eye looking out.

"Paige was the center of our social orbit, a star, and she'll always be missed." Martina said.

I sat up. I'd missed something, although I would have sworn I caught every word.

"What did she say?" I whispered to Jamail, sitting next to me.

"Shhh," he said.

Martina had finished her talk and was already walking back to her seat. I shifted again.

They started calling our names. When we practiced, they told us not to call out or applaud when anyone's name was announced, but of course people still did.

Center of our social orbit. A star. I turned the words over in my head, trying to figure out what it was about them that bothered me. The words were like burrs stuck in my brain, digging their way in, catching.

Drew crossed the stage for her diploma. I heard her brother let out a whoop, and she pumped her fist in the air before she came down the stairs. Her hair was starting to frizz in the heat.

The row in front of me stood and shuffled to the side of the stage to wait for their names. Our row got up and stepped toward the stage. Once I was up, I couldn't help but see the empty seat for Paige a few rows behind mine.

Center of the universe. Star. Planets. The words tumbled around in my head and then fell into place, like puzzle pieces clicking together.

My lungs locked, refusing to do their job. I tried to suck in a breath, but it kept hitching in my chest.

Jamail nudged me in the back, and I half tripped up the steps. I was breathing now, but too quickly. Black dots danced in the corner of my vision. I wanted to turn and bolt, but I couldn't run away. The truth was inside my head, slamming around, trying to get out.

"Relax," Ms. Hunt, my English lit teacher, said to me. She was standing at the edge of the stage, making sure we didn't clump up. "Take a deep breath and enjoy this moment," she whispered.

I didn't even hear my name called. Ms. Hunt gave me a faint push in the small of my back, and I stumbled across the floor. I took the tiny leather folder that held my diploma from our vice principal and then shook both her and Mr. Boyle's hands.

I walked carefully down the stairs. My hands shook, and the faces around me were blurred. It was too hot in the gym. Sweat trickled down my back. Even more tiny black spots popped up around the edge of my vision, and they started to rush in, filling the space. My ears rang.

There was another teacher standing at the side who stepped forward to direct me back when I'd walked past my row, but I dodged him and kept heading for the exit doors. I heard Drew hiss my name, and someone else mumbled something, but I didn't turn my focus from the red exit sign at the back. If I looked away for a second, I was sure I wouldn't make it.

I hit the panic bar and pushed out into the foyer. Now that I was out of the gym, the ringing in my ears was even louder, like a car alarm in my head. I grabbed my bag from the pile in the corner. I started running. The doors to the outside were open, and I flew out as if a killer were on my tail. That thought made me break into hysterical laughter. I tore the flat cap off my head and tossed it aside as I ran through the parking lot. By the time I hit the far side near the playing field, I bent in half, sucking in deep breaths.

Center of the universe.

Planets.

She'd called herself Pluto — for the missing planet. It was a joke.

But you know what else is called Pluto? Disney's cartoon dog. Disney.

Judge Bonnet hadn't killed his daughter. My mom had.

FIFTY

My mom wove her way through the parking lot toward me. She stopped to pick up my cap. I stood there shaking as she drew closer. There was no point in running.

"Are you okay?" She brushed dust off the cap and handed it back. "Did you get too hot in there?"

"It was you." In my mind I'd pictured myself yelling out the truth in her face, but the words came out soft and hushed.

Mom sighed, but didn't respond. She knew I knew.

"You aren't even going to deny it, are you?"

Mom jerked her head toward the playing field and the empty bleachers. "Let's sit down and talk about it."

I laughed. "Are you kidding?"

Mom rolled her eyes, "Candi, there's no reason to turn this into a drama queen situation." She walked past me over to the bench seat. She carefully tucked her skirt under her.

I stood there for a beat, staring at her, but she didn't meet my eyes. I took a few steps back toward school and then stopped. Where I was I going to go? I walked over to her and crossed my arms over my chest. "Why?"

Mom motioned for me to sit, and I sank down on the bench next to her. "Let's just say I had another vision about Paige, about what happened to her," she said. "Do you want to hear it?"

I wasn't sure if I did. "Yeah," I finally croaked.

She looked out over the field. "The . . . person who did this. They didn't intend for it to happen."

I focused on breathing in and out. "You're saying it was an accident?"

"Paige was going to break. No way she would have kept that story going. Once she came back and there was real pressure and questions, she would have given in and left you holding the bag. And if she hadn't, what was her dad going to do? You think he wasn't going to want to know where that money went? You would have gotten caught in the fallout."

Was she trying to tell me she'd done this for me?

"In my vision she said if she went down, so would you." She looked away.

"So—" My breath caught in my throat, and I had to swallow over and over to get control. "So this . . . person confronted Paige, then killed her to keep her quiet."

Mom blinked and then shrugged. "I guess they panicked. Things would have happened fast."

"Detective Jay you said you got the way she died wrong. Why?"

Mom tucked her hair behind her ears. "There's a line between accurate and too accurate."

"Paige was innocent; she didn't deserve to die."

Mom shook her head, her hair flying back and forth. "Paige was a lot of things, but she wasn't innocent. She knew what she was doing."

I pulled off my gown and wadded it up.

Mom grabbed me by the wrist and yanked me so I was facing her. "Stop. I was protecting my daughter. In both our cases, things went farther than we wanted."

I pulled free of her grasp. "I didn't kill anyone."

"Because you didn't have to." Mom pushed the hair out of her eyes. Her hands were shaking. "Paige laughed at you, you know. She had you wrapped around her little finger. You were just a means to her end."

"I thought —" My voice cracked, and I had to pause to clear it. "I thought maybe you had real abilities." A bitter laugh came out of my mouth. "How's that for karma? I made fun of people for believing in me, but I fell for your story."

Mom wiped her palms. "I heard you on the phone. After you left, I went into your room and found the notes and figured out what happened. I realized then I had to do something, so I drove out there. You wrote down exactly where to find her."

Guilt dropped heavy onto my chest. I'd basically drawn her a map to Paige. "I *believed* you." Tears ran down my face.

"You believed what you wanted. You always have." Mom reached up and wiped my cheek. "Oh, Skye, baby. We're going to be okay."

I pulled away from her. "We are *not* okay. There is nothing about this situation that is even remotely okay."

She stood. "Let's go home."

"I don't want to go anywhere with you." Then I turned and ran.

The library was quiet. I went to the bathroom to wash my face. When I closed my eyes, an image of Paige rushed into my head. A hot rush of bile came up, and I spun, slamming the stall door open just in time to vomit the strawberry Pop-Tart I had for breakfast into the toilet. My stomach clenched until there was nothing but sour spit in my mouth. I went back to the sink and splashed more water on my face and swished my mouth out. I threw my cap and gown in the trash and buried them under paper towels. Screw the deposit.

I made it to the reference room by keeping one hand on the wall, as if the library had turned into a boat on storm-tossed waves, but I was the only thing that was unsteady. I sank into a chair and ran my hands over the scarred table. I felt impossibly old. Every joint, bone, and muscle ached. It was as if my entire body were bruised.

I was surrounded by reference books, but there wasn't anything that could explain how things had gone so fundamentally wrong. I wanted to reach back, step by step, and figure out how I'd found myself here. If I could identify what step had led me to this place, then maybe I could figure out what to do next. It was as if I were in the middle of a minefield. My next move could move me to safety or blow things completely up.

How had I not seen it? She must have always suspected something was off. Deep down, no matter what she said, she always knew I wasn't psychic. At first she wanted to believe, but she must have wondered what was happening. Then she did what she always did when she didn't know something — she snooped. I couldn't be sure when she finally put it all together, but it was likely when Paige wasn't at the cabin when I'd predicted she would be.

Detective Jay told me that Mom had made a prediction about Disney. She'd left it general. She hadn't used the word Pluto. She'd seen the notes between Paige and me, overheard our conversations — she would have known the name. She thought of the dog, not the planet. She didn't know it was an alias that Paige came up with — she thought it was a nickname. That's why she mentioned it in her vision — she thought it would be an easy hit. She'd found my hiding places before. She'd listened at doors because she liked to know what I was up to, like a nosy sister.

I pulled out my deck of tarot from my purse and shuffled. The sound of the cards whispering as they touched was oddly soothing. I dealt three cards. I closed my eyes and formed the question in my head. What should I do? I flipped the center card.

The Hanging Man. Appropriate. That was me, the hanging girl, always trying to turn things upside down and see them in a new way.

I flipped the card on the left, five of cups. A card for loss and grief.

I stared at the card still lying face-down. Was I prepared to do whatever the card said?

I flipped it quickly as if I wanted to sneak up on my future.

The Wheel of Fortune. Fortune turns — sometimes it goes your way, sometimes it doesn't.

I tapped the card on the table. It didn't really tell me much. It was all in the interpretation. If I believed in destiny, then whatever I was going to do had already been decided on a cosmic level. What happened next was already determined and there was no point in being anxious or upset, because whatever I did would still lead me to where I needed to be. What happened next had been set out as my future from the moment my mom pushed me out into the world. Instead of fighting against destiny, perhaps what I needed to do was surrender to the universe. Time to stop sitting on the sidelines and join the action.

Or maybe that was just a cheat. Saying it was destiny was a way to justify my own actions. To give me an excuse to do what I wanted.

Fate and destiny might be what you make of them. And what you're willing to live with.

FIFTY-ONE

The apartment was silent when I pushed open the door just before five a.m. After the library closed, I walked for hours, ending up in the Pancake Palace nursing a cup of coffee and a greasy breakfast of eggs and veggie sausage until the waitress started giving me dirty looks. I hadn't wanted to go home, but I couldn't hide forever.

I stepped into the living room. My mom clicked on a lamp next to her on the floor. I blinked in the sudden light.

"You okay?" she asked. She was bundled up in her worn sleeping bag, surrounded by boxes.

I nodded.

Her gaze traveled over me. "Graduation can be overwhelming," she said finally.

I nodded again. A tear fell from my eye, and I wiped it away with the back of my hand. I stared out over the window into the apartment parking lot. The sky was already growing brighter. "You went through my things."

"I've always kept an eye on you. I'm your mom. When you didn't talk to me about things, I paid attention. Listened. Looked around."

I glanced at my mom. "It wasn't just about me, though, was it? If it hadn't been for Paige and your . . . visions, you wouldn't have a book deal or any of it." There it was. My biggest fear. That she hadn't done it to protect me and instead to get what she wanted.

She didn't look away. "And I wouldn't have been able to offer you the money to go away. We'd still be here." She waved her hand to the room around us.

"Still, the way things turned out is good for you."

"Good for us. And this time it went our way; other times it hasn't. Haven't you figured out by now that things aren't fair? Maybe this is just good luck. The wheel of fortune turning in our favor for a change."

I thought of the tarot cards I'd dealt mere hours ago. Was it that easy? Just choosing which way to read the cards, or the decisions we made. We were still dancing around it. If I asked her straight out if she'd killed Paige, she'd tell me. But she might not be honest about why she'd done it. Maybe she wasn't even being honest with herself. My mom was great at the reality that served her best. But if I knew the full truth, I'd have to deal with it. "Paige's dad will go to jail."

She shrugged. "He'll get a trial. With his money, there's a good chance he'll get off."

"What if he doesn't? He could sit in prison for the rest of his life."

Mom sniffed dismissively. "What happens in the court case is out of my hands. The man's a pig. He used his daughter. If he wasn't guilty of this, he had plenty of sins that he was never held accountable for. The idea of him sitting in prison isn't going to keep me up nights." She heaved herself up from the floor. "And speaking of nights, this one is pretty much over. I'm going to put these last few boxes in the car. I want to be on the road before traffic gets bad."

She pulled a fleece top over her T-shirt and yanked her hair into a ponytail. She hefted a box onto her hip and headed for the door. She paused in the doorway. "You gonna help?"

The back seat was packed to the roof. Getting everything in had been a high-tech game of Tetris, putting boxes in different combinations until they all fit. She stopped at Dunkin' Donuts to buy us each a coffee, and the smell of it filled what space was left. It was still so early that we had the road mostly to ourselves. My eyes were gritty from the all-nighter. She'd insisted she'd drive so I could sleep. She'd even tucked a pillow in the front seat for me. I held it close to my face. It smelled like Febreze.

She pulled the car over in front of the police station. People were already going in and out of the building. The tulips that had been in bloom just days ago were already limp and dying. My mom's fingers were white where they gripped the steering wheel.

"You have anything you need to say to the detectives before we leave town?" She glanced over quickly and then back out the windshield. "Any unfinished business? Because once we leave town, it will be hard to come back."

I stared at the door. She was right. There was a limited window of opportunity. Would anything change if I told them what I knew? Paige was still dead. And it was still partly my fault. I could tell myself that I had no idea how things would turn out, but then neither did my mom or her dad. Destiny spun the wheel and did what it wanted, and the rest of us just had to hang on for the ride and do the best we could with the cards we were dealt.

Or maybe that's what I told myself. That if destiny wasn't happy with my decisions, karma would find a way to pay me back.

"Nope, I don't have anything else to say," I said finally.

Mom took a deep breath and popped the car back into drive. "Well then, let's hit the road."

FIFTY-TWO

I stood in front of the judge's desk. I could see the top of her head where her hair color was growing out as she looked over the paperwork. I'd dressed up for the occasion. It wasn't as if it was going to make any difference, but it seemed respectful to make the effort. Now that I was here, I felt nervous, and I had to focus on not picking at the nail polish on my finally grown-out nails.

We'd only lived in Miami a month, but my skin was already a deep tan. I'd gotten used to going from the swampy heat of outdoors into air-conditioned buildings, but it was so cold in the courthouse it felt like there was a layer of frost building up on the skin of my arms.

The judge looked up at me. "It doesn't make any difference, but do you mind me asking why?"

"It was never right. I just decided it was time I do something about it."

She nodded. "Fair enough. Benefits of a free country mean we can all change our names if we feel like it." She winked. "As long as you fill out the paperwork." She picked up a thick fountain pen from her desk and scribbled her signature on the bottom of the sheet before passing it over to me. "You'll need this to apply for a new driver's license and passport."

I looked down at the page as we walked from her office. With a swipe of her pen I was no longer Candi Thorn. My new name was Cate. I liked that it was similar to my old name, but more classic and still unique since it started with a C. I practiced saying "Hi, my name's Cate" inside my head. I stood straighter. A Cate was a different person than a Candi. A Cate could do anything she wanted. Cate Skye Thorn.

Mom linked arms with me as the sound of our heels clicking down the hall echoed off the tile floors. "Let me see," she said. I held out the form, and she smiled. "Looks good. We can hit the DMV on the way home."

"You sure you don't mind?" I asked.

She waved off whatever I was about to say. "Good heavens. I was fifteen when I named you. What did I know? After all, look at the guy I picked to have as your dad, for crying out loud. Clearly making long-term decisions wasn't my gift. No, Cate suits you. A new you deserves a new name."

"A new me," I repeated. I liked the sound of that.

EPILOGUE

Welcome back to Miami Morning. Thanks to Chef Frances for that recipe for the strawberry-blueberry tart. You can bet it will be on my July Fourth menu for sure!

Coming up next, we have the mother-daughter psychic team, Susan and Cate Thorn. Their new show, Psychic Solutions, debuts on this network in the fall. Let's see if these two can find out what the future holds in store for all of us!

ACKNOWLEDGMENTS

I would never get a single word down without a team of people behind me. My friends and family can be counted on to both cheer me on and/or give a kick in the rear as required. Special thanks to: Kelly Charron, Helen Platts-Johnson, and Serena Robar, who all gave early reads. Thanks to Jamie Hillegonds, Joanne Levy, Joelle Anthony, Laura Sullivan, and Lisa Voisin for the extra encouragement. And without a doubt my best publicity is done by my family (special call-out to Mom and Dad), who do their best to get my books in everyone's hands.

I have constant adoration for my agent, Barbara Poelle, who is a bad influence of the very best kind. I am very grateful to have her in my corner. Thanks also go to Brita Lundberg and the entire team at Irene Goodman.

Working with the team at Houghton Mifflin Harcourt has been amazing. Extra thanks go to my editor, Sarah Landis, who makes me a better writer, makes deadlines seem possible, and somehow also makes the entire process enjoyable. Thanks to Ann Dye and Linda Magram in marketing for spreading the word, Lisa DiSarro in library marketing for connecting me to some of my favorite people, the endlessly creative Karen Walsh in publicity, Emily Andrukaitis in managing editorial, editor-in-chief Mary Wilcox, publisher Catherine Onder, Maire Gorman in sales, and Cara Llewellyn in design. And for a cover to die for, hugs and kisses go to Erin Fitzsimmons. For having endless patience, kudos to Ana Deboo, who did the copy edits. For all things foreign, I have relied on Heather Baror-Shapiro, who has been nothing short of amazing.

I learned a lot about how to fake psychic ability from the Committee for Skeptical Inquiry. They do a great conference, and if you're interested in critical thinking — this is the group for you.

At home, I rely on my husband, Bob, for everything from making dinner to doing my website. Thank you. And I need to thank my dog, Cairo, and our new puppy, Gimlet, who provide boundless enthusiasm and love. They can also be counted on to bark while I'm on the phone and to dig holes in my yard.

Lastly, a huge thanks to readers, librarians, and bookstore people. My world would be less enjoyable without you.

TWISTY, SHOCKING THRILLERS

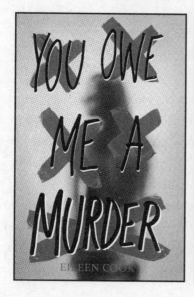

FROM EILEEN COOK

Turn the page for a sneak peek at Eileen's next thriller,

YOU OWE ME A MURDER

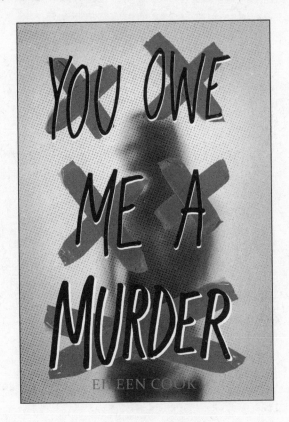

ONE

I plotted murder in the Vancouver airport while waiting at gate D78 for my flight to London.

Based on the expressions of the people around me, I wasn't the only one thinking of how to do someone in. Our flight was delayed and everyone was irritated and restless. The couple at the end of the row were fighting about which one of them had forgotten to lock the bedroom window before they left. Then there were at least a half-dozen people wanting to take out the toddler wearing the SpongeBob T-shirt, who vacillated between shrieking at a decibel normally used to torture dogs and running around slamming into everyone with his grimy hands.

The old guy across from me snarled, baring his yellowed teeth, every time the kid whirled in his direction. You'd think that would freak the toddler out, but it didn't seem to make any impact. Maybe the little boy got his ability to ignore unpleasant things from his mom. She stared down at an issue of *People* magazine, her lips moving as she read, completely ignoring the fact that people in the gate area wanted to club her kid with their roller bags. The only way you knew it was her child was that when he would slam into her, she'd hold out a limp plastic baggie filled with rainbow-colored gummy worms and then drop one into his clutching hand. She was like an apathetic mama bird.

I tilted my head to the side to crack the tension in my neck. I wished I could block things out that well. Instead I found myself continually looking over at Connor. My back teeth clenched, tight enough to crack. Miriam was perched on his lap. I told myself to stop staring, but my attention kept being pulled back. He slid his hand under her shirt and rubbed her back in tight circles. I knew that move. He'd done that to me.

Before he'd dumped me.

Miriam ruffled his hair. He couldn't stand it when I'd done that. He'd push my hand away or duck out of my reach. Connor had gone deaf after a bout of chicken pox as a kid and had cochlear implants so he could hear. He wore his hair a bit shaggy because he didn't like to draw attention to the processor behind his ears. I'd found it fascinating. Not just because it's a pretty cool piece of tech, but also because I wanted to know how he felt going from a silent world to being able to hear. But he didn't like to talk about it, or for me to touch his hair.

Apparently, he didn't have the same hang-up with Miriam. I reminded myself that I didn't care. Connor meant nothing to me now. I swallowed hard.

Toddler SpongeBob slammed into me. His sticky fingers, streaked red and blue from the candy, clutched my jeans. He stared up at me with his watery eyes and then, without looking away, slowly lowered his drooling, slobbery mouth to my knee and *bit me*.

"Hey!" I shoved him hard without thinking. He teetered for a moment and then fell onto his giant padded diaper butt, letting out a cry. I glanced around guiltily, shame landing on my chest with a thud. His mother didn't even look over. The old man gave me a thumbs-up gesture. *Great — that's me, Kim, the kind of person who beats up preschoolers when she's not stalking her ex-boyfriend.* I crouched down to help the kid up, but he pushed me away and returned to running wildly up and down the aisle.

I peered down at my phone, wishing I could call my best friend, Emily. She always knew how to cheer me up. She was spending the entire summer working at a camp on the far side of Vancouver Island. She didn't have any cell service or WiFi, so there was going to be no quick "everything will be fine" text or call. Granted, if I'd been able to reach her earlier in the summer, I might not even have been in this situation at all. Communicating old school — by letters — might be vintage and nostalgic, but it does you no good when you have an emotional disaster that needs immediate BFF interaction.

We'd been friends since elementary school and this was the longest I'd ever gone without talking to her. So far, my summer was proof positive that I shouldn't be allowed to handle things on my own. I fished the last card she'd sent me out of my bag. Inside she'd scribbled, *"I know you can do this! Your trip's going to be amazing!!"* Emily never met an exclamation point that she didn't like. Despite the positive punctuation, I was pretty sure she was wrong on both counts. I felt far from capable, and although the flight hadn't even left, I already hated everything about this trip.

I took a deep breath, counting in for three and then letting it whoosh out. *I can do this.* I wasn't going to let Emily and my parents down.

A few rows over, Miriam laughed, tossing her head back as if Connor had just told the best joke of all time. She playfully punched him in the chest with her tiny little hand. Everything about her was miniaturized. She told everyone she was five feet tall, but she was four eleven at best. She looked ridiculous when she stood next to Connor. He could have put her into his backpack and carried her around like a Chihuahua.

I had to admit Miriam was pretty, other than being freakishly petite. She had long dark hair that could have starred in a shampoo commercial. Her only flaw was that she wore too much eyeliner. She was addicted to the cat's-eye look, accentuating the slant of her eyes. She had a flair for drama; she always made huge gestures, sweeping her arms around, flicking her hair over a shoulder, or talking loudly as if she was constantly trying to make sure everyone could hear her. She was in the theater crowd, so maybe she couldn't help herself.

I never would have guessed Connor would date someone like her: showy. I thought he'd enjoyed that we didn't always have to be talking, but if we did, it was about important stuff: Philosophy. Science. Politics. We met once at the coffee shop in the morning before work and split up the *Globe and Mail*, silently passing the newspaper sections back and forth. He was the only other person I knew besides me who liked to read an actual paper. I'd caught our reflection in the window and thought we looked like adults. Like people who lived in New York or Toronto, with important jobs, a fancy high-rise apartment with lots of glass and chrome, and a membership to the local art museum.

Miriam had no volume control, but she wasn't stupid. I didn't know her well—she hung with the drama crowd—but I wouldn't have thought Connor was her type. I would have seen her liking a guy with an earring and some kind of social justice agenda. She wasn't in the hard sciences but still took a bunch of AP courses. She'd written some paper on Shakespeare that won a national award for English geeks. No wonder I wanted to kill her.

I sighed. I didn't want to kill her, I wanted to *be* her. Miriam hadn't stolen Connor. Someone can't steal what you don't have. He didn't dump me because he'd fallen for her. What had happened between us was complicated. More complicated than I even wanted to admit. He had his own reasons for stomping on my heart. If I was going to take anyone out, it should be him. But no matter whom I blamed, it didn't change the fact that I wasn't looking forward to spending the next few weeks watching the two of them make out in front of me. I shook my head to clear it. As everyone kept reminding me, it would be for only sixteen days.

I closed my eyes so I didn't have to see them, but I could still hear Miriam. Her drama teacher should be proud of how well Miriam's voice carried. She was four feet eleven of all lungs. Her voice filled the entire gate area and spread down the hall like toxic lava. I could tell already that the sound would be like fingernails on a chalkboard by the end of the trip.

The worst part was that I'd pleaded to go. I told my parents if they let me attend, they'd never have to get me another gift. Once Connor had announced he was going — before we'd broken up — I'd been instantly consumed with images of the two of us walking hand in hand through narrow cobblestone streets. The program was advertised as if it were a great educational opportunity, but the truth was, there weren't any real demands. We'd be "exposed" to culture, as though it were a cold we could catch. I didn't really care about the chance to travel, or what I might learn from the sights of London; what mattered was going *with him.* I didn't want him to be away for almost three weeks, doing all these things without me. I loved the idea of starting school in September with the two of us chatting constantly about *"remember the time we were in London?"* until everyone around us was annoyed.

In retrospect, I know he wanted to come because he didn't think I was going. He signed up without talking it over, telling me only after it was a done deal. I pleaded with my parents for days, never admitting that I wanted to go because of Connor and instead laying it on thick how it was a great way to expand my horizons, how amazing it would look on my university apps, and how I'd suddenly developed a fascination with British history, until they gave in.

Then, after things with Connor blew up in my face, I'd begged my parents to let me bail, but they wouldn't budge. They insisted it wasn't the deposit, it was the point. My dad called it a chance for me to "build character." As far as he was concerned, Connor had never been worth my time. He made a snide comment about Connor's overbite, which, coming from a dentist, was some serious trash talk.

My mom had made a dismissive sniff and told me "he's not worth bothering over." She acted as though she didn't like him, but when I'd first told her about Connor, she'd been as excited as me. He was exactly the kind of boy she would have liked at my age, and the exact kind of boy she assumed would never know her awkward daughter even existed. She looked at me differently, as if her ugly duckling had finally hit possible swan status. We went shopping together and got matching hot pink mani-pedis. We'd never gotten along as well as we had for those few weeks.

Then when things went bad with him, my mom acted as if she were the one who'd been humiliated. She might have said she wanted me to go on the trip because it was a chance to travel, but she also wanted me to be the kind of person who held her head high to handle the situation the way she would have done. And I wanted to be that person too — the kind who would have a fantastic time regardless of a breakup and, by the end of the trip, see Connor desperately sorry he'd broken up with me. All while making a pack of new friends.

However, if I was going to go full fantasy, I might as well add in that the queen would invite me to the palace, and Will and Kate would ask me to baby-sit, and Harry and Meghan would offer to hook me up with some minor count or a duke. The truth was, the next few weeks were going to suck.

And I was going to be stuck strapped in directly behind the lovebirds for the entire flight, watching them crawl all over each other in the tiny coach seats. I squeezed my eyes shut as if I could block out the mental image playing on the big screen of my mind. I'd told myself a thousand times since we'd all checked in and I'd heard our seating assignments that I could handle this, but with every second that went by, it was becoming increasingly clear to me that I wouldn't make it. I'd snap somewhere thirty-three thousand feet up and beat the two of them over the head with the in-flight magazine.

Or start crying again. I wasn't sure which would be worse. You would think there was only so much crying a person could do before she got completely dehydrated. I'd told myself I couldn't stand him anymore, so why did my heart still seize and my throat grow tight every time he was around?

I stood up so suddenly that my bag fell to the floor. I snatched it up and strode over to the airline counter. The gate agent didn't look up. She was too preoccupied typing into her computer. Her fingernails, which had a thick layer of bright red gel polish, made a strange clacking sound on the keys. I cleared my throat, but she still didn't stop.

"Excuse me," I managed to get out before she held up a finger to silence me.

She finally finished whatever she was doing and glanced up. "If you're asking about the delay, I don't have any more information. As soon as we get clearance, we'll start boarding." There was makeup creased on her forehead and I suspected she was on her last nerve. She was a walking reminder to never go into a customer service occupation.

I leaned forward even though logically I knew Connor couldn't hear me from where he was sitting. "I wondered if I could change my seat?"

She scrunched up her face. "I don't think—"

"See the guy back there?" I yanked my head in Connor's direction. "That's my ex-boyfriend. We're going to England on a travel program. I'm supposed to sit right behind him." I paused. "For nine hours."

Her perfectly arched eyebrows shot up to her hairline and she looked over my shoulder.

I sensed I was getting somewhere. "He was my first boyfriend." My voice cracked and I had to swallow over and over to keep control. "He dumped me just a couple weeks ago."

Her eyes softened, but she shook her head. "I'm sorry, but I can't—"

"That's his new girlfriend. She used to be my best friend."

The gate agent sucked in a breath and looked over at Connor as though he were something she'd scraped off her shoe.

I felt bad as soon as the words were out of my mouth. Miriam and I had never even hung out before this trip, let alone been friends, but I needed the agent to help me. Desperate times called for desperate measures.

I don't lie to hurt people, or to pull something over on them, but I guess sometimes I . . . make up stories to make myself more interesting. As long as I can remember, I've done it. On the playground in elementary school, I told the other kids that fairies lived in my backyard. In junior high I let everyone think I'd been adopted. I didn't want to lie. I *wanted* to be normal and interesting, but I wasn't.

I hadn't lied with Connor. With him I'd been one hundred percent honest about my feelings, and look how that had turned out.

The agent clacked away on the computer. "Your name?"

"Kim, Kim Maher." I spelled my last name.

"I need your old boarding pass." I slid the limp piece of paper across the counter. She tore it in half as the machine spat out a new one. She passed it over to me with a wink. "He doesn't deserve you. Have a good trip."

The tight band around my chest loosened. "Thanks."

I wove through the crowd clustered around the gate and plopped back down in my seat. I pushed the *New York Times* I'd already read out of the way and pulled out the magazine I'd brought. I hid between the pages, blinking back tears. The gate agent was right. Connor didn't deserve me. It was the same thing Emily told me. But even if I knew it was true, it didn't hurt any less. All I had to do was figure out how to get my heart to catch up to the fact that my head didn't like him anymore.

A girl slid a few seats over to be next to me. "Did she say anything about the delay?" Her English accent made me feel as if I'd dropped onto the set of a BBC historical drama.

I shook my head and quickly wiped my eyes so she wouldn't notice the tears. "No news."

The girl sighed. She pulled her legs up and wrapped her

arms around her knees. She tugged the thin cream cashmere sweater sleeves over her hands. She glanced down at the stack of paper on the chair next to me. "Your *Times*?"

I nodded.

"Did you read the article about the changes to the space program? I saw it earlier this morning."

I jumped slightly in surprise. She seemed like someone who would spot a copy of *InStyle* at a hundred meters but wouldn't know a shuttle from a rocket if she were whacked across the face with one of them. "Uh-huh." I picked up the paper, looking for the Science section.

"I think that's what I like about a real paper," she said. "It's like a knowledge Easter egg hunt. You never know what you're going to find."

I nodded like a bobble-head doll. That was exactly why I loved reading a paper too. "Yeah. Are you into space stuff?"

She shrugged. "Just find it interesting."

I held out my hand. "I'm Kim."

"Nicki." She smiled as we shook. "How come you aren't hanging with the rest of your group?" She motioned to a couple rows over. There were eight of us on the trip and we were all on this flight. A few had busted out cards to play a game on the blue carpeted floor, and the others were clustered around Jamal's laptop checking out his music.

"How did you know—" I got out before she flicked the blue and white STUDENT SCHOLARS FOR CHANGE tag attached to my carry-on. I'd forgotten I was branded. "Ah. I'm not really friends with any of them. There are just three of us from my high school. It's complicated," I said.

Nicki nodded. "Story of my life. I was here visiting my dad, and the reason he lives here, instead of in London with me and my mum, is all sorts of complicated too."

Nicki tucked her hair behind her ears. Her bob wasn't quite long enough, so as soon as she did, the hair fell free and swung forward again. "Sorry, that came out a bit pissy. I just find other people . . . ugh. I don't know. Disappointing." She shoved her hair back again.

"Story of my life," I said, echoing her words. She laughed and it reminded me of scales on a piano.

Nicki tapped the robotics magazine on my lap. "You plan on going into robotics at uni?"

I shook my head. "Not sure. I'm leaning toward engineering, maybe computers."

She waited until an announcement about a flight to Phoenix stopped blaring on the PA. "I'm thinking psychology. I'm interested in research. This is my gap year." She watched the unsupervised toddler fish a booger out of his nose and rub it into his hair.

"What kind of research?"

"Human behavior. I don't have any interest in being a counselor. People blathering about their problems all day would drive me barmy. But I'm intrigued with why people do what they do, why they don't do some things, what they could accomplish, that kind of thing."

I traced the pattern in the carpet with my shoe. Understanding other people was one of the great mysteries in my life. "If you ever figure people out, you'll have to let me know what you discover. Math I can make sense of, but people are more confusing than quantum physics. Give me a robot any day."

She laughed. "Don't give up on humanity just yet. Maybe you haven't met anyone worth figuring out."

The overhead speaker chirped to life. "Attention: Passengers on Air Canada flight 854 to London. Due to aircraft maintenance issues, this flight will be further delayed. We apologize for the inconvenience." The crowd groaned. The screen over our gate flickered and a new departure time, three hours from now, blinked on.

Connor stood and stretched. "Who wants to find a place to watch the Whitecaps game?"

Our group began to gather up their stuff. He was like the pied piper of nerdy people. Everyone was willing to follow him. Miriam walked over toward me.

"Do you want to come?" she offered. Her legs were so small that her size extra small leggings were baggy around her thighs. She must buy her clothing in a kids' department.

"No thanks," I managed to say, willing her to walk away. Or she could disappear completely — I was open to that, too.

"You can't want to hang around here for the next three

hours." Miriam nudged my tote with her foot. "C'mon, we'll all get some fries or something. It'll be fun."

Fun wasn't even in the top ten words that I would think of to describe the situation. "I'm fine," I insisted. It was bad enough that Connor wanted nothing to do with me. It was worse that he started dating someone else right away. It was a nightmare that I was stuck on this trip with them. But her being nice to me was a layer of shit icing on this crap cupcake. I didn't even know how much Connor had told her about what had happened between the two of us. I wasn't sure what I preferred: that she knew and felt pity for me, or that he hadn't told her anything because he didn't think I was worth mentioning. I slouched lower in the seat.

"Leave it — she doesn't want to come. Trust me, no one will miss her with that attitude." Connor strode over and took Miriam's hand without even glancing at me.

I flushed. He was right. I was a walking black cloud of doom. I hadn't bothered to get to know anyone else coming on the trip and now I was going to be miserable *and* alone.

"Gawd, he's a tosser," Nicki said, loud enough to carry.

I wasn't entirely certain what it meant, but it sounded both hysterical and insulting. I burst out laughing.

Connor and Miriam walked off down the hall, the rest of the group following behind them. He glanced over his shoulder at us, and when he saw we were still staring, he whirled back around.

My chest filled with air. I felt like one of those large balloons at a parade — ready to float away. "I don't know what you said, but you're my new favorite person on this planet," I said. I meant it, too. My BFF couldn't be reached except by letter. Emily might as well have been in space for all the help she could give me.

"That guy is a loser." Nicki pulled me from my seat. "I can tell, because as we've already established, I study people. You can pay me back for correctly identifying him as a wanker by keeping me entertained for the next few hours."

"How would you like me to do that?"

Nicki's smile spread across her face. "We're smart women, we'll think of something."